ONE NIGHT
WITH THE MAJOR

Bronwyn Scott

MIX
Paper from
responsible sources
FSC
FSC C007454

This book is produced from independently certified FSC™ paper
to ensure responsible forest management.
For more information visit www.harpercollins.co.uk/green

Printed and bound in Spain
by CPI, Barcelona

MILLS & BOON

First Published in Great Britain 2019
by Mills & Boon, an imprint of HarperCollins*Publishers*
1 London Bridge Street, London, SE1 9GF

© 2019 Nikki Poppen

ISBN: 978-0-263-26895-9

For all those who were told they couldn't,
but found a way anyhow.

Dream big because we're dreaming already.

Chapter One

A tavern on the outskirts of London—
April 1855

Pavia Honeysett needed a man and she had her sights set on that one in the corner, the one in the navy-and-gold uniform with his back to the wall, perhaps out of a soldier's habit, his eyes fixed on his ale, but she could tell even at a distance he wasn't seeing it. His thoughts were far from here.

She studied him from behind the taproom's kitchen door, amid the chatter of the other dancing girls who would be performing tonight. She took in the breadth of his shoulders, the straightness of his jaw. In a boisterous taproom, eagerly awaiting the night's entertainment, he remained apart from the group in all ways: in bearing, in appearance, his clean-shaven jaw and golden hair a sharp contrast to the rough-hewn, home-spun male camaraderie around him. He was alone and he was perfect. It had taken her three nights of dancing in the taverns from Yorkshire to London just to find him. Now she only had to reel him in.

Pavia adjusted the gossamer fabric of her dancing veils one last time and swallowed hard. Now that the moment had come, she was nervous. She reminded herself she should feel lucky, not anxious. This was what she wanted—a chance to claim her own freedom. She'd planned for it since the moment the summons to London had arrived at Mrs Finlay's Academy for Excellent Girls. She'd spent her pin money bribing the Academy grooms for the names of likely taverns where she could dance. This one, the Tiger's Tooth, on the outskirts of the city, was supposed to be her best chance. It hosted nightly dancing entertainments featuring girls of all sorts of backgrounds from all parts of the British Empire. It had been easy to blend into the colourful milieu of dancers gathered in the kitchen waiting their turns to perform.

Applause erupted from the taproom for a dancer who claimed to be Persian. Pavia doubted the authenticity of that claim, but not the girl's appeal. Men would not care with breasts like that. Pavia looked down at her own more modest 'charms' and hoped they'd be enough. One more girl to go and then it would be her turn. Unless… Unless she lost her nerve and slipped out the back door.

No, she wouldn't think such things. It had to be tonight, or it would be too late. Tomorrow, she would be in London and under her father's thumb, a pawn to be used in her father's bid for social advancement. Pavia's pulse began to race anxiously with all that meant. She was to be a virgin sacrifice in marriage to the Earl of Wenderly, a man old enough to *be* her grandfather. Both the men were rich, although her father liked to point out that he was richer by far, but Wenderly had a title and her father, for all the tea in China, quite literally, did not. Her father might be Oliver Honeysett, founding partner of Honeysett and Crooks, the largest importers of English tea, outstripping even the legendary Twinings Company, but he was still a Cit, still nouveau riche, one of the nabobs who'd made his fortune in India. In short, a man who'd worked for his money, a man who could rise no higher in the world without a title and it galled him.

She was to be his way into those lofty ranks of the peerage, the guarantee that if he did not possess a title, by God his grandchildren would. They would be the sons and daughters of an earl. But she didn't want to marry Wenderly. She wanted something different for her life. She wanted adventure, to see the world, to live among her mother's people again in India where she could be wanted for herself. The colour of her skin mattered not at all in the palace of her uncle, the Rajah of Sohra. Here in England, it was the only thing that mattered, the one thing men were willing to overlook in exchange for her father's money or, in Wenderly's case, her virginity. Wenderly was desperate for it, in fact, and that worried her a great deal, especially coupled as it was with the rumours whispered about him behind lace fans at deportment class. It was common knowledge among the girls at Mrs Finlay's Academy who were scheduled to come out that no decent woman would have him. Then eyes would slide her way and the girls would nod to one another knowingly. No decent English girl, that was. But the Indian girl would do nicely. The implication was clear. In their minds, to be Indian in England was to be indecent.

Maybe she *was* being a bit indecent tonight.

Pavia shook her filmy veils loose for fullness and laughed softly to herself at the irony. Tonight those English ladies would be right. She meant to lose that virginity Wenderly seemed to prize so much. In exchange, she would gain her freedom and that was worth any price. It was not a decision she'd taken lightly, but rather a decision she'd been forced to after pleading and begging and appealing to her father's sense of reason failed to produce results. He was set on the match. Not even her mother could sway him. So now Pavia was taking matters into her own hands.

If life had taught her one thing so far, it was that there were no happy ever afters being handed out by handsome princes. If a girl wanted a happy ever after she had to make it for herself, *seize* it if she had to, invent it out of whole cloth if she must. If she didn't, someone else, namely her father, would. Then, it would be *his* happy ending at *her* expense. *That* was untenable. Under no circumstance was her happy ever after the purvey of another, especially not a man. Not her father and certainly not the man he'd selected for her to marry. That's what had happened to her mother—she had been married off to an Englishman and forced to live in an alien culture that had no sympathy for her. Pavia vowed silently once more that such an ending would not be for her.

She fastened the last veil across her face, leaving only her eyes visible as she marked the location of her target. He was the best choice she'd had in the three nights of her journey to London. In the other places her entourage had stopped, the men had been too rough. She might be acting rashly, but she was not without her own cautions. She didn't want to end up battered, or with a disease, or, worst of all, with a child. At least she could control the latter. She had vinegar sponges waiting back at her own rooms in another inn. The quality of her candidate, however, was not nearly as controllable. Pavia sighed. When she'd designed this plan, she hadn't realised how complicated it would be. She'd simply wanted to relieve herself of a ridiculously over-valued English inconvenience.

She considered her candidate one last time as the previous dancer finished. Would he be a decent lover? Would it hurt? The girls at school said it did, but they only had hearsay to go on. The women in her uncle's palace, where sexuality was not nearly as taboo as it was here in England, had told other, more pleasurable stories. Whom did she believe? Perhaps it depended on the lover. This man in the corner looked as if he possessed some honour, but not too much, not enough to make him ask questions, or to make him stay, just enough to keep him from taking extraordinary advantage of her. The way he stared at that ale suggested he was someone who had his own demons to worry about. It also suggested that perhaps the hardest part would be persuading him to take what she was offering.

Pavia bit her lip, considering the option of failure for the first time. In all her imaginings she'd not thought of what would happen if she missed her mark. There was no time to think about that now. She'd fail for certain if she stood here all night. The girl behind her gave her a little nudge. It was her turn. She slipped a pair of tiny cymbals on to her thumbs and forefingers and opened the door. She gave a nod to the fiddler, who moved into a slow tune. It wasn't Indian, to be sure. Irish, perhaps? She didn't care, as long as it had a sinuous, haunting melody made for the undulation of hips and the sway of bodies.

She began to dance, slowly, evocatively, drawing all eyes towards her with the ringing, rhythmic click of her cymbals. She worked through the crowd deliberately, gracing a man here, another man there, with the tease of her attentions. She couldn't be obvious about her target, couldn't race over to him or it would be too transparent. But it must be him. Only the best would do for Pavia Honeysett.

The last made her smile behind her veils. She'd been raised in wealthy privilege, the only child of a tea merchant. She'd been taught to expect the best. Tonight would be no different. A man reached out for her as she passed. She moved beyond his grip, scolding him by turning her attentions towards another. But she understood the warning. She'd teased them with her glances and swaying hips; they would expect her to deliver on those promises. She'd reached the divide between the milieu of the long trestle tables and the soldier's table at the wall. He seemed intent on not looking at her, the only man in the room who wasn't looking. She would change that.

Pavia dropped a veil from the gold-coin belt about her waist, revealing a full glimpse of smooth leg. That got his attention. He was a man, not marble, after all, despite what his chiselled features suggested. She caught his eye and held it—demanded it, actually, with her hips. With a step forward closing the meagre distance between them, she smiled with her eyes, letting him guess at the lush mouth hidden from view beneath the silk draping.

Her candidate was a handsome man up close, golden haired and well kept. A firm mouth went with that strong, straight jaw, topped with sharp blue eyes that matched the strength of him. This was better than she'd hoped for. He'd be moving on, unlikely to linger in London. If she was lucky, he was already on the move to fulfil orders. The world was a big place. They would never see each other again after tonight. But first, she had to entice him and she had only six veils remaining. She couldn't afford to make any mistakes.

Major Cam Lithgow was not a man who made mistakes, but he was making them in droves tonight. The first mistake was coming down to the taproom, wanting to drown his sorrows in ale, only to discover there was live entertainment. He should have left then. Not leaving was his second mistake. His third was making eye contact with the exotic dancer. His fourth was not looking away. How could he? She was dressed in carefully draped veils that simultaneously revealed and concealed the exquisite body beneath, all held carefully in place by a gold girdle that spanned a slim waist and rested on the delicious curves of her hips, jingling provocatively as those hips swayed their promises.

To his dismay, his body was becoming 'interested' in those promises, his mind interested in the dark eyes that held his. He'd not bartered on this when he'd come downstairs to the taproom.

The dancer loosened another veil from her belt with sensual skill, drawing the fabric across her body before letting it pool in his lap in blatant invitation. Behind her there were hoots and catcalls from the deserted crowd. There were growls of disappointment, too. Cam tensed. Jealous, disappointed drunk men were dangerous. Did she understand that? She'd played with them and then turned her back quite literally to choose the one man in the room who was least apt to accept her invitation. They weren't likely to be very forgiving of the slight. Hell, he could see it now. If he didn't claim her and take her upstairs, the taproom would brawl over her, competing for the right to be her second choice whether she wanted any of them or not. And he'd end up defending her whether he wanted to or not because a man of honour could do no less.

The dancer leaned backwards an impressive degree, letting her hips undulate in a sinuous, vertical line, like the hypnotic writhe of a cobra, skeins of silky black hair cascading from beneath the veil that hid her face except for the dark, wide, almond-shaped eyes. The man in him was aroused against his better judgement. She righted herself, her hips returning to a horizontal sway, and she reached for him. More precisely, she reached for his sword, pulling it from its sheathe in a lightning snatch before he could react. He'd let his guard down—he'd thought she was reaching for him or for the scarf in his lap. Now he was unarmed in a potentially dangerous environment.

She leaned backwards again and began the undulation, this time balancing the sword on her hip. Cam held his breath, torn between warning her how sharp the blade was and remaining silent for fear that speaking out would ruin her concentration. Miraculously, the sword lay steady. She became a dervish, then, taking the sword in hand and whirling about, a swirl of colours and veils in time to the music. When the music slowed and the whirlwind abated, his sword was balanced atop of her head. The room was alive now, the crowd clapping to the rhythm of her movements and the music; all of it pushing him towards a de-

cision. Save her from the mob, or leave her
to her self-imposed fate. He'd not come down
here looking for adventure but it seemed adventure had found him anyway.

She turned a fast circle, the sword never
slipping from her head and Cam made up his
mind. Perhaps his mind had already been made
up the moment their eyes had met. Her circle
stopped. He rose and held out his hand. Good
lord, he didn't even know if she spoke English.
This was madness. But he couldn't leave her
here when it was clear she had no idea of how
much danger she might be in from men who
might not hesitate to strip those veils from her,
who might decide to make a plaything of her
for their own amusement, who might not as-
cribe to the idea that a person was a person
no matter the colour of their skin. There were
too many 'mights' for his taste. Too much to
leave to chance.

She dipped him an English curtsy, returned
his sword and without a word let him lead her
up the stairs. How did this happen to him?
How did he find himself in the most unwanted
circumstances? This was not an adventure he
would have sought for himself. He was probably the only soldier in the British army who
didn't *want* to be back on English soil. Bala-

clava had been a bloodbath and he'd been the one to live to tell about it, a prospect so daunting, he couldn't sleep at night—he still woke up screaming about it. But here he was—back in England and with one more responsibility to carry out when all he wanted was to be back with his troops and a life he understood, a life that *pleased* him.

At the top of the stairs, he ushered her into his chamber and shut the heavy oak door behind them. Cam leaned his head against the door frame, closing his eyes for a moment of clarity, savouring the coolness of the wood against his brow. Good lord, he had an exotic dancer in his room. His grandfather would die if he knew. Exotic dancers were not part of his grandfather's plan for him.

Aside from the pleasure that came with the thought of niggling at his grandfather's limited sensibilities, this was *not* how Cam had expected the evening to go. He'd gone down to the taproom in the hopes of forgetting everything, to put off his duty one more day. He could have easily ridden on to London tonight before dark, but that would have meant facing his grandfather, playing the returning war hero and the doting suitor to Caroline Beaufort, his intended, a young woman selected by his grandfather as worthy of a Lithgow with her exquisite looks and immaculate pedigree, but a woman who engendered nothing more than polite interest from him.

It was no wonder he loved soldiering. It was full of the adventures he thrived on—new places, new people, new tasks—where there was little time to spend worrying over the delicate concerns of etiquette, while life here in London spread before him like a vast empty wasteland full of useless occupations. Well, maybe it wasn't quite an empty wasteland just yet. There was still the dancer to deal with. He needed to make it clear to her that she had his protection, that nothing else would occur in this chamber tonight. Despite what his body might have argued, he wasn't in the mood. His mind was too fixed on the things he'd have to do tomorrow, like telling the Duke of Cowden his son, Cam's own best friend, Fortis Tresham, wasn't coming back.

Cam turned from the door, ready to make his pronouncement, and his mouth went dry. His dancer stood before him beautifully naked, her discarded veils at her feet, a tanned goddess come to life with high, bold breasts and a gentle hand over her shy nether pelt, a delicious contradiction of seduction and innocence. Had he really been about to refuse her? His body's reaction laughed at the prospect, but his conscience pricked. How dare he think of pleasure when Fortis was dead.

He strode towards her, purposefully shrugging out of his coat and draping it about her. 'You needn't offer yourself to me. You are safe here.' The coat was big, effectively hiding her, but it did nothing to dampen his response. With her face revealed, she fulfilled the promise of beauty: wide eyes, a full mouth, a delicate jaw that created a heart-shaped face and hinted at English antecedents.

'Do you not want me?' She sloughed off his coat, naked once more, her hands cupping her breasts, lifting them for his inspection.

'It's not that.' Cam was uncharacteristically at a loss for words, he who shouted orders over the chaos of a battlefield. 'It's just that you don't need to feel obliged.' He'd never taken a woman to bed who felt obligated to be there and he wasn't going to start now.

She moved towards him, reaching for the stock about his neck and tugging it free, determined to undress him. 'And if I don't feel *obliged*? Would you want me then?' She smelled like adventure, all citrus and spice, a fragrance of the Far East, a fragrance of happier times, when he and Fortis had served two years for the Crown in India.

Cam swallowed hard. He was starting to lose this fight and maybe he should lose it. Maybe bedding her would help in some way with the grief he carried, a first step back towards living. No, that was ludicrous. He was simply justifying things now to please his body. He put his hands atop hers, stopping them where they worked the buttons of his uniform's waistcoat. 'I don't know who you are. I don't even know your name.' He knew only that she was Indian and English, and beautiful.

She pressed a long, slim finger to his lips. 'No names. It's best that way, don't you think?' He didn't think. He was starting to not think at all.

Chapter Two

'Let me help you.' Her voice was soft, soothing, entirely at odds with the excited turmoil inside her. She'd got him this far, upstairs and into his room. But he'd done nothing to undress himself, so she'd do it for him.

He forgot to restrain her hands this time when she worked the buttons free. She pressed her advantage, slight as it was. 'You came to the tavern to forget something tonight. I saw it in your face out there.' She slid the waistcoat over his shoulders, down his arms and tossed it aside as if she undressed men every night. Pavia pulled his shirttails loose, praying at some point, he would take over. She would soon be in over her head despite whatever theoretical knowledge she had gleaned growing up in her uncle's zenana, but even that was scarce little. She had not been in India since she was twelve. 'You are hurting.' Her hand stopped over his heart. 'In here. I've seen men like you before.'

She had his shirt off him in moments, her hands pressed against his chest. She appealed to whatever sense of fair play he might possess—a trade. 'You helped me down there tonight, now I will help you forget whatever it is that's on your mind.' She raised up on her tiptoes and took his mouth in a soft kiss. 'Then, in the morning, we will be even. All debts between us paid.' Such a bargain should appeal to a military man.

Under her mouth, he gave a harsh chuckle. 'I will never be able to wipe my slate clean again.'

Ah, so she'd been right about the demons. Leave it to her luck to seduce the one man who didn't have seduction on his mind. She twined her arms about his neck. She'd come too far to give up now. 'Then erase it just for tonight.' She whispered the temptation. 'There is comfort here, free for the taking.'

She moved against him, kissing him again as if he'd already accepted her offer, her terms, and this time he gave over. His hands settled at her hips, holding her to him, his mouth opened to her, letting the kiss seduce him, draw him in to the fantasy until he became an active participant, kissing her back, with tongue and teeth at her ear, her neck, the caress of his mouth drawing heady sensations from her—sensations she had not expected. This was meant to be a job. She'd assumed it would be joyless. That was not the case.

The kiss was consuming. Pavia let the world shrink to encompass only this room, only this man, only this time as he took the kiss away from her, making it into his seduction at last, his hand in her hair, gathering it at the nape of her neck, his mouth insistent on hers, and her mouth answering with an insistent hunger of its own. Then they were both falling, to the bed, into the void of the night. Had he taken her down or had she pulled him? She didn't know, she didn't care. He was over her, her body warm as it stretched beneath him, all lush curves and slim lines against the hard muscle of him. The dusky peaks of her breasts arched up to brush his chest, teasing themselves into erectness. Her thighs cradled him, inviting him. This business of lovemaking was easier than she'd imagined, far easier than getting him up the stairs, and she knew she'd been lucky in her choice.

He was a deliberate lover, his body savouring the slow sheathing of itself in hers, making it clear this was not a fantasy to rush. He did not want to lose himself for just mere minutes, but for a night, for hours at a time. She gave a delicate moan beneath him at his first breaching, her body stirring in discomfort and then in accommodation. She arched against him in an untutored squirm that made him laugh, a warm, intimate chuckle. 'Easy now, I know what you want. Be patient. I will take you there.' His mouth hovered above hers, his hand pushing her hair back from her forehead in a gentle gesture as his hips began to move, and his body picked up an ancient rhythm of easement and surge.

She joined him in the intimate waltz, letting him set the pace, letting him drive them towards ecstasy's cliffs as she lifted and fell with him. Her hands dug into his shoulders, her legs wrapped tight about him, holding him close, her body desperate for the promised fulfilment that hovered on the horizon they'd created. His exhalations suggested he was nearly there and she sensed that he was somehow with her and beyond her. When the pleasure took him, she was left alone, that same pleasure eluding her. But she could not complain as his chest heaved and his muscled arms trembled with his release. She had got what she'd come for.

It was done. Completely and *most* thoroughly. Not that she'd been any judge before, but she was now. Her nameless lover had comported himself well. She could have asked for nothing better. Pavia imagined this would become the measure against which any other lover would be compared. He would be measured against this golden-haired, broad-shouldered god of a man who lay sleeping beside her in post-coital exhaustion. She had chosen well. Maybe too well. Instead of leaping out of bed while he slept and running back to her inn a few streets away, she wanted to stay. She wanted to watch him sleep, wanted to trace the musculature of his chest with her finger, wanted to indulge her imagination in guessing his story. Who was he? What was he doing here? Where was he going? Answering those questions broke her rules. No names, no regrets, no tomorrows.

It was the novelty of him that tempted her to linger. She'd not thought a man could be so beautiful. She'd not expected to enjoy his body, seeing it, touching it. It was well muscled and smooth, his chest tanned and devoid of coarse hair, perhaps from campaigns spent sleeping out of doors and bathing in foreign rivers. Pavia let her imagination run wild, shamelessly romanticising the life of a soldier. Not just any soldier, an officer of some rank if she read his uniform aright. There'd been plenty of the East India Company men at their home in India, enough for her to know an officer's uniform when she saw one.

She'd not been prepared either for the surge of emotion the act had raised. She'd expected a messy, painful interlude of grunts and thrusts until the deed was done. There *had* been discomfort, but nothing unbearable and nothing that had lasted once the initial shock had receded, replaced by something, if not breathtaking and heart-stopping, certainly pleasant in its own right. It had been different for him, however. For him, it *had* been breathtaking and heart-stopping. She'd seen it in his face as his release came over him like a wave. A nugget of irrational, womanly pride had formed in realisation that she'd been the cause of it. Whatever had haunted him in the taproom had been temporarily exorcised.

He stirred beside her, his blue eyes searching for her. Somewhere in the room, a log crackled and split in the fireplace. His arm reached for her, drawing her against his side, her head cushioned on the place where his shoulder met chest. This was one more thing she'd not counted on—this easy intimacy of lying naked with a man. She didn't want to question it, didn't want to over think it and become self-conscious.

'I've been to India,' he said in a voice made husky from sleep and waking. 'It's a beautiful place, wild, exotic. Not like here.' His finger traced a slow, idle route over the curve of her hip, raising delicate goose pimples in its wake. 'Where are you from? What part?'

'Sohra.' Telling him that much wouldn't break her self-imposed rules of anonymity. 'Do you know where that is?' He probably didn't. It was a remote principality.

'Hmm. No,' he replied drowsily. 'I was stationed in Madras.'

'Sohra is a long way from there. It's up in the Khasi Hills in the north-east.' She sighed, her own finger drawing a map of her uncle's home on his chest. 'We have green hills, cool breezes and waterfalls.' She sighed. Just talking about Sohra brought its own kind of peace. 'We have root bridges and mountains.'

He chuckled, the sound rumbling his chest beneath her ear. 'I am jealous. Madras was hot and steamy. A man could sweat through his uniform within minutes of putting it on and the streets smelled horribly.'

She raised up on an elbow and gave him a teasing scold. 'You just said India was beautiful. That description doesn't sound beautiful.'

'Oh, but it was. Once I got out of town, the jungle was splendid. The fruits, the animals, incredible.' He laughed in his defence, then sobered. 'It's different than here. Everything here is so...*tame*... Do you miss it?'

'Of course.' She let him draw her back down, but not before the flicker of memory danced in his eyes. She probed it. 'What are you missing? A place? A person?' It struck her too late who that person might be. 'A woman?' A quick spike of jealousy stabbed at her. She didn't want to think about this man with another woman. Tonight, she wanted him to belong solely to her. Yet it was another item unreckoned when she'd concocted this plan. It was supposed to have been simple: find a man, bed him and leave.

He shook his head. 'No woman. A military man isn't very good at making or keeping commitments of that nature. His days are not his own. Nor his life. It could end at any time.' He was warning her to remember what they'd agreed upon. She didn't need the reminder. She'd been the one to set the rules. But it was more than a warning. He was hinting at something larger, something his soul wanted to share. She waited, letting the silence stretch about them. She sensed he wanted to talk, the desire was in him, if only he could find the words. She gave him time and at last the words came.

'My friend was killed in battle, at a place called Balaclava, near Sevastopol. He was an officer in the cavalry, one of the best. I saw him go down. One moment he was waving his sword, rallying his troops, and the next he was gone.' Three sentences was all she would get. Perhaps he, too, was caught in limbo between the freedom of whispering secrets to a stranger to whom those secrets would mean nothing and the need to keep those secrets hidden in order to protect himself. The less they knew of each other the better. It was the deal after all.

'I am sorry.' She said the simple words softly, meaning them.

'Tonight is not for war.' He reached for her, tasting her—her mouth, her neck, the pulse at its base, the swells of her breasts—with sweet, slow kisses as his mouth, his hands, moved down her body. He laved the indentation of her navel with his tongue, his hands at the span of her waist, and then his mouth was in the curls hiding her core, his breath warm against her dampness. 'You've not had your pleasure yet.' Sharp blue eyes looked up at her from their intimate position at her thighs, burning with cobalt desire, for her perhaps, or for smothering the past. It didn't matter to her body which. Her pulse quickened in a way that had nothing to do with her quest tonight, and everything to do with this man staring up at her. 'Permit me?' She might have permitted him out of curiosity alone, but Pavia was well beyond that now. Her surrender was imminent. She was not only curious, but intrigued by this man. He'd become more than a means to an end. No one had warned her about that.

The end was different now than when she'd begun. His wicked tongue licked at the seam of her in proof of that. The end was much more short term; the end was not a blocking of Wenderly's unwanted suit, but something much more pleasurable, much more elusive—the goal was now this pleasure her soldier alluded to. He licked her again and she moaned. She wanted what he'd had. She'd seen his face—she wanted that, too, that sense of being swept away, of being beyond the physical realm. For a moment he'd been transported.

Was it possible for her, too? His tongue found a hidden nub and she cried out her surprise, her enjoyment, the sensation sharper, stronger than before. 'It's all right to let go,' he murmured against her skin. 'You're safe with me. Let the pleasure come,' he coaxed. Her rational mind had no reason to believe him, but her body did. He'd done nothing but respect her since they'd come upstairs.

His mouth took her again and she felt the option to choose slipping away. She would give over to pleasure whether she wished it or not. And she did, her hands fisting first in the linen of the bedsheets and then the thickness of his hair, holding him to her for fear he'd leave her before the pleasure was complete. She would not survive it if he did. She arched into him, once, twice more, sensation driving her to the brink of madness and then to breaking. She felt herself shatter against his mouth, her body shuddering its own completion. *This* was what he'd felt. This was *how* he'd felt. Now she knew. In the swirling kaleidoscope of completion, she felt omniscient, as if she was in possession of great knowledge, of great power, one of the world's supreme mysteries made known to her alone.

Her lover stretched along beside her, his

eyes smoky, his face content. The act had given him pleasure as well. Pleasing her had been important to him. Would all lovers be this considerate? She yawned and he smiled. 'Come and rest.' Against her better judgement she did, nestling into 'her' spot at his shoulder. How quickly she'd become possessive of this stranger's body. What could it hurt to lay in his arms an hour longer? It wasn't as if she could sneak downstairs just yet without being noticed.

Pavia hadn't meant to sleep. She hadn't meant to linger after midnight. But when she woke, it was clear she'd done both. The window showed grey shadows of coming dawn and she knew a moment's panic. She'd slept the night away! Beside her, her nameless lover slept unbothered, his sleeping countenance as handsome as it had been the night before. She had to hurry—hurry to get out of this room before he awoke, hurry to get back to the inn before her maid realised she was missing.

Pavia slid out of bed, wincing at her sore muscles—another surprise. She hastily gathered her veils, quietly retrieving her jingly gold belt. She'd been counting on the darkness to make her less conspicuous walking back. Now

that advantage was gone, too, yet another reason to hurry. A girl wearing nothing but veils
walking through the morning streets was
bound to stand out. She did not want to be remembered. The cloak she'd worn the night before had been left behind in the kitchen. She
took a final look at the man in the bed and
slipped out of the room, closing the door softly
on her one adventure. In the dim hall, Pavia
squared her shoulders, warding off a sense of
melancholy as she left the room and its occu-
pant behind.

She ought to be pleased. Her quest had been
irrevocably successful and now it was time to
go forward into the future she'd chosen for herself; a future that would be somewhat uncer-
tain at the outset and most definitely rocky. Her
father would be furious once she announced
she no longer met Wenderly's marital criteria.
That was a given. But what he would do was
not as obvious. Would he banish her to the
countryside? Force her into seclusion? Would
he send her back to India and be done with
her? She'd prefer the latter. Her uncle would
take her in, she was sure of it. Perhaps her
mother would come with her and they could
both be free. She would hold on to that hope
through the difficult times that would come

first. If there was one certainty at the moment, it was this: things would likely get worse before they got better. But they *would* get better, Pavia reasoned, a little smile teasing her mouth as she walked. It was already better. She wasn't going to marry Wenderly. She couldn't. It was now impossible. She was completely and thoroughly ruined.

Chapter Three

For the first time in the months since Bala-clava, Cam slept. Thoroughly, completely. And, damn it, the price for that sleep was too high. Cam knew before he opened his eyes that she was gone. The room felt different, smelt different; it lacked a certain vibrancy.

Cam gave a groan and opened one eye, hoping his other senses were wrong. But sight only confirmed his disappointment. Her veils were gone. Except for the last mementos of scent, she had vanished with the night. Not that he hadn't expected as much. She'd made it clear there'd be nothing between them beyond the night. Yet, it would have been nice to wake up to her; to the curve of her derrière tucked against him, to perhaps take her gently from behind as she woke, a chance to redeem himself as a lover.

She'd not been with him when release had claimed him alone. Her pleasure had waited until he'd taken her with his mouth, determined that she know the joy of release with him. It was a point of pride that his lovers found their pleasure, too. That the pleasure had initially eluded her had come as something of a surprise to Cam. He'd not been prepared for that. Everything leading up to his climax had suggested that moment would be jointly shared. Except for her eyes. Damn it, he should have put more credence in her eyes.

Even now in the grey coolness of morning, the heat of the night was etched on his mind with startling clarity. Her body had welcomed him eagerly, but her eyes had been dark and knowing, and not nearly as pliant, or as hot, as the rest of her. There'd been reserve in her gaze, a piece of her that she'd held back. And in the heat of the moment, Cam had wanted to claim it. Even now, he could recall that fierce surge of possession with warrior-like sharpness. He'd wanted that one piece of her, wanted to know what it was that she held back and why. And he'd set out to conquer it, driving himself into the oblivion of lovemaking, urged there by the arch of her body, the sounds of her mouth as he thrust into the tight, wet heat of her. The tightness had been exquisite, shaping itself around him as he moved within her. But despite his intent to conquer, to claim, that one piece had remained in abeyance, reserved from the encounter. For all his skill, he'd not been able to coax it forward. Despite the encouraging mewls and the subtle urgings of her body, he was alone when his release had come, pulsing, hard and sweeping, leaving him spent and, for a precious amount of time, too replete to think of the world beyond their bed, too replete to worry over what had gone amiss.

This morning, he *still* felt too replete to worry over her flight from his bed. Why had she flown? Had she taken anything with her? He wondered vaguely if she'd robbed him while he'd slept and Cam found he didn't care. He had few items of worth on his person save his ring, a watch and his officer's gorget. He had his sword, of course, which would fetch a good amount. He rather hoped she hadn't taken that. It would be hard to explain how he'd lost it. He had a money clip in a pocket of his coat. But money was replaceable.

Cam reached a long arm out and lifted his coat from the floor, feeling for the money clip, half-hoping it was gone. At least then he'd know she would be able to purchase some security, pay rent, buy food, buy clothes if she needed them. Perhaps she would not have to dance in taverns where men tupped her with their eyes. His hand closed disappointingly around the clip. All was intact.

Cam sighed, questions filling his head. Where would she go? What would she do? Would she be safe? These were new questions. He'd never given much thought before about such things. Then again, he was not inclined towards lightskirts as lovers in general. Continental widows who loved their freedom were more to his taste when it came to assuaging physical need. But last night had somehow transcended the usual satisfying of his carnal appetites. Worrying over his absent lover was a distraction he needed to set aside. He could do nothing for her and other business called today.

He squinted towards the window, testing the brightness. It was well past dawn. Past time to get on with the day and the unpleasantness that waited. Cam threw back the covers and swung his legs out of bed. He stretched, arms over his head, rotating side to side from the waist. He rotated to his left side, then to his right, then halt—what was that on the bed, revealed only when he'd thrown back the covers? The pale stains of sex and blood on the sheets were unmistakable. He'd bedded enough women and seen enough blood to know. There were only two conclusions he could draw from that and one of them seemed too far-fetched to even consider: his dancer had been a virgin. Virgins didn't dance in taverns, didn't take arbitrary strangers upstairs for the night. Yet his body remembered the exquisite tightness of her, the hesitation before her hips had taken up the rhythm of his. He remembered, too, the provocative shyness of her when she'd stood before him naked, perhaps defiant instead of bold. Then, there had been her one hand, protective and shielding, giving her the air of innocence.

It had been coyly done, but even now with blood on the sheets, he couldn't quite convince himself it was more than an act simply because it didn't make sense. What did make sense was the other, more practical conclusion. She'd got her menses in the night. Not that it mattered. She had vanished completely. He would never see her again, even if he wanted to. To his surprise, he *did* want to. She'd captivated him with her passion, her beauty, with the concern he'd seen in her eyes, as if he wasn't just another customer. *'You are hurting, in here.'* Cam's eyes quartered the room looking for a token of her presence, a scarf left behind, a coin dropped from her belt. Anything that offered insight into her identity. But there would be no glass slipper for him, no way to trace her.

Just as well. What would he do anyway if he found her? He was here on leave. He had duties to carry out. He would go back to Sevastopol as soon as his leave was up in August. It was time to get on with those duties. Cam mapped out the day in his head. He would send for his batman, who had chosen to bed down in the stables, eat breakfast, shave, dress and then, when the hour was decent and he could put it off no longer, he would call on the Duke of Cowden.

'Fortis is dead, Your Grace.' As it turned out, there was no decent hour at which to tell an ageing man his son had been killed. Cam stood ramrod-straight at attention, bringing all his sense of military ceremony to the announcement. Cam would honour his fallen friend with every ounce of pomp and pride in him. Fortis's family deserved as much and Cam had promised. It was not a promise he'd ever thought to keep. They'd been half-drunk the night he'd made the pledge years ago in

India on their first posting. They'd been immortal then.

The Duke of Cowden received the news with as much aplomb as it was delivered with, but it was a Herculean task for them both to maintain the stiff upper lip demanded by social etiquette—an etiquette that maintained a man did not fall apart over loss: loss of money, loss of life, the loss of a child. A man carried on.

'Will you join me in a drink to him, then?' Cowden moved to the side board holding a cut-crystal decanter full of brandy. His hand trembled as he poured. Cam moved to take the tumbler before the older man could drop it. He'd not seen Cowden in nearly eight years, not since Fortis's hasty wedding to Avaline Panshawe, a marriage Fortis barely acknowledged. Cowden's hair was white and his face was lined, although his back was straight. He was still a tall, commanding man if one did not look too closely, but the age was showing in small ways: the shaking hand, the long pauses before he spoke.

Cowden raised his glass, his voice firm. 'To my son, Fortis, who lived as he wanted and died as he wished.' They drank, long, deep swallows to cover the emotion. It was exactly how Fortis had wished to die: in the saddle, in the heat of battle, exhilaration thrumming through his veins. Cam hoped it had lived up to Fortis's expectations.

Cowden refilled his glass and gestured to a chair, his tone shifting. 'There, now that's done. We've fulfilled our social obligations. Perhaps you would sit and tell me the details, tell an old man about the last moments of his son's life?' Grey eyebrows lifted at the request, his blue eyes not as sharp as Cam remembered them. The Duke had always been a formidable figure to him, but a friendly one. Cowden was older than Cam's father, but younger than his grandfather. He'd been a happy medium in Cam's life while he was growing up. He'd always been welcome at Fortis's home. He'd never thought he'd have to repay those years of kindnesses like this.

'Should we call the others?' Cam made a gesture towards the door of Cowden's study. 'Should we include them?'

Cowden shook his head. 'Let them think Fortis is alive awhile longer. Besides, you needn't sanitise the details with me,' he offered knowingly. 'The news will be upsetting enough as it is.' The whole Cowden crew was in town at the moment even though the Season would not be fully under way for a few weeks yet: Frederick, the heir, who had always been so jealous of Fortis's freedom to serve his country; Helena, his wife, and their five boys; Ferris, his wife, Anne, and new baby, and Avaline, Fortis's widow—a woman Fortis had spent only three weeks of married life with before he'd returned to his troops. Had he loved Avaline? Had Avaline loved him? Fortis had said little of his marriage. But Cam knew she had written to him dutifully for seven years. Cam did not relish telling her the news.

He sat, thankful for Cowden's offer of informality. He could be himself here. He could be a friend, talking to another about a mutual friend instead of being the officer. He would return the Duke's gift with the very best of Fortis: stories of Fortis in camp, how well his men liked him, how well the other officers respected him, the brilliance of his strategies, the successes of his warcraft, his daring in the Battle of Alma, the one preceding Balaclava. No father could be prouder. No friend could be luckier than to have Fortis by his side. In truth, it felt good to reminisce this way, to remember Fortis as he'd been in life with someone who knew him well.

'And at Balaclava?' the Duke asked at last, too sharp to overlook the one omission in the tales Cam had so carefully chosen. Some of the elation the stories had created ebbed from the room. 'All that brilliance, all that courage, could not save him?'

Cam shook his head ruefully. 'It was a series of missteps from the beginning. Raglan should have been using the cavalry to cut off the Russians at the Causeway, but he refused to take action.' Fortis had been furious at the Lieutenant General's refusal to put the Light Brigade into play. 'Major General Cardigan was angry by the time he saw the Russians going after our cannon. He might have stood around all day while others saw action, but he would be damned if he would hold back his troops while the Russians stole our guns off the ridge.' There had been other mistakes, too. Like sending the note for permission to strike with a messenger who believed too heartily in what a mounted cavalry could do and there'd been a mistake in the route Cardigan used. They should not have cut through the valley. That route had drawn the fire of the entire Russian army. 'Fortis was ready for the charge. He was magnificent on that stallion of his, his sabre overhead as he called his troops to him. We were the right flank, the second line.' Cam let the euphoria of battle fill him as he told the tale, how they'd driven through the Russian artillery, how they'd persisted, meeting the Russian cavalry in combat, pushing them back. There had been heady moments, glorious moments! He would not forget how gallant, how fearless his friend had looked. But they hadn't the strength or numbers to hold the position. They'd been forced to withdraw.

Some of the euphoria let him. 'We took the worst of it in retreat, in my opinion. We couldn't withdraw to safety. That's when Fortis fell.' When had Fortis realised they'd crossed the valley of death? That the mission was impossible? That they might have achieved smashing through the lines, but that victory was their very downfall. They were exposed with no hope of shelter.

'The papers said only one hundred and ninety-three returned,' Cowden said quietly, reverently. 'That fifty-five of the Fourth's regiment were killed and four officers.' But not Lieutenant Colonel Lord George Paget, or Major Camden Lithgow. Guilt swamped him for having survived.

'Yes,' Cam replied sombrely. Six-hundred-and-seventy-three men had charged the valley. He'd been one of the one hundred and ninety-three. He still grappled with that reality. How was it that he'd emerged unscathed while those around him fell—officers, good men who knew how to handle themselves in battle—cut down while he had not a scratch? No one could explain it, not the generals who had sent him home, not the priests who'd prayed with him over the dead and now he had to explain to the Duke of Cowden. Why had he lived when Fortis had fallen?

The Duke shook his head and put a fatherly hand on his leg. 'No, don't do that. Don't blame yourself for being spared. At least one of you lived to come home and tell the tales. Fortis was a soldier. He knew the risks. He embraced them.'

Cowden drew a breath to ask the only question that remained. 'Did you see the body?'

'I saw him fall. He was only a few yards away from me. Khan, his big black, went down. The Russians shot his horse out from under him.' Perhaps a horse had made a difference. Perhaps that was why he'd survived. Cam and his strong grey stallion, Hengroen, had both remained miraculously intact. 'I pushed towards Fortis the moment I saw.' Cam remembered turning Hengroen towards the fallen Khan, but he couldn't get close; it was an impossible horizontal movement in a vertical charge. All around him, men and horses were falling, blocking his way. He could do nothing but push forward.

'And afterwards? Did you see his body then?' Cowden pressed. It was the question Cam didn't want to answer, a question that raised all his old hopes and fears when it came to Fortis—that somehow Fortis had survived, that he wasn't dead.

'No, Your Grace, I did not. I had orders to carry out and there was…difficulty, shall we say? Afterwards. The British army does not accept defeat without placing blame.'

A little light of misguided hope flared in Cowden's eyes. Cam had been prepared for this even before Cowden uttered the words, 'Do you think there's a chance…?' He let the words drift off.

'No, Your Grace, I do not. Four hundred men and horses were slaughtered. I saw him go down in impossible circumstances.' Cam looked down at his hands and swallowed hard against the lump in his throat. 'I know what you're thinking. That Fortis was strong enough, canny enough to survive. I thought it, too. For months I hoped. When things settled, I scoured the countryside every chance I got. It was winter, it was cold. I asked at huts and in little villages if anyone had nursed a wounded man.' He paused, remembering the desperate months of searching, of hoping and all the emotions that went with alternately experiencing intense hope followed by the intense grief of disappointment. There'd be a possible story in a village that only turned out to be someone else. Towards the end, he'd been drunk quite a bit of the time and bitter. It was not the proudest chapter in his life. He still cringed to think about it, embarrassed by his grief and his inability to manage it. The army had been embarrassed, too. He knew why he'd been sent home. In their opinion, he'd become a danger to himself and perhaps to others. He did not want to fuel such a disastrous hope for the Duke.

'It's been seven months, Your Grace. If I thought there was any hope left I would not have come home.' He would have found a way even if it meant desertion. The army had wanted him to go home sooner, but he'd refused, citing the difficulties of winter travels. He'd bought himself a little more time until finally the Major General had insisted he go home and recover before he shot someone by accident or himself on purpose. The latter was more likely. He'd got the gun as far as his head on two occasions.

Cowden smiled. 'Of course. Forgive me, I am a foolish old man.'

'And I was a foolish young one—there is nothing to forgive.' Cam returned the smile. 'We both loved him and we will miss him. Always.' He was just starting to accept that part, that his life would go on and Fortis would be with him in his heart. Maybe some day there would be peace along with that knowledge. But it would not be today.

Cowden drew a deep breath, steadying himself. 'Are you ready? Let's go tell the others.' He clapped a hand on Cam's shoulder. 'You've been very brave in coming here. I know it was not easy. You have your own grief to deal with. You and Fortis were close, like brothers.' Cam thought he detected a warning in that statement, that the Duke sensed he wasn't dealing or hadn't dealt sufficiently with his own grief. The Duke would be right.

Cowden peered at him with kind eyes. 'You're a soldier just like Fortis. I can see you want to be with your men far more than you want to be here in London. But don't underestimate the power of being home, Cam. Whatever you may think of him, your grandfather will be pleased to see you.'

It was technically true. His grandfather *would* be glad to see him, but not in the way Cowden meant. Not in the way of an elder family patriarch affectionately welcoming home the returning, youthful branch of his family tree. His grandfather would be glad to see him because of what Cam could do for the family. That was as far as his grandfather's affections went, for any of them. The old man simply wasn't capable of love.

Chapter Four

The old man was, however, capable of a great deal of other things. Cam made his bow at four in the afternoon to his grandfather in the Earl of Aylsbury's elegant pale blue Louis XV drawing room with its elaborate cornice work and gold leafing. By eight o'clock that evening, a family dinner, ostensibly in his honour, had been instigated with the best china laid out— his grandmother's favourite Colandine pattern by Primavesi and Son in Cardiff blue, along with the very best wines —his *grandfather's* favourite, the Chateau Margaux Bordeaux— and the best guests which included, not surprisingly, the Beauforts and their daughter, Caroline. By the end of the evening, Cam had an appointment to take Caroline out driving the next day and to escort her to a musicale the next. Everything was playing out just as he'd imagined it would. There were no surprises here. Just expectations. And he was meeting them all.

'We'll have a grand time, now that you're home.' Caroline smiled over her shoulder as he helped her with her wrap in the hall. The long evening was finally coming to a close. 'There are so many entertainments this year. Mademoiselle Rachel will be performing at the St James's Theatre in June...'

Cam did not hear the rest. Out there in the world, men were dying defending British interests abroad, dying to help their country build an empire and influence the world. In his estimation it was a noble legacy. Those lives had purpose. They were fighting for something, but was that something nothing more than the preservation of a life filled with the minutiae of looking forward to the talent of Mademoiselle Rachel treading the boards? It seemed an unfair trade. Surely there was more to life than the one depicted and acted out by Caroline Beaufort? He'd been in London less than a day and he was already itching to leave. The months of his leave stretched before him like an eternity. Today, he'd taken his first steps into the wasteland he'd imagined last night.

The thought of last night prompted a smile.

What was his nameless lover doing right now? Then the smile faded. Was she dancing for another? No, he wouldn't think of her like that— dancing with her veils, enticing another man. He would remember her as distinctly his. He would remember the way she looked, arching into him, her eyes wide as pleasure took her, the little sounds she made. She'd been as honest and open in her expression of pleasure as she had been in her nudity.

Caroline thought the smile was for her. 'I am glad you're home, Cam.' *Cam.* That was new, as was the possessive way she held on to his arm and both set off alarms. Before, such a confession from her would have been accompanied by maidenly blushes. Tonight it was not, a reminder that she was not a shy maiden any more, no longer a debutante of eighteen, but a woman of twenty-one who was in her third Season.

'I will go back to the Crimea in a few months. I am not home for good,' Cam reminded her with a polite smile. He was already counting the days. His men needed him and he would continue to look for Fortis. He would do it discreetly this time. If Fortis was dead, he *would* find him—a body, a grave, anything to bring closure to that tragic day in Balaclava.

Despite his counsel to Cowden, Cam wasn't willing to give up until he had proof. Here in England, he was too far away to be effectual. He'd written letters and made enquiries, but it wasn't the same as being on the ground. He didn't want to be at parties, wasting his days with nothing when there was even the smallest chance Fortis might be out there, struggling to survive while he drank champagne. Cam pushed back the memories. Not now. He didn't want to think about them here in front of everyone, people who didn't understand what it meant to go to war.

Caroline trailed a well-manicured finger down his sleeve, oblivious to his pain. 'Perhaps going back is not a foregone conclusion,' she purred. 'Maybe we will find you a reason to stay this time.' The message was clear. There was a new enemy that demanded his attention right in front of him. Caroline had grown bold indeed. And why shouldn't she be bold? She was not panicked she'd been out for three Seasons. Her family and the Lithgows, through his grandfather, had an understanding. She was to marry him. It was an understanding she'd been raised on and never had reason to doubt. The entrance hall of his grandfather's home was no place to raise those doubts. So,

Cam bent over her hand with a gallant smile and wished her goodnight.

Would he do it? Would he, like Fortis, marry a woman of his family's choosing and simply leave her behind, going back to his old life as if nothing had happened? Or would his family demand he resign his commission? Would he do that, too—give up his career and his choice in order to marry and live the life the family wanted for him? Or would he refuse to marry at all? To refuse his family and the Earl was no small thing. As far as he knew, no one had refused his grandfather in Cam's lifetime. Not his uncle, the heir, or his father. To what benefit would such a refusal be? What would be worth refusing the family and all the financial and social support that went with it?

That night, Cam dreamt quite pleasantly of his Indian girl, his secret life, his last adventure before falling into the abyss of the London Season. In the days that followed, filled with routs and parties, and Caroline clinging to his arm as if he were already hers, it was comforting to think of his dancer out there in the world somewhere. He thought of conversations he would have with her. He talked to her in his head the way he'd talked to her that night, confessing what he had confessed to no other. Perhaps if she were by his side instead of Caroline Beaufort, the magic of the Season would be restored.

The two women could not be more different: Caroline with her blonde paleness and penchant for tradition and correctness; his dancer with her toast-coloured skin and dark eyes and sensual boldness. Cam imagined her dressed in a fine ballgown, with jewels glittering at her neck, and he wondered what she'd think of the Season. Would she think it silly like he did? Or would she see the enchantment? In short, she became a fantasy of the ideal, the perfection of beauty and companionship—giving all to him while demanding nothing in return. It was a harmless fantasy. He could imagine all he liked. There was no chance of the fantasy being realised.

'I cannot marry Wenderly.' Pavia stood before her father's desk of polished Indian rosewood, her shoulders straight, defiance coursing through her veins. She had made this argument before, only this time the outcome would be different. This time she had leverage.

'Wenderly is an earl.' Her father glanced at her mother, his eyes pleading with her to intercede, but her mother had launched a subtle rebellion of her own and refused to come to his rescue. He was on his own. One arranged marriage in the family was enough, her mother's posture seemed to say. 'He is highly placed in society.' Pavia knew this argument of her father's well. 'You would be a countess. Your son would be an earl when Wenderly dies, which can't be more than seven to ten years in the waiting.' Leave it to her father to look at all angles, distasteful as they were. 'You will be a rich, young widow, able to pick her next husband.'

How like her father to assume there would be a next husband. For all his innovation in business, he lacked a certain creativity when it came to imagining a woman's life without a man beside her. She supposed to his balance-sheet-driven mind the deal looked acceptable, sustainable.

Pavia looked down at the fawn medallion woven in the Kashan carpet to hide her disgust. Minimum input, seven years, maybe less, and then maximum output to her benefit in her father's eyes. She would be twenty-five, maybe twenty-eight. Not even thirty. But those seven years between now and then stretched before her interminably. Her father was assuming she'd survive them intact, mentally, emotionally. Her father was also assuming his numbers were right and Wenderly wasn't endowed with supernaturally long life. Her father was just as confident in Wenderly's demise as he was in the outcome of this conversation. He was going to win. It was the thing he did best: winning at all costs. And it had cost him plenty over the years, even if he couldn't see it.

Pavia knew her father was not concerned about the cost of her rebellion. He viewed these arguments as a temporary unpleasantness between them that would end with her capitulation and the complete return of his wife's loyalty, something he'd always taken for granted. As for herself, Pavia knew differently. This would not end well for him. She played her ace.

'You don't seem to understand. This is not an issue of wanting to. I *cannot* marry Wenderly. I no longer meet his marital criteria. I am not a virgin.' She would never forget the silence that followed her statement. It was an expensive ace, not only in its acquisition, which had cost her the most valuable thing a young woman possessed by society's standards, but also in the damage such acknowledgement would do to the inner workings of her family. It would positively cleave a chasm between her and her father.

In truth, the beginnings of that chasm were already there and had been ever since Pavia had realised she was nothing but a pawn for her father to use in the advancement of his ambitions. This would merely widen that chasm. The wedding negotiations with Wenderly had been a start, making it impossible to avoid what had already been the truth: at some point, she'd ceased to matter beyond being a placeholder for him, the face of his fortune. It had been this way ever since they'd returned to England. Now it had become a conflict that caught her mother in the middle—between a husband who wanted his wife's loyalty and a daughter who wanted the same.

Her father's eyes glinted dangerously, his voice razor-sharp. 'Who? Tell me who and I will see that he answers for this on the field of honour.' Of course that would be his first response—his first concern was always for appearances. How would this look to the public? What would people think? She should not be surprised. And yet, it stung that his first concern was not for her, even if that concern came with anger.

Pavia did not flinch. 'I do not know his

name.' It was not a lie and she was glad for the truth. It would protect her from the guilt of dishonesty and it would protect her lover's life. Images of his strong, glorious, well-muscled body came to mind. She pushed them away along with dangerous thoughts. It had occurred to her fleetingly on the walk back to her inn that it wouldn't be impossible to find her lover. She knew the colour of his uniform, had some idea of his rank. She could go to the military offices at Whitehall and make enquiries. No. That was not what she'd promised him or herself. One night only. There were many reasons for that precaution and this was one of them. She did not want him to face her father at twenty paces for her folly. Her father, even at forty-five, was still deadly with a pistol.

Only now, when he'd been denied a victim, did he direct his attention towards her. 'You ruined yourself to spite me? Turned yourself into a Jezebel as part of this temper tantrum of yours? Do you know what you've done? What man will have you now? And you've ruined this family.' Her father's anger rumbled near the surface. 'All my life, I have worked for our family and in one instant you have destroyed it.' It was a visible struggle to deny his temper free rein. Pavia did not think she ever recalled him being this furious. He pushed his hand through his hair. 'Perhaps Wenderly can be duped.' He gestured to her mother. 'Sabita, you have to fix this. There must be some female trick to create the impression of virginity.'

Pavia froze. Her father meant to go through with it. If he did, her sacrifice would be for naught. She'd risked herself, brought conflict to her family, all for nothing. And she'd have to sustain the lie. She had not counted on this. She exchanged a quick glance with her mother, although she doubted there would be much hope there. Her mother would be just as mad as her father.

Her mother's dark eyes held hers for a moment and then flitted away. 'Wenderly isn't the only peer on the market this Season,' her mother offered. Pavia opened her mouth to protest. She didn't want to marry Wenderly, but that didn't mean she wanted to marry someone else either. Her mother slid her a stern look that said they would talk later. Pavia wasn't fooled. When that conversation happened, her mother would do the talking. She would do the listening. 'What is all your money worth, Oliver, if it can't buy your daughter a husband? Surely your fortune can buy more than a middling earl.' It was subtly done, the comment a compliment and a challenge. Her mother was a master when she chose to exert her influence. It was a choice she seldom made these days. England had beaten her down, changed her as it had changed her father. They'd been a different family in India.

Her father's face became contemplative. Her mother smiled and pressed her argument softly. 'There are two marquises and a duke hunting brides, and there are other earls desperate enough for funds to even look towards American brides. They'd be more than happy to take your money and overlook such a little thing as the lack of a maidenhead if their bride can keep a roof over the manor and claim English blood at the same time.'

'It's a slim field,' her father mused, not liking the odds.

'Slim for others, perhaps. But no one's bank account can match yours and your daughter is beautiful,' her mother responded smoothly. 'Besides, Wenderly was no challenge for a man like yourself. Aren't you always saying never take the first offer? Catching a husband isn't much different than selling tea.'

Her father glanced at her mother who gave a small, imperceptible nod of encouragement. 'All right,' he said with an infrequent smile.

'We shall go fishing, one last time. Draw up a list of the eligible men and we'll see what can be done. We'll need an invite to the Banfields' ball in a couple weeks. It's the most lavish entertainment this early in the Season. Pavia will need a gown that is equal to it. Get it ordered early so it will be done.'

Pavia smiled, careful not to betray her sense of victory. It wouldn't be her fault if those gentlemen her mother spoke of didn't come up to scratch. She had won. But she was acutely aware she'd only won time. Still, anything could happen in those precious weeks.

'You betrayed me.' Her mother glided into her room without so much as a knock and shut the door behind her, dismissing the maid with a flick of her hand. She could be imperious when she wanted to be. Once a princess, always a princess.

'He's the one who has betrayed us,' Pavia argued. She'd been expecting this conversation and she was ready. 'He wants to sell me to the highest bidder. Are you willing to let him do that? Wenderly is an old man with perverse tastes.'

'A woman must marry, Pavia,' her mother snapped. 'Whether she likes it or not, she is nothing without a man. She has no money, no shelter, no status. Nothing with which she can protect herself. It's not right, but it's reality. What do you think happens to you without a husband if your father withdraws his protection?' Her mother was furious.

'This is not the Middle Ages,' Pavia protested, hurt that her mother hadn't sided with her immediately. Surely her mother saw the injustice of the situation?

Her mother sat at the edge of her bed, her voice quiet. 'Your actions do not endear me to him. I had one job and that was to raise his child—a beautiful, obedient girl who would be a credit to him and help him advance his position in the world. I have failed.' That silenced Pavia. She hadn't thought of it like that. She'd thought only of what the arrangement with Wenderly meant to her.

'I wish we were in India, with Uncle, like it used to be. I don't know how you bear it.' Pavia huffed. 'Why don't we go? Surely Father wouldn't care if we went? We mean nothing to him, just chess pieces to move around his board.' She searched her mother's face for guidance. 'How do you stand it? So far from home, so far from your family?'

'Your father and I complete each other,

Pavia. *Dher aham prithvi tvam.* If I am the sky, you are the earth. People change over time. Perhaps he is not the same man I married, but he is still the man I am married to. A wife stands by her husband. My brother made this marriage for me in good faith that I would be provided for and I have been. I want for nothing. I would not shame my brother by returning to his palace.'

'But what about love?'

'Love is only one thing to build a marriage on and sometimes love alone is not enough. There are other things that matter, too. Surely you don't believe in fairy tales, Pavia?' Her mother was unrelenting.

'No, not fairy tales, but marriage should be reasonable, mutual, at least.' How could she believe in fairy tales when her mother had left her home to follow a husband halfway around the world who had no time for her? Who was always gone, leaving her alone in a strange country?

'It can start that way, but things do not always go as planned.' She reached for Pavia's hand. 'You blame your father for too much. He didn't understand how difficult it would be for us here.' She smiled softly.

'We had so much hope. When we came to

England, he had already made his first fortune. You were twelve and we were naïve. We thought we could throw money at our obstacles and they would dissolve. He bought this house, then the estate in the country. He sent you to Mrs Finlay's. He gave us all the trappings of nobility. When that was not greeted with acceptance, he worked harder, made another fortune and then another. But nothing changed. I was not invited anywhere. I have not become the great hostess he wanted. He wanted London at our feet and he didn't get it. I failed him, but he has another chance through you.' She paused. 'I just want you to understand why he pushes so hard.'

'You shouldn't have to justify his failings to me.' Pavia rose from the bed. She would never be as tolerant, as forgiving, as her mother, nor would she be as accepting. 'I'm not like you. I don't want a marriage of convenience to a man I have to make excuses for. I want to be free. I want to go places and see things. Women can do that now, Mother. The railway is opening up travel like never before. The world is changing.'

'Not really, it isn't. Have you not heard a word I've said?' Her mother sighed. 'I love you and I want you to be safe and cared for. What about the Marquis of Chatham? He seems like a tolerant man. Perhaps Wenderly was not the best choice, but you are safe from him only if you can bring another lord up to scratch. Don't waste this chance, Pavia. And for heaven's sake, don't fall for the lie these modern women portray in their pamphlets. Don't believe for a minute that you are free. A woman alone is never free. She is in constant danger. The sooner you understand that, the better. Now, let's talk about a gown for the Banfields' ball.'

Chapter Five

The Banfields' ball went down better with champagne. Cam grabbed another flute from a passing tray, adeptly trading his empty one for a full. It was a move he'd perfected over the last two weeks—weeks filled with entertainments like this one, each event grander than the previous as the official opening of the Season drew closer. That opening was so close now, the Banfields' ball might be considered a soft open for the festivities that would soon be underway. Everyone who was considered anyone of importance for this Season was here tonight, doing one last dress rehearsal, the diamonds brighter, the dresses whiter, the smiles wider. Even the ballroom itself seemed to glitter with a sense of its own self-importance: chandeliers from the Venetian masters, the slim Ionic-styled columns framing the ballroom wrapped in elegant swathes of shimmering pale rose silk and white roses everywhere. Out on the dance floor, Caroline swirled by in a froth of ivory and pink skirts on the arm of a young, but financially disadvantaged viscount's heir. She flashed Cam a smile. He raised his glass in salute and drained it, his eyes already roving the room, searching out a footman with a tray. Ah, there was one! He moved to swap flutes, a low, familiar chuckle erupting behind him.

'Easy there, soldier, don't you think you've had enough? You'll be too foxed by midnight to take the lovely Miss Beaufort in for supper.'

'That's the point.' Cam laughed, turning to shake hands with an old friend. 'Sutton Keynes, what brings you to town? I thought you never left Newmarket these days.'

Tall and immaculately turned out, Sutton looked far more like a gentleman tonight than the dairyman he aspired to be. One would never guess he spent his days mucking around in camel stalls. Sutton shrugged evasively. 'I had business in town. Uncle is at it again, another one of his crazy schemes to see me wed. Best to nip that in the bud before the Season heats up.' It was said jovially, but Sutton's eyes were tired and his mouth was tight. Cam wondered if there was something more serious at play this time. Ever since he'd known Sutton back in school, Sutton's uncle had been, well, odd to say the least. 'Nothing I can't handle, of course,' Sutton added and then lowered his voice. 'I heard about Fortis. I am sorry. Is that the only reason you're home?' He nodded towards the dance floor. 'Miss Beaufort grows lovelier every year. Your grandfather certainly knows how to pick them.' The mechanics of the arrangement were an open secret between Cam and his friends.

'Then my grandfather can marry her.' Cam swallowed the contents of the icy flute whole. Damn, the glasses were holding less and less as the night wore on. Either that or he was emptying them faster.

'Your grandmother might have something to say about that,' Sutton joked to take the acerbic edge off his comment, but his voice was low when he spoke again, invoking all the privacy that could be mustered in a ballroom. 'So, is it the match you're opposed to, old friend, or the way it came into being? Caroline is as good a choice as any and better than most.' Sutton paused. 'Unless, of course, you have someone else in mind?' Images of his dark-eyed dancer swam in his mind. Cam pushed them away. He didn't want to think of her tonight, not when such images could only serve to torture him with reminders of what he couldn't have.

'There is no one else.' Cam infused his words with a sense of finality. He wanted to move away from this avenue of conversation, but Sutton seemed determined.

'What if there was someone else? What if you went to your grandfather and said, "Here's who I want to marry"?' Sutton surveyed the ballroom. 'Granted, it might be difficult this year. There's not much to pick from in the way of outstanding catches. There's the usual milieu of grasping gentry, baron's daughters and such. That won't impress your grandfather. But...' Sutton's voice picked up a tempo of excitement '...Endicott's last daughter is out this year. I think there's been an Endicott girl on the market every year since we came up, poor man.'

'I don't want an Endicott girl.' Cam shook his head.

'Well, there are only two viscounts' daughters and one daughter of a marquis this year. People are saying it will be a bloodbath, the three of them will make rutting stags of us all.' Sutton took another sip of champagne, his glass still half-full. 'There is a Cit heiress, though.' He raised his dark eyebrows. 'That should make things interesting. She's the only child of Oliver Honeysett, the tea merchant. He's made it clear he wants a title and is willing to pay for it. His fortune would keep a man in horses for life.' Sutton calculated everything in horses, or camels. The man should have been a Bedouin. 'Of course, you don't need the money, but plenty of these fellows do. It's always interesting how that dilemma plays out,' Sutton commented neutrally.

Cam didn't respond. He eyed his empty glass and sighed. 'It doesn't matter, Sut, they're all the same. This year, last year, next year. They're all the same. Every girl, every night, every ball, all the same.' It had taken coming home to really see that. He'd been gone from London for seven years and he might as well as not been. Nothing was different. The routine was the same, even the balls were the same. He went to the same places, saw the same people. Men's trouser legs were a bit narrower, but, other than that, sameness permeated everything and it was suffocating him like a stock tied too tight. Even now, he had the sensation that he couldn't breathe.

Across the room, a ripple shifted the crowd as the dance ended and couples walked back to their groups, new pairs drifting on to the floor.

It was the flash of turquoise that caught his eye, bright and vibrant, and Cam's eye riveted on it. Turquoise and dark hair, both a striking contrast against the pale palette of ivories and creams and blondeness around him. It was enough to capture his attention and to recall the memories he'd been trying to subdue all evening. 'Who is that?' Cam gestured with his flute. Maybe someone new to hold his interest was exactly what he needed, someone to replace his dancer in his fantasies.

'You have good taste.' Sutton followed his gaze. 'It must be all that time abroad. That is the tea merchant's daughter, our richest, most controversial prize of the Season.'

'Because she's a Cit? One would think we'd be more progressive these days. If we can power steam ships and run an empire, surely we can broaden our minds about social class.' Good lord, the champagne was starting to take effect. His tongue was looser than a Covent Garden whore.

Sutton laughed. 'It's all about self-protection and you know it, Cam. People think if we let everyone in, the peerage would mean nothing and we'd be useless. But that's not the problem with her. I dare say most would make an allowance for the Honeysetts in order to get their hands on all that money. Lord knows the aristocracy needs it.' He dropped his voice even lower. 'It's her breeding, I'm talking about. Society is uncomfortable with the fact that her mother's Indian. She's a mixed-blood heiress and society has no idea what to do with her.'

'Society had better get used to it. Empires by nature are not homogenous.' Cam couldn't keep the disgust out of his voice. The colour of someone's skin should not determine their value. He thought of his dancer and the leers men had cast her in the tavern, and the disregard he'd feared they would show her without his protection.

'True enough,' Sutton agreed. 'We're seeing more and more of that as the empire expands— wealthy men marrying abroad and bringing their children home, only to discover England doesn't want them. They're trapped between worlds.'

Cam's heart went out to the heiress. The Season must be torture for her, knowing that no matter how much money her father had, her antecedents would be held against her, weighed against access to that fortune. The girl would never truly know if she was appreciated for herself. 'I want to meet her,' Cam said, the decisiveness clearing the fuzziness of his head.

The request stunned Sutton. 'I've only met her once, last week at the Haverfords' rout.'

'Good. Then she'll remember you.' Cam made a forward motion with his hand. 'Lead on.'

'It won't do you any good,' Sutton argued as they wove through the crowd. 'Rumour has it, she's nearly engaged to Wenderly.'

'Wenderly?' Cam's eyebrows shot up. 'Is he still around? The man must be nearly sixty. I'd think a widow would be more his sort.'

'Well, you'd be wrong,' Sutton said over his shoulder. 'He's got a taste for virgins these days.'

They approached the heiress's little court from the side so that she was turned away from them. The crowd parted to make room for the newcomers and Cam stood back, waiting for Sutton to make the introductions.

'Miss Honeysett, a pleasure to see you again.'

'Mr Keynes! How good to see *you*. How is your camel dairy?' she effused with genuine sincerity in a voice that held notes of the familiar, the smoke of it, the soft intimacy of it, sending a ripple of awareness through Cam.

'My dairy is fine, how kind of you to remember.' Sutton bowed over her gloved hand.

'I have a friend with me tonight who would like to meet you. May I introduce you? Miss Pavia Honeysett, this is Major Camden Lithgow, lately of the Fourth Queen's Own Hussars, although he's not in uniform tonight as he's home on leave.'

Cam stepped forward, his gaze locking on Miss Honeysett for the first time. He stalled, barely hearing Sutton finish the introduction. His heart pounded hard. The room seemed to spin either from champagne or from the shock of a fantasy come to life. His mind grappled with the enormous improbability of it all. After weeks of wishing for it, his dark-eyed dancer was here.

He was here. Pavia froze, barely remembering to extend her hand, so intent was she on his face—a face she'd studied intimately in the dark, a face she'd committed to memory. Only now the face had a name: Major Camden Lithgow. *'Enchanté,'* Pavia murmured automatically.

Mrs Finlay's academy had done its job with years of drills to help protect against unnerving circumstances. Perhaps he wouldn't recognise her. It was a short-lived thought. The sharp look of shock in his eyes said he remembered her quite well. He'd not expected to find her here either.

'The pleasure is all mine.' His eyes lingered on her, full of memories and questions even as he delivered that wickedly wrapped double entendre. In the world beyond Cam Lithgow's broad shoulder, the musicians struck up the beginnings of a dance. She was caught off guard, but Cam took advantage. 'Might I hope you are free for the waltz?' She was envious how quickly he'd recovered his aplomb while she was still wallowing in stunned surprise.

'Absolutely.' She took his arm and let him whisk her away to the dance floor and whatever privacy they might find there. It was the perfect short-term remedy. They would be seen, but not heard.

'You were not a dancer like those other girls that night.' He wasted no time, his hand at her waist, moving them into the waltz as he began his interrogation.

'No.' She was breathless as they took the first turn, the speed of his pace perhaps akin to the speed with which his mind was working, sorting, as she was, through the surprise and the facts. 'I was not supposed to see you again.'

'Nor I you, yet here we are, dancing again,

but in very different circumstances,' the Major said tautly.

Pavia lifted her chin defiantly. 'Here we are, but it changes nothing. I am not asking you to claim a previous association with me. In fact, I'd prefer you didn't.' Never mind that she still dreamed about him at night, that he, nameless as he'd been, had somehow managed to imprint himself on her heart, on her mind, in that short time. She knew now she'd never be rid of him.

'I know.' His blue eyes narrowed, fixed on her in a piercing cobalt stare. 'My friend tells me you're engaged to Wenderly.' He paused, perhaps considering that piece of information, and her mouth went dry. Did he know she'd been a virgin? Would he put the pieces together? Would he be angry? She didn't want his anger. Even now, her body thrilled to the feel of his hand at her waist, of his hand in hers, the weight of his gaze on her, things she'd never thought to experience again.

'It's a possibility.' Pavia was careful with her words. She couldn't risk him saying otherwise if it came up in casual conversation at his clubs.

He arched blonde brows in doubt. 'Truly? Does the earl tolerate such liberal behaviour in his fiancée? Does he know you dance in taverns and seduce men in their chambers?'

Pavia froze him with a stare. Scolding him silently for such crassness was the only recourse open to her. She could not plead it was only the one time or he would know her secret and he would know she'd used him. But it sat poorly with her to let him get away with thinking what she'd done with him was habitual. 'That was one night out of time. It is best we forget about it,' she said tightly. 'If we don't acknowledge it, it is as if it never happened.'

'Of course, if that is what you want. You have nothing to fear from me. Your secret is safe.' But Pavia thought she detected a shadow of disappointment as he reassured her. 'I won't be in London long, just until my leave ends in August. I will rejoin my troops in the Crimea. Don't worry London is large. We needn't encounter one another again.' He smiled, but it was not warm. 'I won't be home for a long while then. If ever.' He *was* angry. There was a coldness to his words as the dance ended and he escorted her back to her court.

So it was done. Her fantasy had come full circle as his broad-shouldered back walked away from her, swallowed up in the crush of the ballroom as best it could be. Major Lithgow was taller than most, his hair brighter than most. Pavia was certain she could find him in any room if she looked. She could not look. It would do no good to torture herself with looking. A hundred questions had gone unasked during their waltz. The less she knew of him the better, the harder it would be to find him. He was not an acceptable substitute for Wenderly or for the other titled gentlemen she was supposed to be chasing. He was a military officer of some rank and respect, but he did not come with the title her father coveted. He would say she could have any officer. There was nothing special there. She had to give the major up.

'Miss Honeysett, I believe this dance is mine.' A wheat-haired man of respectable height and impeccable dress bowed before her, his eyes crinkling at the corners as he smiled, confident in himself and his appeal.

Pavia returned the smile of the only Marquis out wife-hunting this Season. 'Yes, I believe it is.' Beyond him, she caught her father's eye and nod of approval. And beyond her father was the golden head of Major Camden Lithgow, a pretty blonde beside him, her hand on his arm, her face laughing up at him, her body leaning close as if they were long acquainted and easy with one another. The sight riveted Pavia with a surge of irrational, jealous anger. How dare he! How dare he what? How dare he do exactly as she'd bid him and forget her?

Only there was no forgetting, was there? He knew that woman and she knew him. Quite well. Their body language suggested a history between them. No wonder he hadn't flinched at her request to forget their night. He'd hardly want the pretty blonde with him to know such a thing.

'Ahem.' The Marquis smiled again, revealing straight white teeth as he attempted to reclaim her attention with a compliment. 'I have been looking forward to this dance all evening.'

Pavia gave herself a mental scold. She needed to focus. This was a man to bring up to scratch. It shouldn't be too hard; he was thirty-five, needed to marry and he was penniless—penniless enough to overlook her antecedents in exchange for a fortune.

'As have I,' Pavia lied smoothly and laid her hand on his sleeve.

Chapter Six

She wanted nothing to do with him! The thought still rankled a week later. It didn't help that for a girl who'd claimed to dismiss him, she was everywhere. Cam couldn't go to a musicale, a ball or a sailing party without her being there. So much for the idea that London was a big place. He couldn't seem to avoid her. Worst of all, she'd grown an appendage otherwise known as the Marquis of Chatham. She was on his arm, laughing, smiling, entrancing. Chatham was clearly smitten with her. Today was no different. She was dressed in a day gown of simple white muslin with a square neck and tiers of ruffles at the hem and charming Chatham effortlessly.

'It seems Wenderly has some competition,' Cam remarked drily to Sutton from their vantage point at the Countess of Claremont's Richmond picnic. Caroline and the others in their group had wandered off a short distance to view the river, giving him a few minutes alone with Sutton.

Pavia and Chatham had wandered off on their own somewhere too, he'd noted, and the thought sent a hard surge of *something* through him. There were only so many things two people stole away on their own to do. Hot images of their one night swam to the fore followed by a bolt of undeniable jealousy. Had Chatham kissed her yet? Did he, too, know the sensual press of her lips, how she moved her whole body into a kiss? The way her breasts felt pressed against one's chest? Of course, she'd been naked then, naked for him. Irrationally, he wanted to be the only one she was naked for, the only one she kissed like that.

'And Caroline?' Sutton asked rather bluntly, breaking into his thoughts. 'Does she have some competition as well?'

Cam shot his friend a hard stare. 'What the hell is that supposed to mean?'

Sutton chuckled. 'It means you haven't been able to take your eyes off Pavia Honeysett since the Banfields' ball.' Sutton cocked his head, considering. 'Nor she you, I think. She watches you when you're not looking.' Sutton plucked an orange from the basket on the blanket and began to peel.

She watched him? Cam schooled his features into bland neutrality, careful not to give away any reaction as to how that made him feel. A schoolboy exhilaration shot through him. He'd laugh at himself if Sutton wasn't already doing it for him. He was twenty-eight and a soldier who'd seen the world. He was well past the crushes and infatuations of a green boy, yet here he was, fantasising about a woman he couldn't have. 'So, she's decided to go to the highest bidder?' Cam asked, definitively forgoing a response to Sutton's question.

'I think that's what her father has decided,' Sutton replied evasively.

Under other circumstances, Cam would find little to dislike about Chatham. The man was an excellent horseman, a solid marksman who responsibly held his seat in the House of Lords and kept a superior wine cellar. He supposed women found the Marquis attractive in other ways. He was tall and kept a clean, well-tailored appearance. He would, indeed, be an extraordinary catch for a Cit's daughter. She would be able to vault to the top of society's rungs with such a marriage.

'She won't get a higher bid than that.' Cam

couldn't keep the despondency out of his voice. He couldn't compete with the Marquis. He'd never before felt any lack in his assets. He had a comfortable income, a small manor house in Little Trull in Somerset, which he never visited, political connections through his grandfather and opportunities to use those connections if he ever left the military. But those assets paled in comparison to what a marquis could offer, even one in financial straits. And yet she looked at *him*.

Cam rose from the blanket, feeling suddenly restless. 'I'm going for a walk.' He needed space. Perhaps if he had a moment's privacy he could regain perspective. He felt as if he hadn't had a moment to breathe on his own since he'd been home. His days and his nights were filled with family and the family's plans for him. There'd been dinners and parties, and councils with his grandfather and his father, like the one this morning before he'd set out for Richmond, only this time Caroline's father had been there, too. It had been conducted pleasantly enough. No one was putting his thumbs to the screws. But the message was the same: It was time to make the engagement official. Caroline had waited patiently through three

Seasons. It was hinted that she'd even passed on other offers.

Cam *did* feel guilt over that. It was not only his future at stake, but hers. He would have a future if he married her or not. Men had choices. Women did not. Caroline was counting on him. He was stealing her best years, her best choices while he deliberately procrastinated on a marriage he didn't want. If he was any sort of gentleman at all, he'd marry her now or cut her loose in order to give her this Season. Cam prided himself as a man who knew his own mind and acted on it. But he also prided himself on being a man of honour and responsibility. He knew and did his duty. It was something the military had instilled in him as much as his grandfather's sense of familial loyalty had. Only now, the two were in conflict. To do his duty meant not standing up for himself. But to stand up for himself sacrificed duty and family. It was an untenable situation to be in.

Cam took long strides into the trees bordering the picnic ground, leaving behind the white canopies on the bluff and the merry sounds of laughter and conversation. There would be silence in the trees. Maybe even solutions. If not solutions, perhaps a chance to accept what must be and come to terms with it. He wouldn't be the first gentleman to make an arranged marriage. If only it were as simple as logic made it out to be.

The Marquis was the logical choice. He was taken with her, Pavia knew. He was intrigued even. He'd shown himself to be an intelligent man and a sincere one. He might not draw her eye in a room, as Camden Lithgow did, but he was not unattractive and he would fulfil all her father's requirements. In that, the Marquis of Chatham far outstripped even Lord Wenderly. Not that she'd ever planned on marrying him. Originally, she'd thought only to buy some time, pursue these other worthy gentlemen, then simply fail to bring them up to scratch and worm off the hook. In the three weeks since she'd made that deal with her father, things had changed. She needed to marry quickly. She might be pregnant. In fact, as the days went by, she was convinced there wasn't any 'might' about it.

Pavia excused herself from the small group under her picnic pavilion, asking discreetly for a moment of privacy. The smell of ham sandwiches had not set well with her stomach and that realisation set her nerves churning. Further proof that what she'd believed had been a reliable preventative had apparently held some flaws. Her sponges had failed.

She made it to a stand of trees before her stomach gave out. She wiped her mouth with a handkerchief and leaned against the sturdy trunk of a thick English oak. Despite her careful plans, her great attempt to escape Wenderly had gone awry in the extreme. Not only had she encountered her stranger again, she was pregnant with his child. If there was a silver lining, it was that she was beyond Wenderly now. But she was not beyond the Marquis, not if she moved quickly. They could be married by the end of June and first babies were often born early. Her father would have all he wanted and she would have escaped Wenderly, although she would not have freedom. She would still be tied to a man.

Oh, heavens! What was she thinking? Pavia let out a deep breath, trying to calm herself. She felt sick and clammy, her pulse erratic. Not all of it was to blame on the ham sandwiches. One lie always led to another. If she trapped the Marquis in marriage, she would have to sustain the lie for ever. She would steal his right to an heir of his own blood by foisting a bastard on him, *if* the baby was a boy. If it was a girl, would the lie matter any less? This was despicable thinking. A life was a life and a lie was a lie. The Marquis was a good man. She'd seen the decency in him. He did not deserve to be drawn into her tangle. She could not do that to him, but if she didn't, what became of her?

Her mind drifted to another man and another plan, a more honest one albeit more difficult. What if she told Major Lithgow about the baby? Would he marry her? Did that help her cause? Her father would be furious, his plans entirely thwarted, but her honour and that of her child would be salvaged, perhaps even her freedom in some form. He was only here on leave. She would be on her own after that and a married woman had far more freedom than an unwed girl. But words like *trap* and *renege* came to mind. She didn't want to trap anyone, hurt anyone, but something had to be done and soon before there were no more choices.

She wiped her palms on her skirts, wishing for some cool water. She could speak with the Major today. He was here. He seemed to be everywhere these days, and always with the pretty blonde from the Banfields' ball. That was another consideration. Who else would be hurt if she told the Major? Would she be stealing another girl's beau? Another girl's hopes?

Her future? Marriage was serious business to the beauties of the *ton*.

There was a rustle and crunch behind her. Pavia startled. Someone was in the little woods with her. She turned, a hand already attempting to smooth her hair and restore her appearance.

'It's only me, Miss Honeysett.' Major Lithgow strode forward, his golden hair bright even under the dim canopy of the trees. His gait was easy and he was dressed immaculately in white-and-cream-striped trousers topped with a short blue-wool shooting jacket that brought out his eyes, but for all the ease in his stride, there was a disquiet about him and it touched her as it had in the room above the tavern. Suddenly, her troubles were no longer centre stage.

'Are you well, Major?' She stepped towards him, her hands outstretched.

'Why would I not be?' he answered, refusing her hands.

'You seemed sad. I thought perhaps you were thinking of your friend again,' Pavia replied honestly.

She felt his keen gaze take her in. 'Perhaps I should be asking you the same question. Are *you* well, Miss Honeysett?'

She managed a smile. 'I am fine now. I just needed some air.'

'We're already out of doors, Miss Honeysett. I suspect there is plenty of air at a picnic.'

'I meant a moment alone, if you must know,' Pavia snapped, more short than she'd intended. Her mind was whirling with decisions. She had him alone, *now*. When would that happen again? This might be her only chance to tell him.

He gave her a short, curt bow. 'I am sorry to have intruded then, Miss Honeysett. If you are not in need of my services, I will excuse myself.'

She put out her hand on his arm as he passed. 'Please, wait. I was rude, I am sorry.' She searched his eyes for forgiveness, but found none. His body was tense, his gaze shielded. This was not the man she'd known. That man was in hiding, a reminder that the man who stood before her was still a stranger despite their intimacy. It was almost enough to dissuade her from her course.

He halted and waited for her to go on. 'There is something I need to discuss with you.' His true self flickered behind the shutters of his eyes. She had his attention, she needed to make the most of it. 'Are you committed to anyone?'

she rushed on, stalling his usual response. 'I know you've told me that you are not, but I don't think that's true. The blonde girl, who is she?' Her words were inadequate for the questions she really wanted to ask. *What is she to you? Does she hold your heart? Do you hold hers?*

'What does it matter? You said you wanted no connection to me.' He reminded her she had no right to those answers. She had no claim on him. Any claim she might have had, she'd willingly given up in the Banfield ballroom at her own behest. If she wanted to establish any claim, she'd have to make the first move without those answers. It would be a blind leap of faith.

Pavia studied him. 'Can I trust you, Major?' She thought so, if for no other reason than ruining her would result in ruining himself. If he told anyone what had transpired and then refused to marry her, shame would fall on him, too. He'd survive it, though. Men always did.

The hardness in him softened. 'I give you my word. Whatever secrets you wish to impart will be safe with me.' She knew it to be true, so far. He'd said nearly the same words to her on the dance floor at the Banfields'. Even so, there was a sense of checks and balances between them. He couldn't ruin her without ruining himself. She supposed he could have blackmailed her for her wealth. He had not. At the ball, he'd simply given her what she wanted: the pretence that they'd never met, that they were strangers. Of course, she'd be naïve to assume that concession was entirely altruistic. Being strangers suited him. What she had to tell him and what she wanted from him today might not suit him as well.

Pavia held his eyes and gathered her courage, her hand tightening on his sleeve. 'I ask about the young lady because what I am about to tell you will affect her, too, if she has aspirations in your direction.' She drew one more breath. 'There has been a consequence from our night together. I am pregnant.'

Pregnant. With his child. The announcement blasted past the shutters of his eyes. There was no hiding the range of emotions he felt in those initial moments: confusion, disbelief, mathematical calculation, questioning— was it his? But he knew it was. The sheets had told the story, only he'd misunderstood that story until now. She'd been a virgin after all. Why would a girl with prospects do such a thing?

Wenderly. He recalled Sutton's words, offered in passing about Wenderly's penchant for purity and the last piece of the puzzle fell into place, the answer to the question: why would a gently bred girl with high expectations be dancing in a tavern? He knew now. To escape an unwanted marriage to a lecher. Wenderly would not have her ruined. It was a naïve, risky plan. Had she not seen the flaws? One need not announce to Wenderly that she was ruined. Being ruined was no guarantee. There was no reason to disclose such a thing to Wenderly until it was too late for Wenderly to renege. And of course, there was this risk, too—that in escaping one marriage, she'd found herself trapped in another. And she'd trapped him as well.

'You used me,' Cam ground out once the flurry of pieces in his mind settled. 'And now you want marriage? I assume that's why you're telling me?' *Marriage.* The word could put a pit in his stomach faster than anything else. There'd already been one discussion of marriage today. He wasn't ready to marry. There were things he still needed to do, *wanted* to do, such as return to the Crimea and his work there, his search for Fortis. Marriage and the military could not co-exist. His grandfather expected marriage to be the end of his military career, that he would come home and turn to a life of politics, serving the family interests. Pavia Honeysett would expect no different. She would want a father for her child, someone who wasn't a continent away being shot at on a foreign battlefield.

Her chin went up in a show of brave defiance. 'I am telling you because you are the child's father and you have a right to know. What you do about it is entirely up to you.' Marriage meant giving up for good on Fortis. Marriage meant choosing between Fortis and a wife. That decision had been easier when the wife in question had been Caroline Beaufort. But now, standing in the glade with beautiful, defiant and, yes, scared Pavia Honeysett, a woman who stirred him, a woman who carried his child, the decision was not an easy one. This was not only about marriage. It was *beyond* marriage. He was going to be a father. The kind of father he'd be started right here, right now with the decision he made. His mind made all nature of rationalisations in those few seconds. Perhaps there was a way to have them both; perhaps she could come to the Crimea with him. Some officers' wives did. He didn't let his mind move on to think about the logistics of moving a wife and a baby into a war zone. Perhaps she'd prefer to stay behind and raise the baby at his home in Little Trull. But those were questions for another time. He had to move forward, believing those details would sort themselves out as he and Pavia decided what their marriage would look like. All that was certain for now was that he would not abandon his child.

Cam reached for her hand. It was cold in his grip and it occurred to him how frightened she must have been, not just today, but for some time now as the reality of her situation settled on her and how alone she must have felt. 'You needn't worry, Pavia. I am no cad. I will marry you, of course. My child will have a father, a name, and you will have a husband.' He felt her fingers curl into his and saw the faintest of smiles on her lush mouth and knew he'd brought her relief. 'I will speak to your father tomorrow. I can obtain a special licence. We will be wed as soon as possible.' With luck, she was no more than six weeks along. An early arrival would be easy to explain if they wed soon enough.

'You are generous and kind. It is more than I deserve and less than what you deserve.' Pavia looked down at their hands, joined together. 'I didn't mean for this to happen. I took precautions, but they failed.' Cam understood. She wanted to give him absolution. 'None of this is your fault, it's mine. All mine. I didn't think it would turn out like this.'

'And yet it has. Now I am the only one who can do anything about it.' He gave a short bark of laughter. 'I came into the woods wishing for solutions. I did not expect to find them in this manner, but I've found them none the less. The questions I came seeking answers for have been settled and yours have, too.'

'Yes, my questions have been settled, but at great expense. I have upended your life. The girl you were with, will she be disappointed?' The comment touched him. It spoked well of Pavia that she showed concern about another even in the midst of her own crisis.

'Caroline Beaufort? I imagine she will. But she is pretty and wealthy. She will recover,' he answered directly. 'You will have to give up the Marquis.'

She met his eyes and nodded. 'There was nothing decided in that quarter.' But the fact remained that they were both giving up a lot. They were trading arranged marriages to partners hand-picked by their families for a marriage of convenience to a stranger neither barely knew except for one night of madness. The thought would be overwhelming if one dwelt on it, so Cam opted for more practical manoeuvres—action.

He took Pavia by the arm. 'Now that's settled, we need to get you cleaned up. There's a stream nearby, where we can wash your face. Were you ill? Is that why you came into the woods?'

'Yes, a bit of delayed morning sickness,' Pavia admitted with a hint of embarrassment tinging her cheeks.

'Don't worry, we'll have you looking fine in no time.' Cam helped her wash her face and restore her hair with a comb from his pocket until she looked presentable. No one would ever guess what had happened in the woods.

'Thank you.' She handed the comb back to him and he tucked it away, understanding she was thanking him for these small kindnesses as well as the larger ones he offered her today.

He squeezed her hand, an unexpected rush of emotion tightening his throat. 'This time tomorrow everything will be all right, Pavia.' It felt right to use her name, right to hold her hand and to offer comfort. Perhaps it was nothing more than the pleasure of having someone to take care of again. In the military he had troops to care for. Since he'd been home, he'd had no one to look after, no one to lead. And yet, perhaps this was something more than filling a void. Maybe it was a sign of how things could be between them, the first step on the road to the intimacy of the marriage they would share whether either of them had planned it or not. He'd entered the glen with despair, but he was leaving it with a spark of hope.

'I want to believe that.' Pavia said softly.

'If you can't believe my words, believe this.' He leaned in, capturing her mouth in a soft kiss full of promise and full of reminders of what they'd once shared. They would have passion between them and a baby. It was a start, Cam thought.

'Go back to the party, Pavia,' he whispered. 'I will come for you in the morning. Put your affairs in order.'

It was an interesting choice of words. It was what people did when they prepared to exit this life. Their old lives were dying. Tomorrow, their new life, whatever it might be, would begin.

Chapter Seven

'I am going to marry Pavia Honeysett.' Cam stood with ramrod-straight, military precision before his grandfather's desk in the Earl of Aylsbury's study and voiced the words with all the conviction at his disposal. If his grandfather sensed any weakness, he would exploit it to the extreme, as would his father and his uncle, who flanked him on either side in tall, leather wing-backed chairs. Cam had no illusions his family would respond well to this announcement. It was a deuced situation to be in, to have to advocate so thoroughly for a position one had only barely been able to comprehend hours ago.

Cam had given himself the night to grapple with the news before approaching his family. He would need all his wits and all his patience this morning. He had a plan, he needed to hold to it no matter what threats and obstacles they put in his way, just like any other campaign he'd waged on the battlefield—his child was depending on it. His toes curled inside his boots as the reality swept him again. *He was going to be a father.*

'The hell you are, boy.' His grandfather didn't waste time with more subtle arguments. 'We don't need her money, she has no connections of value to us and, even if she did, she's a half-breed.' He thumped his fist on the desk. 'What we need is the alliance with Caroline Beaufort. You've dithered enough in that regard. Clearly, you are ripe for marriage if you're so eager to throw yourself away on the Honeysett chit. We can announce your engagement to Caroline tonight. You can wed in June, the first big wedding of the Season. Your grandmother and mother will be in alt planning it and I'll sign over that property in the Lake District you're so fond of as a wedding gift, eh? You can take Caroline and honeymoon there.' This was always his grandfather's strategy: to sweeten the angry pot with a treat, a tempting morsel that made acceptance seem reasonable. His grandfather smiled and put his hands palms down on the desk, a signal that business was completed to his satisfaction. 'I think a toast is in order, gentlemen.'

'No, we are not done here.' Cam interrupted abruptly. 'I am marrying Pavia Honeysett. She is carrying my child.'

'Says who?' His grandfather did not blink at the disclosure, although his uncle and his father shifted in their seats, an uncomfortable look passing between the two brothers.

'Pavia herself,' Cam answered steadily. 'She has no reason to lie. With her money, she could surely aim higher than a man with no title.' And surely she'd wanted to, intended to, until she'd discovered herself pregnant. The Marquis of Chatham was evidence of that. She'd pursued him up until she could not pursue him any longer, when proof of her situation had made itself entirely clear.

His grandfather considered this, tapping his index finger on the polished surface of the desk. 'I don't doubt she's pregnant. Are you sure it's yours?'

Cam's fists tightened at his sides. It took all of his patience not to leap the desk and plant the man a facer, grandsire or not. 'You will not speak of her like that.'

His grandfather gave a condescending smile, offering an aside to Cam's father. 'The cub grows claws, Eustace. You've raised a fiery one.' Then to Cam, 'How do you know it's yours? I hear she's dangling after the Marquis of Chatham. Perhaps it's his? As you say, it hardly makes sense that she'd claim you're the father when she could marry higher. Unless...' The Earl's eyes narrowed critically. 'Chatham has refused her and now she's trapped, desperate to pass that baby off on whomever she can find. Those nabob types are always looking for a way in.' He slid a look towards Edward, his heir. 'This is how the aristocracy dies, my son, polluted by poor marriages.'

Cam couldn't resist. 'I thought it was from refusing to adapt to times. Closed systems atrophy.'

His grandfather's blue eyes shot him a hard look. 'You haven't answered me. I am afraid, for the sake of the earldom, I must insist, Camden. Tell me, how do you know it's yours? A girl like that will say anything.'

'Because she was a virgin when we lay together.' It took all his willpower to say the words like a man and not like an embarrassed boy. It was rather difficult to put this part of his life on display in front of his grandfather, his father and his uncle. It was one thing to know they all knew he wasn't untried. He'd been in the military for ten years after all. But to discuss it and his partners openly was another thing.

His grandfather's eyebrows raised in displeasure. 'Did we not teach you better than that, Camden? A virgin? Really?'

'You did teach me better, sir. Which is why I am offering for her now. A gentleman protects a lady's reputation with his name and that of his child's,' Cam said firmly. 'I am obtaining a special licence and we will be married as soon as possible. I am standing here today to inform you of the news. Do not confuse that with asking for permission. I am far from the age where permission is needed. How you react to the news is up to you.'

'Cam…' his father broke in, a warning in his voice.

'No, Eustace,' his grandfather interrupted. 'Let the cub be clear on what his defiance will cost him. We will not acknowledge her. If she comes to town, flaunting the Lithgow name, we will give her the cut direct. She is not allowed to claim any ties to us. As for you, cub, you will not support a wife not of my approval on any allowance from the earldom. I will cut you off, effective as of today, and there will be no support of your candidacy for a seat in the Commons from us.'

This was expected, but not less hurtful because of it. His family was stepping away from him, distancing themselves, as if he'd not shared a lifetime with them, and his father sat silent while it happened, refusing to champion his son. 'I wouldn't want it any other way,' Cam answered with steely certainty, not if they were unwilling to acknowledge his wife, his child, his choice. 'Those plans were your plans. My plans are somewhat different.'

'And the tea heiress's plans?' His grandfather chuckled coldly at that. 'Do you think she wants to spend her life following the drum? Chasing you around Europe, hoping you don't end up dead and leave her stranded in some godforsaken part of the empire with a babe on her hip and no decent way to support herself?' He pointed a long, bone-thin finger at Cam. 'Don't think we'll take her in if you die.'

'I wouldn't want you to. Do you think I'd want my child raised in this loveless mausoleum of a home?' He needed to leave. His anger was starting to brim, all the old frustrations of being under the thumb of his family coming to the fore. Cam turned on his heel and stalked out of the room.

'Young man, you have not been dismissed!' his grandfather's voice boomed.

Cam paused and turned back, a cold smile on his face. 'Yes, I believe I have.' He straightened his shoulders. He should have done this years ago, asserted his right to manage his own life. Freedom was starting to feel good. Already, he felt lighter, more directed. He had the freedom now to claim a life of his choice. Only, it wouldn't be a life truly his own. His life now belonged to Pavia, to his child. Some might say he'd traded one responsibility for another, one family obligation for another. Cynics would say that choice had come with too great a cost.

His father caught up to him in the hall, a hand on his sleeve. 'Wait, Cam. Don't do this. If you walk out the door...'

'There will be no walking back in,' Cam finished the sentence for him. 'I didn't think there would be.'

'I need you to see reason. You're not thinking clearly.' His father's eyes weren't filled with concern, though. They were filled with contained anger. Anger at his son. This was not a plea. It was a scolding.

'I am thinking like a father, like the father I wish to be,' Cam retorted. He gestured towards the study. 'You did not stand up for me in there. You have never stood up to the old man. You let him plan your life, pick your bride and you were willing to let him do the same for your own son.'

Something dangerous passed across his father's features. 'It is how things are done in successful aristocratic families. We are lucky to have a patriarch who has survived so long to give this family direction.' His father grabbed his arm. 'Cam, look around. There are families losing everything these days. The peerage is under attack. In a couple of generations it could be gone.'

'Because it chooses not to adapt, Father. Times change. People must change, too,' Cam answered, wrenching his arm away.

'What about your mother? This will break her heart. You are her only child.'

Cam was ready for this, too. Long had his darling mother been a pawn in these battles of power, leverage for coercion and compliance. 'She will always be welcome in my home, as will any of you. She can choose to come and visit her grandchild.' Would she? Was his mother capable of an act of defiance? Was his father? Such an act seemed in doubt based on this morning's performance. 'Grandfather might be banishing me, but I am not banishing you.' The import that this relationship was only one way now came with a sharp realisation. Was this the last time he'd see his family? He'd often had that thought over the years each time he deployed. How ironic if it turned out not to be a foreign bullet that ended their contact but a simple civic matter of matrimony. But he couldn't let it weaken him. He'd made his choices; now they'd have to make theirs. 'If you'll excuse me, Father, I have a bride to collect. I'll send my valet for my things this afternoon. He'll bring word when the ceremony is to be in case you change your mind.'

At that, his father let him go. Of course. His father had never fought for anything. Not for him, not even against him. His father had sat there today and let the Earl malign the mother of the earldom's first great-grandchild and then cut his grandson from the family. Cam took the front steps rapidly, wanting to be away from this place.

Today and always, his father had been the picture of a perfect second son. He'd done his time in the military with an aplomb that matched Cam's own career, come home and married dutifully, served in the House of Commons protecting the family interests and watching the heir's back. No one would say he was a weak man. His opponents in the House found him a formidable champion for his causes. But today, Cam had seen his father in a true light—a man who put duty first, a man who was willing to sacrifice his own son in homage to that duty.

It was a rather sobering realisation to fully understand he was just a piece on a chessboard to Aylsbury, a knight to command, to be used in service to the family as Aylsbury saw fit and nothing more; he was not a beloved grandson, or a treasured son. Just a piece to be used for the greater good of the earldom. Cam swung up on his waiting horse and gave a last look at the Aylsbury town house with a vow to do better. He would not make his father's mistakes. His child would be treasured. His child would know a father's love and a father's devotion to the *person* that child was and not as a placeholder in a legacy.

'This is the best you could do, Pavia? A grandson of an earl? A major in the Hussars?' Oliver Honeysett sneered over the rim of his teacup while his wife, Sabita, kept her eyes downcast, perhaps in embarrassment over her husband's flagrant and rude bluntness, a bluntness that both shamed Pavia and insulted Cam. 'This is not what was agreed upon. A marquis, Pavia. You said you could deliver a marquis,' her father said, spearing Cam with his dark eyes. The man should meet his grandfather. They would get on famously.

Pavia was not intimidated by her father's outburst. She moved to speak, but Cam reached out a quiet, silencing hand and took her own, letting the gesture speak of their unity. He would be damned before he'd make his wife have to defend herself while he sat silent beside her. 'We are anticipating a blessed event and wish to be married well in advance of it.' He would be delicate even if her father was decidedly not.

Pavia's mother gasped, a sound of utter surprise. 'Darling, is it true?' Her dark eyes came up to take in her daughter's gaze with a mix of joy and hurt—she hadn't known, yet the thought of a child pleased her, softened her, even as she realised she had not been confided in during this recent crisis. It was another reminder to Cam of how much Pavia had shouldered on her own in the past few tension-ridden weeks. She'd been entirely alone in her anxiety, her fear, her uncertainty.

There was no joy, however, from Oliver

Honeysett. The thought of soon becoming a grandfather did not soften him. Perhaps it did not even occur to him. The man exploded from behind his desk. The rant that followed was not unlike the rant Cam had heard earlier from his grandfather: that this betrayal was a deviation from the grand plan; Pavia had shamed him, had selfishly set her needs above the family's. 'And you, Major Lithgow, you are nothing more than a fortune hunter,' Honeysett accused, the vein at his temple throbbing. 'You will not inherit anything on your own, so you thought to move on to an innocent girl with a pile of money.'

'I am sorry you think that,' Cam replied evenly. He was not about to disabuse the man of the notion this was a situation of his own making. He would not transfer the blame to Pavia by telling the man his daughter had danced half-naked in a taproom. Acknowledging the realities of the situation could change nothing. In truth, it didn't matter who'd started this gambit. He and Pavia were in it together, now.

Cam was more than happy to bear the brunt of Honeysett's cruel words if it spared Pavia. She was dressed prettily in an afternoon gown of white muslin with large green leaves appliqued at the hem and a green ribbon in her hair to match, but she was already pale beneath the tan of her skin and her eyes were tired. He wondered if she'd been sick again this morning.

'I don't want your money.' The words were boldly spoken from a man who'd just been cut off from his own resources Cam knew exactly how much it cost him.

That took some wind from Honeysett and Cam knew he'd just neutralised the man's last weapon. Her father had thought to bring him down with that dart. A fortune hunter would have been cowed. Still, Honeysett was determined to brazen it out. 'Good. You won't get a penny from me, Lithgow.'

Cam managed a smile not unlike the one he'd used on his grandfather. 'I am glad that's settled, then.' He rose and held out his hand to Pavia. 'We will be going now. I have a special licence and we'll be married in the morning.' He'd ridden to Lambeth after leaving his grandfather's in order to prevent his grandfather from any chicanery that might forestall his ability to acquire the licence. 'You are welcome to attend, or not. We will remove to the country for a honeymoon. I have a place outside of Taunton in Little Trull. She will be well cared for.' The last was said with some bravado of his own. Some way, somehow, he would see that last come true. He had not thought about the particulars involved in taking a wife, not past acquiring the licence, claiming Pavia from her home.

Honeysett speared his daughter with a challenging look. 'You've heard the terms, girl. If you go with him today, those terms will apply to you. No money, no welcome in this house. Do not come running to us when he leaves you for a new tour of duty, or when he insists you accompany him to some far-off land. Are you truly willing to give up all of this?' He waved a hand to include the luxury of the town house, the fine silk of her gown and her mother's. 'Everything you have, you owe to me. He cannot provide all this for you.'

Silence stretched between them, father and daughter, eyes locked in quiet combat. Then Pavia rose, giving Cam the first glimpse of her strength, her fortitude, even her stubbornness in the face of adversity, and Cam understood how incredibly hard all this must be for her. 'No, thank you, Father. You have provided all this for me, I will not argue that, but your price is too high.' Cam understood that price. He had walked out on his family, too, but he had his career, his gender to fall back on. She had nothing, and no one, but him—a man she didn't know. A stranger who had given her a child. She was trusting him with everything. Damn it all, he would be worthy of that trust.

His hand curled around hers in solidarity. 'Are you ready, my dear?'

'Yes, my things are in the hall. I had my maid bring them down.' Her head was high, her voice steady, but her hand trembled in his. Her strength was not limitless.

'Then let us go, Pavia.' He turned to usher her out.

'Are you truly taking her out of this house?' Honeysett stuttered in disbelief, perhaps realising for the first time that his rant had no power over her, over *them*.

'No, Father. He is not taking me anywhere. I am going of my own accord,' Pavia interrupted before Cam could answer.

Honeysett rose, a big, hulk of a man. For a moment, Cam thought he might have to fight him. 'How dare you...?'

'My child will have a name,' Cam said fiercely, meeting the tea merchant's stubborn gaze one last time before he escorted Pavia towards the front door and down the steps. Reality swept him as he helped her mount his horse and swung up behind her for the short ride to Grillon's. What a day they'd had. They'd been disavowed by their families, cut off from the social and financial supports that had been so naturally part of their worlds for so long. They were absolutely and entirely on their own—all three of them—and it was only noon.

Chapter Eight

⁓⁓⁓⁓

They were on their own. Completely. A reminder that was driven home by the empty chapel in which they wed the next day, Cam in his uniform, burnished and brushed to perfection, she in a carriage ensemble of forget-me-not blue. Pavia had half-expected her father to burst in to protest the marriage, but no one came to stop them. Neither did anyone come to bless them, a point made evident by the absence of a wedding breakfast. There was a definitive lack of fanfare as they went straight from the chapel to Paddington Station and boarded the train for Taunton as if it were another, ordinary day.

All these reminders should have pointed to how daunting their decision was: two people forsaking their families, choosing to cling to each other, strangers. But instead of daunting, Pavia had found their adventure a unique kind of exciting; a mixture of disbelief and fantasy as she'd walked down the aisle to Cam; reality suspended as the countryside flew by outside the train. Everything about the last twenty-four hours had been exciting in the extreme—these things happened in books, not in real life, and yet they were happening to her.

She supposed it was a little like eloping. Exhilaration could carry a girl quite a long way. All the way, in fact, from London to her wedding night in a manse outside Taunton with a man she hardly knew.

What little she did know of him was due to the immediacy of their situation, which had thrown them together like two survivors lost at sea. They were forced to rely on one another. But that glimpse, brief as it was, of her new husband had been...*intoxicating*. Romantic even. It almost made her believe fairy tales *did* come true. He'd looked so very handsome in his uniform this morning as he waited for her in the chapel. Soon, he would come to her by candlelight.

Pavia hummed to herself in the soft glow of the master's suite, unpacking a few essentials, including a white-lawn nightgown embroidered with tiny pink flowers. She'd done the work herself, part of an assignment at Mrs Finlay's in inevitable expectation for this very night—a wedding night, the attainment of which was the academy's yardstick of success. Mrs Finlay's girls were educated and prepared to make the best matches. She wondered what Mrs Finlay would think of this one?

Pavia shook out the gown, anticipation and an odd sense of anxiety making her fingers tremble as she thought of the intimacy to come. She wouldn't have to wait much longer. It was already late, their train having been substantially delayed in Didcot to take on special cargo. Full darkness had caught them as they'd made their journey by carriage from the station in Taunton to Cam's home outside the town.

Cam. The simple word evoked a certain, intimate thrill. He was 'the Major' no longer, but her husband. A husband who was, at present, out seeing to the horses. Pavia laid out her brushes on a console against the wall, working quickly and fumbling in her haste. She knew what his gesture meant. He was putting the horses away to give her time and privacy to prepare for the night ahead. His efforts would be unnecessary otherwise. Under regular circumstances there were servants to see to the master's horses. He would be back soon and she needed to be ready. The room was ready, but she wasn't, not mentally or physically.

Pavia worked the fastenings of her carriage ensemble, hands clumsy. She was thankful for the foresight of choosing a travelling costume she could get in and out of on her own. There'd been no maid at the hotel last night or this morning and she'd been unsure of what she'd find here. Finally free of her outfit, Pavia slipped the lawn nightgown over her head, shivering a bit in the coldness of the room. She brushed out her hair. She would wear it down tonight, loose and flowing, instead of her usual plait. In any case, she wasn't sure her hands could handle the braiding.

She shouldn't be nervous. There was nothing to be nervous about. They'd been physically intimate before, naked with one another before. There would be no secrets between them when the time came, yet her hands shook and her body trembled. Pavia picked up the candleholder and surveyed the room. It was spare, holding just three pieces of furniture in its big space: the console, a bureau and the enormous carved-oak four-poster bed that dominated the room's centre. She headed there, slipping beneath the covers for warmth.

They smelled musty, but tonight the scent only added to the mystique of her adventure, like the Gothic romances the girls at Mrs Finlay's passed around after lights-out: a dark house, a hasty marriage, a stranger for a husband. In the novels, the heroine was always frightened. She'd thought those girls incredibly silly. In hindsight, she thought she might have misjudged them. She wasn't 'scared', per se, but she was definitely anxious.

From downstairs came the sound of the door closing and the clomp of boots on the steps. Her husband was coming. A tremor of excitement and nerves raced through her, her body remembering the last time they'd shared a bed, her mind reminding her of the import of tonight: her wedding night. The night she gave her body to a man for ever. Until death. Was Cam Lithgow worth the trust she gave him? The power she gave him? A power she'd not wanted to surrender to a man?

She might not know Cam, but she knew enough to know he was honourable and kind, and fierce, as a warrior should be. He'd stood up to her father's threats. He had stood up *for* her and it had been magnificent. No one had ever stood up for her before. He'd been a gentleman the night before at the hotel, engaging two rooms for them and seeing to her every comfort before going out to finish his business. He'd returned and shared a private dinner with her in her chambers before retiring. Part of her had been disappointed by that honourable disappearance and yet she understood the reason for it. He would treat his wife with respect. And he had, from sending up breakfast the next morning, to carrying her over the threshold of their home when they'd arrived in Little Trull, tired and weary from the emotions and travel of the day. The door had stuck. He'd had to kick it open but he had persevered to make the homecoming as perfect as possible.

The bedroom door opened and her husband's broad shoulders filled the space that had seemed so large moments before. His gaze swept her, taking in her hair, her night-rail, the bed and all it stood for. What they had done together before could not compare to the significance of what they'd do in this bed. Consummation would bind them together.

Cam nodded towards the dark hearth. 'Shall I start a fire, first?' He seemed relieved to have something to do with his hands. Perhaps he was nervous. It calmed her a bit to think that her husband was affected by the moment, too.

He lit the fire, squatting on muscular

haunches, and then rose. He turned towards her, his gaze finding her again in the firelight, then slowly, deliberately, he pulled his linen shirt over his head, exposing a lean expanse of abdomen. He pushed his trousers down over slim hips until he was wholly revealed to her, letting her look her fill at her golden demi-god of a husband before he slid beneath the covers and came alongside her, drawing her close with a kiss.

'You're shaking, Pavia. Are you nervous? There's nothing to be anxious about,' he whispered against her lips.

She wrapped her arms about his neck, smiling to quell those nerves he mentioned. 'I memorised every inch of you as you slept that night. I thought you were the most perfect man I had ever seen, yet you've outdone yourself tonight. Perhaps it frightens me to think such a man is mine.'

'You have it wrong, my dear. I am the lucky one…' Cam stroked her cheek with gentle knuckles '…to have such a beautiful bride.' The heat of his body warmed her, calmed her and she felt his strength in those moments, the strength that protected her and their child. She was safe with him.

'Shall I prove it?' he whispered huskily, his

kisses tracing her jaw, her throat, the patch of bare skin above the bodice of her nightgown, all the while heat was gathering and pooling low in her belly, want overcoming her nerves.

'Yes,' she answered breathlessly, her body open to him as if he'd always belonged there with her, in her. 'Prove it to me.' In bed they would be safe. They needn't think about what they'd done or what it had cost them. If they thought at all, it would only be to note the price had been worth it for this.

Cam ran a hand along the pretty embroidery of her nightgown. 'We'll start with this. It's lovely, but it will have to go. Tonight, I want nothing between us.' He reached between her legs and gathered up the hem of the fabric in one hand and worked the gown up over her body, over her head, tossing it to the floor. She'd spent hours on the embroidery. Mrs Finley would have a fit if she knew how carelessly discarded the gown was. But there was no time to protest.

Cam sucked at her earlobe with a growl that sent a ripple of white-hot heat, primitive and fierce, through her, her mind running riot at the thought of him ripping her clothes off. That would be a wickedly delicious fantasy to play out, embroidery be damned.

'Good God, you're even more beautiful than I remembered.' He reared back on his haunches to look at her, his eyes going dark to a shade of midnight, his voice a rasp of desire. He touched her then, a hand to her breast, a thumb rubbed across a dusky nipple in a manner that made her breath catch and her pulse race, her body remembering the last time he'd put his mouth on her and she'd nearly screamed. His body was remembering, too.

He was hungry for her, she could see it in his eyes, and she was hungry for him, for another chance to claim what had eluded her before. Cam came over her, his command for consummation a whisper against her lips, 'Open for me.' And she did.

He took her then, in a possessive thrust, the muscles of his arms locked taut and strong above her, her legs wrapped about him, holding him to her, urging him on. Desire rose deep within her, unwilling to be held in check this time, unwilling to be denied its full pleasure. This time, there was no reason to hold back and Pavia did not. She gave herself over to the loving entirely, her back arching, her hips thrusting up to join his, her hands fisting in the sheets as passion swept her, pushing her along to the shattering cataclysm, and this time that cataclysm claimed them both. His heart thundered against hers, his breath hard at her shoulder as he poured into her.

Good lord, was there anything on earth as grand as this? This was ultimate completion. Ultimate peace. For these moments all was right with the world. She'd never felt anything like it. She was reluctant for it to end, for Cam to withdraw, leaving her body empty of him. She wanted him back almost immediately.

'My wife is greedy.' Cam laughed. 'But I'll be ready soon enough.' He drew her close and she curled her body against him as he rested.

'I see the changes in you already.' His voice was a baritone caress in the candlelit darkness. His hand gently cupped her breast. 'You're fuller here.' He trailed a featherlight hand down the curvy silhouette of her, resting on her hip. 'And here, too. Very feminine, very alluring.' He kissed her. Oh, she loved those kisses! 'Only a discerning lover would notice, only a man who has memorised every inch of you.' He gave another one of his warm chuckles. 'You were not the only one who was making mental pictures that night.' This, Pavia thought, was how they'd build their own history, collecting the memories and turning them into stories. They would build their history one tale at a time, telling it over and over until a solid truth emerged. What would that truth be? Strangers who fell in love at first sight? Or strangers forced to wed?

Cam's fingers flexed at the curve of her hip. 'I thought you were the most beautiful woman I'd ever seen, the most intriguing, a veiled mystery I was compelled to solve.'

He pushed her gently on to her back. 'And have you solved me?' She looked up at him, his blue eyes dark with want.

'Oh, no, you're an even greater mystery than you were before, like a maze where the closer you get to the centre, the further away it seems to go,' Cam whispered at her ear, his palm warm on her stomach. 'You were far less complicated as an exotic dancer.'

'And you were far less complicated as a stranger I would never see again.' Pavia laughed.

'Neither of us were what we seemed,' Cam murmured. 'I never dreamed you were a tea merchant's heiress.'

'Nor you the grandson of an earl.' Somewhere in the back of her mind it occurred to Pavia that those monikers no longer applied to them. She was an heiress to nothing now and his family had disavowed him for his choice to wed a mixed-blood daughter of a commoner. Tonight, drunk on desire, she saw only the freedom such a predicament afforded. In casting off her former life, she'd cast off both chains and limits. She was free to become whoever she liked. *They* were free to become whoever they wanted to be *together*. There was infinite possibility and potential in that.

Cam's thumb stroked softly over her belly. 'But here we are, with a child between us. It's hard to imagine he's in there.'

'Or she.' Pavia yawned the correction. She was getting sleepy, the tolls of the day catching up with her at last. Not even exhilaration could outrun sleep for ever.

'Or she,' Cam acceded. 'It doesn't matter, as long they are healthy.' He sighed. 'He *or* she,' he added before she could scold him again, 'will be here for our first wedding anniversary. We'll be a family, a good family. I've learned a lot since coming home about the kind of father I want to be.'

What a perfect note to drift off on, to begin a new life on: to fall asleep in the arms of a man who embraced his impending fatherhood, unplanned as it was, with the same passion he brought to bed as a husband, yet another un-looked-for role his honour had required him to take on. Perhaps it would be enough to overlook other truths: that they were strangers to one another, that they would not have chosen each other of their own accords. That, in securing their freedom, they'd cost each other everything. Perhaps if he loved the baby enough, it wouldn't matter if he loved her, or she him. The love they each held for the baby would be enough to keep them together, enough around which to build a good life together. They had respect, passion, honour and a child between them. That was a great deal more than many people ever had. She had not gone looking for him or this path she was currently on, but she had found Prince Charming in disguise. What could possibly go wrong?

Chapter Nine

Pavia woke in a beam of sunlight and stretched, her body contentedly sore, a delicious reminder of the night before. At the memory, she put out an arm and reached for her husband. But her hand came up empty. He was gone and the bed was cold with his absence. He'd was not only gone, he'd been gone awhile.

The realisation was enough to prompt her to open her eyes, to push herself up gingerly against the pillows and survey the room. What had been Gothically romantic in the dark last night was starkly spare and disappointing in the morning light. The few pieces of furniture the room possessed were well used, marked with scratches and dents, the small carpet by the bed well worn. She sneezed. The covers were still musty, only now that mustiness served to turn her stomach. She needed toast and perhaps some tea to settle it. Pavia reached for the bell pull next to the bed. They'd been alone last night, but surely the help had come up this morning to resume work. Surely her husband would not have left her alone.

After ten minutes of waiting, Pavia wasn't sure either of those assumptions were true. She shut her eyes against the roil of her stomach, willing it to calm. Perhaps the bell pull didn't work. She was going to have to go downstairs herself.

Once the nausea passed, Pavia carefully levered herself out of bed and slipped on a dressing gown she'd unpacked last night. She tied the sash tightly, catching sight of her nightgown, still on the floor where Cam had discarded it. *That* made her smile, made her warm with just the memory of his hands on her body, skimming, caressing; his mouth kissing.

She wasn't smiling several minutes later, however. Getting downstairs on a nauseous stomach had proven to be the thirteenth labour of Hercules. It was something of a victory that she'd made it to the foot of the stairs without casting up her accounts. Now she held on to the newel post for dear life, feeling sticky and clammy as another wave swept her. 'Is anyone here?' Pavia called out. There was no answer. The house seemed preternaturally quiet. In her parents' home, there'd always been servants about, there'd always been movement. One was never truly alone. Pavia could not remember the last time she was alone. At home she'd been surrounded by servants. At Mrs Finlay's Academy she'd been surrounded by other girls. In her uncle's zenana, she'd been surrounded by her mother, by other women and children. But here, she was alone. This house was *still. Empty*, except for her. The feeling was unnerving.

Pavia took a deep breath. At least no one would see her wandering about in her nightclothes. Her mother would have had a fit. Mrs Finlay would have had a fit. A sudden surge of tears threatened. She was alone in a strange house and feeling sick. She pushed the tears back and took herself in hand. She needed a plan. Doing something always helped in a time of uncertainty. She would find the kitchen and perhaps some bread.

At least that wasn't hard. The house, it turned out, wasn't all that large, only twelve rooms in total; in addition to the rooms above, there was a nice-sized front parlour, a dining room, an office for the master of the house, a small sitting room for the lady and the kitchen. Pavia dragged a finger over the butcher block, picking up dust. The kitchen hadn't seen use in a while. Then it hit her what the dust meant: there were no servants. No one was coming. No one had been here for a very long time. What had Cam said? He hadn't been home for six years?

Her stomach growled, hungry and nauseous all at once. Pavia pressed her palms flat against the surface of the big work table to stave off the panic. Tears threatened again. The exhilaration of the two previous days was non-existent now, the thrill of an adventure gone. The reality of what she'd done settled on her mercilessly. She wanted her mother, desperately. Her calm mother, who worked tirelessly behind the scenes of her father's busy life, who never showed her temper. Her mother would know what to do. Her mother would take her in her arms and smooth back her hair and tell her everything would be all right. But things weren't all right: she was alone with a strange man, in a strange place and it would be ages before she saw her mother again.

Had her mother felt like this when they'd come to England? An outsider in a foreign land? She'd known nothing of the culture or the people. She'd had only Pavia's father to rely on. *You have Cam* came the quiet prompt of her conscience. Yes, she had Cam, wherever he was. Right now, having Cam wasn't worth much. The enormity of what she'd given up when she'd defiantly stormed out of her father's house on Cam's arm began to swamp her. Exhilaration could not keep the loss at bay.

Pavia shuffled to the front parlour and sank down on a threadbare sofa, a puff of dust rising from the upholstery as she sat, miserable and hungry. What had she done? Was it just last night she'd thought nothing could go wrong? Now nothing seemed right. Pavia shivered and wrapped the faded red throw over her. She would rest a bit and then she would pull herself upstairs and dress. She would need to walk into town and find a way to purchase food. She had some coins in her trunk. Just the task of hauling herself upstairs seemed daunting. Going into town, *finding* town seemed superhuman at the moment. *You'll feel better after a rest*, she reminded herself. The morning sickness never lasted more than a couple of hours. Pavia yawned. Perhaps when she woke, a walk would be the perfect thing to restore her spirits.

* * *

Cam returned to the house shortly after ten o'clock, a basket of food supplies strapped to his saddle. It had taken longer than he'd planned to get what he needed. He tied his horse outside and pushed at the door with his shoulder. It would need some work right away. It had stuck last night, too. He'd been forced to kick it open in order to carry Pavia over the threshold. But he'd been determined to keep at least one wedding tradition.

It was the least he could do to make up for what must have been a very plain, uneventful wedding for her. No one had come. He'd not expected anyone to, but the look on Pavia's face as she'd walked down the aisle, fleeting as the look was, suggested she'd not really believed her family would desert her. Whatever disappointment it had brought her, she'd hid it well. She'd been beautiful, radiant, all day. Nothing had outwardly dampened her spirits: not the anti-climactic trip to the noisy train station, or the long delay in Didcot, or the arrival to a closed-up house in the dark.

Cam stepped into the narrow hall of the manse, using a foot to shut the door behind him. He hoped the house by daylight hadn't daunted her. He'd wanted to be back before she woke, but it hadn't been possible. He caught sight of her in the parlour and smiled. His bride, asleep under the red throw, her dark hair spilling over the edge of the sofa, long and silky. Then he caught sight of her face and his smile faded. She was pale and there were dried tear tracks on her cheeks. Had she been sick this morning? He was struck with remorse. He hadn't remembered. He hadn't thought about her being ill and alone in a strange place. He should have waited to go into town until after she woke.

Cam put out a hand on her leg and gently shook her. 'Pavia, wake up, I've brought breakfast.' Was that the right thing to say? Weren't pregnant women always hungry? He didn't know. In fact, this morning, he was suddenly feeling very much at sea. He had a pregnant wife and no idea what to do with her, apparently. He'd left her alone and now he didn't know whether or not to offer her food. Perhaps the food would just make it worse? For a man used to commanding men and making split-second decisions in the heat of battle, this was unknown territory. He was not used to uncertainty, to not knowing exactly what to do in any given situation.

Cam knelt beside the sofa and smoothed

back her hair. She was beautiful and she was his. She was trusting him to take care of her and the babe. He would figure this out. 'I have apples and cheese, some fresh milk, eggs, a rasher of bacon, some bread, ham, butter *and* jam,' he tempted.

Her eyes fluttered open and she smiled expectantly as if she could already taste the hot, melted butter spread on warm bread. 'Toast? With jam? It sounds delicious.' One would have thought he'd promised her the finest of French crêpes with crème fraiche and berries. Then she sighed. 'I am sorry you had to do it. I was going to go for food after I rested, but I fell asleep. Not a very good start to being wifely, letting my husband go out for food while I laze away the morning.'

Cam leaned forward and kissed her forehead. 'You are expecting our child. No apology necessary. I can't say I made the best starts at husbanding either. I left you alone to wake up in a strange place. Were you ill this morning?'

'Nothing I couldn't handle.' Pavia sat up, carefully. 'I'm pregnant, Cam. I am not an invalid.'

'I don't know much about pregnancy. It doesn't come up often in the Hussars.' Cam chuckled, but it wasn't all that funny. Not to him anyway. He was used to being competent, knowledgeable. But he was out of his league at present. The nearest he'd been to pregnancy was Fortis's brother Frederick's ever-expecting wife, Helena. Even then, that was just through letters sent to Fortis. He'd been abroad for all five of her pregnancies. It was a rather stark reminder of all he didn't know about his role as a husband and a father-to-be.

He was feeling decidedly awkward when Pavia laughed. 'Me either. It's my first time, too. We'll learn together. Now, how about that breakfast you've promised me?'

In the kitchen, they managed breakfast, but just barely, relying heavily on Cam's military campfire cooking skills. To her credit, Pavia tried her best, but after burning the toast twice in an effort that took half the loaf, she was on the verge of tears before Cam intervened. 'It's harder than it looks,' he assured her. In the end, they put a creditable meal of scrambled eggs, toast and bacon on the butcher block, but reality was sinking in. Pavia was no cook. She'd not been raised to be. She'd been raised to prepare menus *for* a cook, not to execute those menus. She'd been raised to run a house, not to clean one. And neither had he. He knew how to ride, how to shoot, how to fight, how to manage men. None of their skills would be very useful here in his twelve-room manse.

'We'll need to hire some help.' Cam took a bite of eggs. They couldn't live on camp food for ever. 'I didn't keep anyone on after the last time I was home. It seemed pointless, knowing I would be gone indefinitely. There's just a man in the village who looks in on the place from time to time.' He was regretting that decision in hindsight. He'd had a good look around this morning. So much needed to be done. He'd let the place go in his absence. But he'd never thought he'd be bringing a wife here, raising a family here. The vow he'd made himself on the steps of the Honeysett town house was starting to seem impossible. He'd made a muddle of taking care of his new bride so far.

Pavia looked up from her buttered toast, her dark eyes wide. 'Can we afford to hire help?'

Can we? Her simple words warmed Cam inexplicably and diminished some of his doubt. He reached across the butcher block and grasped her hand. 'We are not paupers, Pavia. We will live in comfort, if not luxury. We could hire a housekeeper-cook from the village to come in during the day and a gardener to help with the grounds a few times a week, and a boy for the stable.' Certainly not the corps of servants their fathers' homes boasted. Cam thought it best not to mention that. It did no good looking to the past. It was gone, for both of them.

Pavia nodded, assured by the idea of a cook-cum-housekeeper. 'Why are you smiling?'

'Because we're having our first household discussion as husband and wife.' Cam's thumb ran over her knuckles in a small caress. 'We're making decisions about how to run our household and how to manage our expenses.' It was a good beginning, he thought, and a very different start than any he could have imagined. He definitely couldn't picture himself and Caroline discussing the household in the kitchen. Then again, they'd have had a score of servants to wait on them, a London town house of their own, courtesy of his grandfather, and it would already be staffed and stocked courtesy of Caroline's mother. There would have been no decisions to make, no authority to wield. For a man used to doing both, it would have been an empty transition from son to head of his own house.

Pavia held his gaze. 'You're thinking of her, aren't you?' Her hand tightened inside his grip. 'I've cost you everything, haven't I? Money, a home, servants, every privilege.' She tried to pull her hand away, but Cam held firm.

'I was thinking of her,' he replied honestly, 'and how glad I am that it's you I'm with, how glad I am to be here, a complete master of my future. Pavia, you haven't cost me everything, you've *given* me everything I've ever wanted.' He bent his forehead to hers. 'I know it's not easy, but I think we've made a fabulous start. We might not be great at cooking—' a seductive smile flirted on his lips '—but we're good at other things and we have all our lives to sort out the rest.'

Her arms went about his neck as her voiced teased with feigned naivety. 'What other things do you mean?'

Cam kissed her earlobe, breathing in the jasmine scent of her. 'Things that happen in the bedroom. Maybe the kitchen just isn't our room,' he murmured. He wanted to scoop her up in his arms and carry her upstairs, lay her down on those dusty covers and make love well into the afternoon. But his bride had other ideas.

'And maybe the kitchen could be,' she whispered against his lips. 'We just need to practise.' She disengaged from him long enough to come around the butcher block. Her hands went to the waistband of his riding breeches, working the fastenings open and sliding his trousers past his hips, as she held his gaze with a hot, wicked glance, once more the dancer he'd met in the tavern. There was an innate boldness to her that more than compensated for whatever she lacked in expertise.

Cam was already hard with imagining, with desire, when she bade him sit on the edge of the slab and, with one last, hot look, took the long length of him in her hand and began to stroke. Good lord, he wouldn't last long at this rate. She kissed him hard on the mouth, as her hand moved on him. 'My only regret,' she whispered huskily, 'is that the butcher block is too high to use my mouth on you.'

Cam groaned. He was going to lose it, right here in the kitchen if she kept up that talk. Already, he knew he'd never walk into the kitchen and see it the same way. Her thumb stroked the tip of him, tender and teasing, bringing his desire to a boiling roil of heaven and hell. He strained against the motion of her hand. 'Cup me,' he instructed hoarsely. And she did, her other hand reaching for the hidden sac beneath his phallus, her fingernail tracing the sensitive seam of them until Cam was reduced to the most primitive of exhalations as he shuddered, his body wanting release and yet refusing it, struggling to prolong this pleasure, to hold on to any small amount of control he had left. But she wrested that from him, too, until all he could do was let the climax envelop him as she held him, his head buried against her shoulder. They stayed like that for a while, his head against her, his arms wrapped about her waist, her hand on his exhausted member.

'Did you like it?' Pavia whispered as his breathing settled.

He laughed softly. 'No honeymoon to the Lake District could be finer. We'd be limited to one room there.'

Pavia shook back her hair. 'One of the benefits, I suppose, of not having any servants. We have the place to ourselves.'

Cam raised his head and gave her a considering glance. 'One of the benefits. Another would be the ability to wear one's dressing gown downstairs without drawing undue notice.' He tugged at her sash, his desire stirring once more. 'Your turn, wife. Up on the butcher block you go. There's a recipe I want to show you that involves jam.'

Chapter Ten

'Tell me about the house, Cam,' Pavia asked dreamily, as Cam licked the last of the jam from her breasts. It had been a rather erotic breakfast despite its ignominious beginnings.

'I've never lived here. This house used to belong to my great-aunt Lily, my grandfather's sister. It was a holiday retreat for her and her husband, Elliott.' Cam passed her a napkin. 'But I spent summers here, when I was younger and Grandfather allowed it. After I turned fourteen, it was simply not good enough for Grandfather.' Cam leaned against the butcher block, watching her, his blue eyes contemplative, remembering.

'Why wasn't it allowed?' Pavia used the corner of the napkin to wipe a spot of jam from his mouth. She liked this light intimacy, these quiet conversations.

'It embarrassed my grandfather that they didn't have anything grander, but Lily would always say, "Why? It's just the two of us and it's close to the river for Elliott's fishing".' Cam smiled. 'I loved being here. It was different than anything I'd ever known. The house was warm and cosy, full of overstuffed chairs and braided rugs. A boy could run and play without fear of knocking over precious knick-knacks or being yelled at for making too much noise.' He grinned. 'Do you want to know a secret? Great-Aunt Lily and I would bake biscuits. We'd roll out the dough right here on this very butcher block. I think I ate more of it than we baked.'

'It wasn't like that at home, I take it?' Pavia gave a soft laugh, 'I'm imagining you as a little boy with dough on your fingers. Were you a darling or a terror?'

'A darling. Aylsbury wouldn't have it any other way even if I wasn't an heir. I was top of my class in mathematics and history at Eton. I studied very hard for that. Grandfather was proud, of course. I distinguished myself quickly in the military. He is also quite proud of that. It's all a credit to the Aylsbury name.' Cam said it all lightly, wryly, but Pavia sensed the bitterness beneath. He'd given his life in service to his family, making them proud. All for what? At the first sign of disobedience that family had abandoned him—they couldn't even be bothered to come to his wedding.

'And now this,' Pavia said softly. His world had been perfect until she'd interrupted it.

Cam drew a breath. 'Yes, now this. The golden child has displeased the dynasty.' He grinned as if to say he was unconcerned by what his family thought. She wondered how long that nonchalance would last. His hands bracketed her hips as he leaned forward, eager to dismiss the unpleasantness of his family. His forehead touched hers. 'What about you? Were you an angel or an imp?'

'An angel. Did you really need to ask?' she teased, but she was decidedly uncomfortable with the subject. Her childhood had been different by English standards and that was putting it mildly.

'And?' Cam coaxed. 'You have to say more, I told *you* more.'

'You will think my upbringing scandalous,' she warned. 'Maybe it's best you don't know.'

Cam kissed her eyelids. 'I want to know everything about you. What's the fun of marrying a stranger if you can't uncover them?'

'I think you've uncovered quite a bit already.' Pavia laughed.

'Tell me, Pavia. I promise not to be scandalised,' Cam begged, his blue eyes dancing with irresistible mischief.

'All right. Remember, you promised,' Pavia said sternly. 'I lived in the zenana at my uncle's court in Sohra with my mother and all the other women and children. My father was gone on business, travelling all over Asia, making his fortune.' She watched his face for a reaction. 'Are you scandalised now, like every other Englishman who doesn't truly understand the function of a zenana?'

'Hardly,' Cam assured her. 'You forget, I've been to India. I know what is real and what are the fictions. Now, I believe I promised to show you the house. Let's start in the dining room.'

The dining room was empty, no table, no chairs, no hutch for dishes. It was just a space, until Cam began to talk, walking her about the room, painting her a picture with his words. 'There used to be a rosewood table with six chairs, here in the centre. Aunt Lily had a hutch against the wall over there where she kept her silver candlesticks and china with pink roses painted on the edges.'

The room came to life for her as Cam talked.

Pavia could see the table with a white cloth, the pretty dishes and the candlesticks; it was a homely image. Something tugged at her heartstrings. They would create such images here, too, for their child, for each other, perhaps. It would take a while. Today, there wasn't even a table to sit at and, even if there was, she hadn't the faintest idea of what to cook.

Nostalgia softened Cam's eyes when he looked at her. 'I have mostly good memories of this room and the meals we shared in here. Dinner was far more informal here than it was at home.'

'Mostly?' She teased softly. 'What does that mean?'

Cam lowered his eyes and let out an exaggerated breath. 'It means there's something you should know. Something that you might find shocking.' She could tell from his tone, he was having fun with her, paying her back perhaps for over-dramatising her earlier confession. 'I hate green beans, passionately, all because of what happened in this room.'

She played along, a smile flirting with her mouth as she gave a dramatic whisper. 'What happened in this room?'

'I'd been taught to eat the food I liked least first, so I could enjoy the rest of the meal without the unlikeable food hanging over me,' he explained. 'One evening, the Hughleys came to supper and Mrs Hughley brought green beans, which I have never cared for. I ate them first, of course, since that was the rule, only to have Mrs Hughley take note at how fast they'd disappeared. She said, "Oh, you liked them so much, here's another helping".'

'Oh, no, what did you do?' Pavia waited breathlessly for the conclusion. Her husband was a born storyteller, entertaining and funny— what an interesting and delightful revelation to make.

'I ended up having to eat both servings to be polite. It was the last time I used that strategy. But to this day, Mrs Hughley thinks I love her green beans.'

The last caught Pavia's attention. 'She still lives here?'

'Oh, yes. Most folks in Little Trull have never left it, never been more than ten or fifteen miles away from home. It's different now, for my generation. The train makes it possible for people to travel about the country if they wish. Many don't wish to. Some of the boys join the military and see a bit of the world. Most don't. Most take up their fathers' occupations.'

Pavia looked down at her hands, the mirth of his story fading. 'Then I will be quite foreign to them. What will they think of their hero coming home with an exotic bride?'

Cam took her hands. 'They will love you.' But secretly, Pavia worried. What would these people think of their baby? She had been protected by her father's money. What would protect her child? Society could be cruel to those who were different. Could she count on Cam to be their champion? It was simple to say one thing when honour was easy. What would he say when the sacrifices never ended? She searched her husband's face. Did he understand life wasn't like a military campaign? It didn't have a definitive beginning, end and outcome. The battle he'd fought to marry her would be just one of many and they would never end.

She squeezed his hands and smiled. 'I hope you're right.' He had to be. She'd staked everything on it.

That first morning established a rather decadent routine in the days that followed: intimate breakfasts in the kitchen in their dressing gowns, Cam standing behind her, one hand at her waist, the other covering hers on the handle of a skillet as he taught her how to scramble eggs and turn the toast, his mouth at her ear, her neck, stealing kisses. Breakfast itself was a time to talk, to plan their day, which involved a tour of some part of the house or the property.

Technically, they were making lists of supplies needed to make the house habitable: curtains for the front parlour, furniture, carpets. Nothing too luxurious, but enough to see the house made comfortable. More importantly, though, they were learning one another. Planning the house gave them time to share, to know one another, to rub off the strangeness of being together, to dream together. This house was becoming 'theirs', a blank slate they were imagining together. It might not be an elegant town house in Mayfair, but it was theirs and they were determined to make a family home, full once more of braided wool rugs and comfortable furniture, a place where their child could run and play as Cam had.

The house was full of happy memories for Cam, but Pavia was learning her husband had other memories, memories he preferred to keep hidden. Her husband didn't sleep well. Too often at night, she woke to find him absent from their bed, pacing in front of the windows, his torso bathed in moonlight, the deep look on his face suggesting he wanted to be left alone. So she did. She would respect his privacy and hope that, in time, he would come to her with his troubles.

Meanwhile, their week passed amiably. They'd saved the sitting room at the back of the house for last and Pavia approached this final room with trepidation, knowing that it signalled the end of the honeymoon. It had been seven days since Cam had brought her here. They were out of spaces.

'I loved this room best.' Cam came up behind her as she surveyed the space, his voice quiet at her ear. She was getting used to this; the ease with which he touched her and held her was yet another product of this nearly perfect week. They'd begun to figure out how to be together in and out of bed. There was much to be thankful for, but always the blemish on the edges of Pavia's happiness was the fear of reality. They would have to leave this world soon and rejoin the real one. There would be more tests, harder tests. But those could wait, just a day longer.

Pavia sank back against him, resting her head on his shoulder, and craned her neck upwards to smile at him. Like the other rooms, this one was empty now, devoid of even a single chair. 'Tell me about this room, then.' This, too, was part of their ritual; Cam's stories of his childhood visits here.

'Aunt Lily and I would curl up in this room on rainy days and she would read to me.' He pointed to the fireplace with its painted-white wood mantel. 'There was a big, overstuffed chair near the fire, done in a red-checked upholstery.' Her husband was smiling now as he told the tale. 'It was old even then and it sagged a bit, but there was room for two of us in it. To this day, I have never since sat in a more comfortable chair.'

'Your great-aunt sounds like a lovely woman.' Pavia was already envisioning a rug and two chairs at the hearth.

'She was. I have fond memories of her. I was thrilled to receive the property when she passed. I think my grandfather was hoping it would simply disappear after she died, or that I'd sell it. After all, what does a travelling military man need with a property? But I kept it, although there was never time to visit.'

'I'm glad you kept it.' Pavia turned in his embrace, hugging him close. 'It will be a wonderful home for us.' She looked up at him and he smiled down at her, a different smile than the one he wore reminiscing about Great-Aunt

Lily. This was a wicked smile, one that said they wouldn't be decorating much longer. His hands flexed at her hips.

'I can see our children now, playing on the carpet with a ball and jacks, laughing. You in a chair, a book in hand or maybe some needle-point, relaxing by the fire of an evening. Me in another chair, just there, pretending to read through the newspaper, but really I am looking over the top of it, watching you and wondering when I can have you again.'

It was a warm image, an inviting one, a glimpse into a future they had not yet created. 'Children? That might be presumptuous given that we haven't had the one yet,' Pavia teased.

'I am not an advocate of only children, having been one myself. I don't think it has much to recommend it. You wouldn't mind? After all, you're an only child, too.' Cam sobered suddenly, a line creasing his brow. 'We're both only children. I just thought of that. Our children won't have any aunts or uncles.'

Or grandparents at this rate, with both sides having refused to acknowledge their marriage. Their children would be born into a contentious, difficult family situation, whether she and Cam willed it or not. That die had already been cast. Pavia shoved the thoughts away and smiled brightly, determined to think only of the present. There were enough troubles in the immediate future without borrowing more. 'No, I wouldn't mind.' There were other interesting aspects of the image he painted, full of underlying assumptions they'd not yet talked about like his military career and their income. But Pavia pushed those thoughts away as well. Rome wasn't built in a day and neither was a marriage. They had hurdles enough to face and they would face them in due time. They would not conquer the world today.

She took his face between her hands and kissed him, meaningfully.

'There's no furniture in this room, Pavia,' Cam cautioned, divining the message of her kiss correctly. Several of their planning sessions had ended like this—a kiss, a caress and then lovemaking on a worn piece of furniture. It had become their ritual just assuredly as scrambling eggs in their dressing gowns.

'Are we dogs, marking our territory?' Cam laughed.

'Dogs!' Pavia shook her head and wrinkled her nose in distaste at the metaphor. 'Hardly. We're christening each room. That's a much more civilised concept.'

He nipped at her neck. 'Where shall I take you, then? The floor?'

'There's four good walls. Pick one, Cam.' She sucked at his earlobe. 'But hurry.'

He chuckled. 'Because walls are so civilised, my dear? Are you sure we aren't dogs?' But he was already lifting her, her legs already about his waist as he backed her to the wall, his dressing gown already open.

'Civility is overrated,' Pavia murmured huskily, clinging to him. She didn't mind. There was nothing terribly civilised about the wall or about her husband thrusting into her, hard and hungry, nor was there anything civilised in the thrill of moaning her pleasure as he took her. Passion was a glorious, greedy thing, Pavia had discovered in the early days of their honeymoon. Once one had it, one simply wanted more. Thankfully, Cam was an inexhaustible lover.

Too bad the house wasn't as inexhaustible. They'd run out of excuses to live like romantic hermits. Perhaps Cam felt it, too. There was an edge to his lovemaking this morning. It was rougher, deeper, his groans more primal than usual. Not that she minded. The desperate razor of sex matched her own feelings. Sooner or later, they'd have to emerge from their cocoon, an eventuality that grew closer with each passing day. Pavia gripped him tight, her body overriding her mind, her thoughts, as Cam drove them relentlessly towards pleasure, towards forgetfulness. As long as they were in pleasure's grip, they didn't have to think, didn't have to plan, or reckon with the outside world. He came into her, hard, once more. She shattered with an unrepressed scream and a selfish wish that it could it be like this for ever. No worries, only pleasure.

Cam held her against the wall for a long while afterwards, their bodies still joined, his head on her shoulder, in no hurry to leave her. 'I love the way you smell. Jasmine and lemongrass and what else? There's something else there.' He breathed deep at her neck.

'Citrus,' she whispered. 'I mix it myself.'

'Yes, I can smell it now.' Cam sighed, his body shifting, a sign his muscles were tiring of the position at last. 'I have an idea. I know a place where there are wildflowers you can pick. There's no jasmine, of course, but you might discover a new scent you like. Shall we take a picnic and go? We'll take a honeymoon from the honeymoon.'

'Right now?'

'Well, yes, since I have to put you down anyway.' Cam gently disengaged and her legs unwound from their post at his hips.

Chapter Eleven

A honeymoon from the honeymoon was most apt. Pavia took Cam's hand and let him lead her down the sloping path beside the waterfall to the pool beneath. 'It's like our own Paradise,' she murmured softly, unwilling to break the silence around them. That silence was penetrated only by the trill of kingfishers hiding in the trees.

Cam spread out a blanket and deposited the basket. 'My great-aunt brought me here once. I've never forgotten it.'

'Thank goodness, there are no signs. One would never know it's here.' Pavia settled her skirts about her, breathing in the fresh air.

'It's supposed to be enchanted. There are stories of the waters having magical powers to restore youth.' Cam leaned back on his elbows. 'Do you see the island in the middle of the pool? It's a love heart. We can walk out to it if you want.'

Her stomach took that moment to gurgle loudly and intrusively. 'It seems I'm hungry all the time, if I'm not being sick.' Fortunately, the morning sickness had not become a regular occurrence. She hadn't been nauseous since the first day of their arrival.

Cam reached for the basket. 'Maybe we should eat now. Ham sandwich?' He passed her one of the sandwiches they'd made together in the kitchen before setting out.

She bit into it with relish, tasting the sweetness of the meat and the soft cream of the cheese. 'These are so good.'

Cam's eyes were on her, a smile on his lips. 'Enjoy it. That's the last of the ham until we go into town.' It was meant as a tease, but the words shifted the ease between them. 'Perhaps we should arrange for that cook-cum-housekeeper to start work when we go into the village?' Cam asked neutrally.

She met his eyes, her own response reluctant. She knew what that meant. An intruder in their little world. But she couldn't argue with it. 'I suppose we should. We can't live on ham sandwiches and scrambled eggs for ever.' She tried for a laugh but managed to conjure tears instead. Sweet heavens, what was she crying for? Over a ham sandwich? Over her husband wanting to hire help? It was nonsensical. Those were not reasons to cry. She brushed at the ridiculous tears and got to her feet.

'Pavia?' Cam reached for her, but she shook her head.

'I'm sorry, I need a moment.' She moved to the edge of the pool to collect herself but it wasn't long before Cam's arms were about her, pulling her close.

'I've upset you.'

'No, it's nothing. I am just being silly.' She dashed at the tears. 'I know we have to rejoin the real world some time.' She tried for a smile. 'We're out of rooms to plan and food to eat.'

'But you wish we weren't?' he asked.

'Yes.' Pavia sighed. 'This has been nice. I don't want to give it up.' She paused. Her words didn't do the sentiment justice. 'We are not so much strangers any more, are we? I don't want to lose that, Cam.' That was her real worry. What would happen to this fragile, precious 'togetherness' they'd cobbled, once the world intruded with its opinions?

'We won't,' Cam insisted. But how could he be sure? She wished she had his confidence.

'The world will test us. I am not entirely

English and I don't look English.' They'd not talked of that. It had never been an issue between them, but the world would notice and make them accountable for it. 'People will cut us.'

'People have already cut us—*family* has cut us.' She felt Cam's shoulders lift and fall in a shrug of dismissal as if those things were of no consequence. She could not dismiss that reality so casually.

'Cam, it is not so easy to be alone, to be shunned by everyone from butchers to dressmakers.' She'd not forgotten how hard it had been when her family had first arrived. Not everyone was eager to serve her mother.

'You are borrowing trouble, Pavia. That hasn't happened yet and maybe it won't. Perhaps the rest of the world is less judgemental than the *ton*. Besides, once they meet you, they will love you.' She wished she shared Cam's optimism but she'd seen how London responded to her mother when they'd first arrived and how they'd responded to her. If not for the buffer of her father's money, they'd not have been welcomed. She didn't want to argue, so she let it go. They would see soon enough what the world had in store for them.

'We'll have to start wearing our clothes

more often, with help under foot,' Pavia said with a disappointment that wasn't all feigned. She would miss these heady days of discovery, of pleasure. These days gave her hope as to what they could be to one another. Never mind that they'd started as strangers. They might, in time, become something more. This week had demonstrated the potential was there, if they had a chance to explore it. One week was hardly enough to build something that could stand up to the outside.

'I suppose we shall have to concede on the clothing.' Cam laughed softly. 'Will you come back and finish your lunch?' He took her hand. 'I don't want the ham to go to waste.'

Pavia let Cam lead her back to the blanket, let him tell her tales of English fairies and the magical powers of the waterfall, but the ambiance of the day had ebbed and she never quite got it back. Still, her new husband's optimism was much appreciated. She yawned and Cam patted his leg. 'Come, lay your head on my lap. I'll keep guard so that no one invades our fairy glen.'

Invasion would come, though. His bride was not wrong on that account. They had to surface from playing honeymoon house and join the real world. Cam stroked Pavia's hair, watching the soft rise and fall of her as she slept. While she was worried about what the world would tempt them with, he was worried about the threat from within. What would they do to themselves?

They had yet to discuss the future. The present had been full of enough hurdles to negotiate, the most important being that his child and its mother had a name, that they were protected from society's slander. But now that was accomplished and it was time to turn thoughts to what next? They had a home. His child and his wife would have a roof over their heads no one could take away. But would he be there with them? Would he share that home with them? Would he even have a choice?

These thoughts had niggled at the back of his mind all week as they'd gone through the manse, making their lists, imagining their home. His leave only lasted until August. He would be expected to rejoin his men and take up his command in Sevastopol. When his child came in January, he would be a continent away, isolated by snow and ice. It could be spring before he had word of the child's birth. Unless…

Unless he gave it up. How could he be the father he'd vowed to be if he was absent, engaged in a career where the goal of any encounter was to simply survive until the next time he was shot at? He'd never thought of his soldiering career in such dreary terms before. No one else had ever been counting on him the way Pavia and his child were. But what of the search for Fortis and what of his men? Staying here meant ending his personal mission to confirm Fortis's death. He would have to rely solely on letters, which would take weeks to travel. Time would be lost, time that might be crucial in locating Fortis if he was still out there. If he did not continue that mission, who would? No one else believed there was a chance. It was a deuced difficult spot to be in, having to choose between one's best friend and one's family. Both deserved his loyalty, but only one could fully have it.

In the trees a kingfisher trilled. He should give up the military, at least the active part of it. Perhaps he should write to his commanding officers and start the process of seeking out a desk job, something safe and staid in London. The train made London closer these days. Perhaps they could even get a small house in the city. There were new suburbs, respectable homes in Bloomsbury they could afford on his salary. They could spend the holidays and summers here in Somerset.

It was a difficult sell, though. He'd worked hard for his career, for his rise up the chain of command. It was no easy thing to contemplate limiting himself to a desk and paperwork. And yet, it must be done if he wanted to see his child born, to see his child grow to adulthood, to take care of his wife. Pavia stirred in his lap and something fierce woke within him. He loved his friend, but he would not make Fortis's mistakes. Fortis had been an imperfect husband. Cam would not leave behind a widow. He'd seen Avaline's face the day he'd told her the news. Whatever their marriage had been, she'd been truly devastated. Never mind they'd lived apart, separated by Fortis's career and perhaps more, for the years of the marriage. As long as Fortis had lived, there'd always been hope he'd come home, that maybe this time he'd choose to stay, that they could start over. Now Avaline was alone, her position in the world insecure. Perhaps it was a blessing there'd been no children for them. That meant one less person affected by Fortis's death. Cam would not choose such a destiny for his little family.

He looked down at his wife, sleeping in his

lap. He let the newness of that word 'wife', and all it entailed, sweep through him. He was a married man now. He made a private pledge. His family would be provided for. If that provision came at the expense of having a desk job, of watching others march out for glory, then so be it. His family needed an income. The military was the only way for him to provide it now that his grandfather had stopped his allowance and there was no bridal dowry. He'd not expected one and Honeysett had made it plain none would be forthcoming. Still, the facts were that he and Pavia had gone from being a very wealthy young couple to a young couple living on a major's salary, which was just about right for a twelve-room cottage and a couple of servants—a far cry from town houses and summer estates, and scores of help.

When would Pavia miss it? All the luxury of her father's home? All the trappings of the life she once had? When would *he* miss the military life? When would they come to resent each other for what this had cost them? That was what Cam feared more than he feared any cut direct from a society he had little use for. He didn't want to hate his wife. He didn't want his wife to hate him. This week had been full of joy and hope, as long as they didn't look too far ahead. He wanted that joy to last, wanted to get to know this woman. Those things took time. Real friendships were forged with history that bound them together. They were not instantaneous things. He hoped they would have that time.

The child will bind you together, his conscience whispered. *There will always be that and that will be your comfort and hers. You will look at that child sleeping in the cradle, toddling on the lawn, catching their first fish, and in all those moments you will be reminded that it was worth it. Whatever sacrifices are made, they will be worth it for those moments, for that life.*

The litany brought peace. Yes. He was a husband now, a father now. Whatever needed to be done would be worth it. Resolution settled firmly on Cam's shoulders. There were plans to be made and people to meet. It was time. The next day was Sunday. The future would begin tomorrow whether they were ready for it or not.

Chapter Twelve

❧❧❧

Sunday church was as good a time as any for building their future and perhaps a better choice than most, Pavia reflected as they took their seats in the pew at the village church amid not-so-covert stares of interest. Or, maybe, Sunday was more ominous. The irony was not lost on Pavia. She and Cam were beginning the work of integrating themselves into the community of Little Trull on the day of rest. She hoped it was not an ill portent. She slid a secret glance at Cam and squeezed his hand in solidarity.

They sat seven rows back from the pulpit, trying not to be overly conspicuous, while the Vicar preached on the importance of loving thy neighbour. Of course, in a small, tightly knit community, any newcomer was bound to stand out as a matter of fact. When those new-

comers were young newlyweds, one of whom
had once hailed from these parts as a child
visitor, the usual amount of interest permitted
over a stranger escalated to a fevered pitch.
Pavia thought the Vicar did an admirable job
of keeping his congregation's attention focused
where it should be—on the pulpit. If his sermon was slightly shorter than normal, it was
a wise shepherd who knew the patient limits
of his flock.

'Therefore, Children, as the world grows
larger it also grows smaller, with distances
spanned in remarkable speed,' the Vicar concluded. 'The words of St Matthew's Gospel
remain more important than ever. "Love thy
neighbour".'

A fortuitous message for today, Pavia
thought. The man couldn't have known they'd
be there. *They* hadn't even known they'd be
there until yesterday's decision, made over
ham sandwiches at the fairy falls.

The service was nearly over. She wouldn't
have minded a longer sermon today. Now only
the benediction stood between them and the
satisfaction of congregational curiosity. Cam
gave her a private smile. He looked handsome
today in his Hussar's uniform of dark blue
wool and gold braid, his hair brushed back

in thick, shiny waves. She knew Cam was as anxious as she. She'd awakened in the night to find him pacing by the window. She'd wanted to go to him, but she'd sensed his distress and opted to leave him alone, still clinging to her earlier hope that men like her husband would ask for help when they needed it.

They rose with the others and shuffled into the aisle, queuing to greet the Vicar at the door. She was conscious of Cam's hand at her back, ushering her before him, his touch giving her extra confidence, a reminder that she was not alone. They were together in this. Whatever anyone said or thought of the other, they said or thought of them both. She could get used to that—the unwavering, unshakeable strength of such a person beside her. She knew how potent such a characteristic was. It was not the first time he'd displayed it. She'd had a taste of it the day he'd come for her at her father's. Today, the hand at her back said, to her and to others, 'you are mine', '*she* is mine'. Once, she would have despised that message, seen it as high-handed male proprietary behaviour that claimed a woman was a man's possession. In this room full of strangers, she understood that message anew. It was not about the possession of property. It was a message of protection, a reminder to others of what her due was and what might be forfeit if that due was not rendered.

She hoped there would be no need to claim that forfeit today. She'd dressed carefully, too, wanting to be the equal of Cam's brushed and polished uniform. She'd chosen a white summer muslin, with embroidered wildflowers in a riot of summer pinks, greens and yellows at the hem. She'd done them herself as part of her trousseau at Mrs Finlay's. A hat and delicately embroidered lawn shawl completed the ensemble, with her dark hair fashioned into a twist low on her neck beneath the hat's brim. It was a very English outfit.

She wanted to be a credit to Cam today. He had such optimistic hopes about their first outing. It was natural Cam would. He'd spent time in Little Trull. He'd never been shunned. Wherever he went, doors had always been open to him as the grandson of a powerful earl. Despite her father's money, her world had been very different. Her father's money had to oil hinges on doors that had opened for Cam without protest. Sometimes, that money was used to force those doors open when a polite knock did not work, like the door at Mrs Finlay's Academy, a school famed for its exclusivity and its ability to attain the highest matrimonial prizes for its pupils, boasting among its storied matches Helena Colbert to the Duke of Cowden's heir. Mrs Finlay's had not wanted a nabob's half-breed daughter mixing with the aristocratic elite. Would Little Trull feel the same way? And this time, she wouldn't have her father's money to change their minds.

They reached the front of the line and Vicar Danson shook Cam's hand with enthusiasm. He was an older man with friendly lines about his eyes. 'We are so happy to have you with us, Major. What a delight to know that Mr Elmsworth and Lady Lillian's home will be occupied again.' He chuckled and turned warm brown eyes to Pavia. She drew a breath and waited. This was the moment of truth. Perhaps even now, the congregation was watching for the Vicar's reaction to set the tone. 'Mrs Lithgow, I hope you didn't find the place uninhabitable?' he asked sincerely. He gave her a wink. 'If so, we'll have to scold your husband and teach him better manners. If you need any stories about him as a young lad, remember I know them all.' He tapped his temple with a knowing finger.

'I am pleased to have a home of my own,' Pavia answered with a truth she'd discovered throughout the week. As they'd made their lists and plans, the empty house had wormed its way into her heart. It would be their place, a home they would make themselves.

'The place does need some work,' Cam admitted. 'My bride has been good-natured, to say the least.' He gave her a lingering smile with the compliment, letting everyone see his open affection for her. But even as beautiful as the moment was, a testimony to newlywed happiness, Pavia felt doubt edge her bliss. Cam had orchestrated this occasion, with his uniform, his bearing, the touch at her back. Was this statement orchestrated, too? Was it genuine affection or was he playing for the crowd? Despite their growing closeness, Pavia wondered—was this real or was it show? Something done because it must be? Because Cam's deep-seated sense of honour demanded it?

'We will have the place set to rights in no time,' the Vicar assured him with a fatherly clasp on the shoulder. 'And, my dear Mrs Lithgow, my wife will waste no time calling on you. She's always looking for someone to add to her committees.'

'I will look forward to it.' Pavia smiled, feeling one hurdle was conquered. Surely, it was a good sign if she could charm the Vicar into acceptance.

'She's delightful and polite, Major. I am happy for you both.' The Vicar smiled again and offered Pavia his arm. 'Let me introduce you two to everyone. Come with me and we'll make the rounds.'

People were eager to meet them as the Vicar led them from group to group beneath the shady oak trees in the churchyard where the congregation gathered to socialise. Men were keen to greet 'the Major'. Older men reminisced with Cam about his great-aunt and uncle. The younger men were drawn to the uniform, wanting to talk politics about the Crimea and the situation at Balaclava. Pavia wondered if it bothered Cam to speak of it. Their wives and daughters came with them, some of them interested in meeting the Major's wife. Some were shy, some wore their disapproval of a 'foreign marriage' in their eyes. Others, like the Brownings, were more open in their dislike.

'Welcome home, Major.' Mr Browning, straight-shouldered and white-haired, shook Cam's hand solemnly, but barely spared Pavia a glance. 'I am sure you are glad to be back on civilised ground again. Foreign climates can be difficult. I'm surprised you'd want to marry a reminder of all those tribulations.'

Mrs Browning gave Pavia a cold stare. 'Especially when there are so many good-looking English girls who would make splendid wives.' Beside her, Mrs Browning's unmarried daughter blushed with lowered lashes.

'Well, my wife has stolen my heart,' Cam affirmed in stern tones meant to remind anyone who disagreed that he would champion her. 'If you will excuse us?'

The Brownings were not alone. The Stiltons made no secret of their dislike either. 'How dare you marry the enemy, when so many good English boys have died over there. Killed by fevers and heathens just like her.' Pavia found herself taking a physical step back in the wake of Mrs Stilton's quietly voiced accusation, which was no less vitriolic for its lack of volume.

Help came from an unlooked-for corner. A blonde-haired matron swept in, looping an arm through Mrs Stilton's. 'There, there, Hetty. We all miss your Jonah,' she consoled. 'He was a good lad, but it's not Mrs Lithgow's fault. That was nearly twenty years ago. She had nothing to do with it.' The blonde smiled apologetically at Pavia. 'Your gown is lovely—did you do the needlework yourself?'

'Yes, I did,' Pavia answered, grateful for the change in conversation.

'It must have taken hours,' the woman said admiringly. 'We simply must have you on our committee.' She moved away from Mrs Stilton and slipped her arm through Pavia's. 'I want to snatch you up before Vicar Danson's wife claims all of your time.' She laughed heartily. 'I'm Letty Weldon, head of the church blanket committee. Come and meet the other ladies.' She drew Pavia towards a group of women gathered beneath one of the shady oaks and, within moments, Pavia was engulfed in the friendly group. The committee, it turned out, made blankets from local alpaca wool to welcome all the newborns in the parish, each blanket embroidered with the baby's name and date of birth as a keepsake. 'We also do baskets for the mothers,' another matron explained, 'full of food so their families won't starve while they rest.'

An older matron slid her a friendly look. 'With a handsome husband like yours, we'll be making you a basket within the year, I'd wager.' It was meant as a tease, but Pavia blushed, giving away the truth of it.

The matron clapped her hands with delight. 'Oh, like that, is it? Already expecting? How delightful!' Another hurdle fell, despite the negativity of the Brownings and Stiltons. Pavia could hear it collapsing in her mind. She had never met earthy women like these in England, women who weren't afraid to talk about life. In their own way, they reminded her of the women from her uncle's zenana. There was nothing like a wedding, a pregnancy or a baby for breaking down barriers. These were universal experiences that bound women together regardless of geography and culture.

By the time Cam came to collect her, she'd been inundated with advice on everything from managing morning sickness to the household budget. There had been some unpleasantness today, but there were also many who welcomed her with polite promises to call, or invitations for her to visit their husbands' shops in the village. It was a start. She could cultivate relationships from those offerings and she would, for Cam's sake, and for the sake of her child.

But as well as the outing had gone, Cam seemed tired and drawn on the walk home. They walked mostly in silence. She hoped he was pleased with the morning, and pleased with her. 'Success can be overwhelming.' Pavia ventured once they reached home and the sanctuary of their bedchamber. 'I don't know if I dare trust it.' She shut the door behind them and leaned against it, watching her husband. He sat down on the bed, tugging at his boots. His face was pale.

She went to him and took hold of the boot. 'Let me do this. Are you all right? Did something happen? Did I do something wrong?'

He reached a hand to her check, a brief, tired smile on his face. 'You were brilliant. Everything went as I hoped it would for you.'

She held his hand a moment longer at her cheek. 'You're warm. That uniform must be ghastly to wear in the heat.' Then, she set to work on loosening his collar. 'Everyone was impressed with it, though.' She tried to tease him into a better humour. 'Especially the ladies.' She paused and added, 'The men were impressed, too, I think.' She rested her hands on Cam's shoulders, touched by all today had cost him. 'You wore it to impress them, didn't you? To remind them of your station and, by extension, mine?' It was a gallant sacrifice to make considering the discomfort. But it was not entirely a physical discomfort. 'Was it difficult to talk of the war?' Pavia enquired softly, recognising the extent of the effort he'd made today. She helped him with his coats and hung them over the chair. Cam stretched out on the bed, his long body filling it. He was looking cooler now in just his shirt and breeches.

'Yes.'

That single word of admission moved her. It took a brave man to admit his limits. But more than that, Pavia was moved by the motives behind what he'd done—he'd pushed those limits for *her*, for *their* chance to win acceptance. It was another reminder that whether or not she'd married a man who loved her, she had married a man who would be loyal.

Pavia sat on the bed beside him. 'You did it for me. And now you've stirred your demons.' She smoothed his hair back from his forehead. 'I remember that first night in the tavern. I watched you from behind the kitchen door and I thought then, there's a man with troubles.' He'd shared some of those troubles with her that night. Perhaps he would do so again if she was patient. This was not like trading childhood memories and stories as they walked through the house. Talking of these troubles, of the war and his lost friend, was different— riskier, darker, more exposed. Pavia took his hand, lacing her fingers through his, and waited. Her husband was a man who shared very little of his deepest self. He protected his private self. He needed time to find his words.

'There's rumour that Raglan, our command-ing officer, will resign his commission over the bungling at Balaclava.' Cam sighed. His free hand rubbed at his temple, massaging. 'It hardly matters what he does now. It can't bring the others back. He never should have been in charge to start with. He knew nothing of tac-tics and strategy.' There was a fierce, desper-ate edge to his voice.

'And now your friend is dead,' Pavia em-pathised softly. He'd spoken of that friend once before and she'd sensed the deep grief he car-ried over that death, a grief he held on a tight rein. She'd forgotten that in the whirlwind of their marriage. Perhaps he had, too, and today had brought it all roaring back to the surface. The grief was still there, the pain still there.

'Yes, dammit! Fortis is dead because a stu-pid man gave stupid orders and no resignation can change that.' Cam winced against the pain, this time clearly a physical pain. Her stubborn husband had a headache.

Pavia rose and went to the console acting as a dressing table. She might not be able to cook, but she was good with herbs and medicine. She opened a small travelling kit and took out a vial. She pulled the stopper and sniffed, then tried another one until she found the oils she wanted. She mixed droplets in with the water in the basin, a pleasant smell filling the air as she soaked a towel. She wrung it out and brought it to Cam, placing it on his brow. 'This will help. It's lavender and rosemary with a hint of basil mixed in.' She sat down again and took up his hand. 'Basil is supposed to bring happiness. It seems like you need some of that today.'

'Do you know what else would make me happy?' Cam asked, eyes shut. 'You, laying down beside me. Tell me how it is you know so much about herbs and oils. I don't want to think about war any more.' Or his friend, Pavia divined. He needed to talk about it, though, or it would continue to haunt him. But perhaps not today. Perhaps he'd suffered enough for one day. So Pavia loosened her gown and lay down beside her husband, running her fingers through his hair.

'In the court of the Raja of Sohra, the women are very beautiful and skilled in the ancient arts. I learned them at my mother's side. I learned to distil oil from flower blossoms. I learned that it took one thousand orange blossoms to make neroli.' She regaled with him tales and uses: that the precious neroli oil soothed nerves, that lavender relieved stress and soothed skin burnt by the sun. 'And frankincense helps with meditation,' she ended softly, noting the smooth, slow rise and fall of his chest. He would have some peace now and so would she, snuggled against his side. A wifely peace. The kind that came from caring for another.

This was a new kind of intimacy for them, one that didn't involve sex. They'd relied heavily on the pleasure they found in bed to establish common ground. There, they knew one another. It was outside the bed that they were most exposed, most vulnerable, where they knew the least of the other. Today had been a first test of sorts for them as husband and wife. Not just the public appearance, but what had happened afterwards. He'd been the vulnerable one then. This was the first time since she'd known him that Cam had allowed himself to need her.

Since the day she'd told him about the baby, Cam had been in charge, shouldering the burden of their situation. He'd been the one to make arrangements: the hotel, the special licence, the train, the house. He'd even been the one to get food supplies and do the cooking this first week. He'd donned his uniform and given her every social advantage he could offer today should she need it. But this afternoon, he'd needed her and it had made her feel good, like a partner in this unlooked-for marriage instead of something fragile to always be protected and cossetted.

'This is just the start,' Pavia whispered to her sleeping husband. 'I will show you that I can be a wife worthy of your efforts. I will learn to clean for you, to cook for you, to keep your clothes, so that when you go out, everyone will know you have a good wife.' It would be hard. Her failed attempts at toast were proof housekeeping wouldn't come easy, but she'd have help. This wasn't the sort of housekeeping she'd been educated for at Mrs Finlay's, but she would learn. It would be her gift to him, in return for all he'd given her. Many marriages were built on less.

Chapter Thirteen

Cannon ripped like wildfire through the valley. Around him, horses and men fell with shrieks and cries. The Light Brigade had chased the Russians back to their lines, but now the survivors manned the guns once more, firing anything they could lay their hands on, not caring if their makeshift ammunition hit the Russian cavalry that still fought in the field. Yards from him, Fortis waved his sabre, gathering his riders to him. Cam did the same, spying Paget riding towards him, urging retreat. He wheeled his horse about once, looking for his men. Cannon boomed again, spraying the ground with grapeshot. Twenty feet from him, Fortis's horse reared and fell, taking Fortis with him. The Russian cavalry surged towards his fallen friend. Get up! His mind shrieked. Get up and fight! But Fortis didn't rise.

'*No, Fortis!*' *Cam tried to turn his horse, tried to push through to his friend, but Paget was there, forcing him back, blocking the route to where Fortis had fallen.*

'*Don't be a fool, man, look to yourself!*'

'*Fortis!*' *he roared, but even his horse knew better than to stay on the field where there was only indiscriminate death…*

'Cam! Wake up!' A hard shake called him back to the waking world. 'You were having a nightmare.'

Not *a* nightmare—*the* nightmare. He was covered in sweat, his breathing uneven. He recognised the symptoms. It was the first time since their wedding that he'd dreamed of Balaclava.

Pavia was beside him, the room flooded with the light of early evening, concern etched on her face. 'I'm fine,' he mumbled grumpily. His mind had betrayed hm. He was a soldier. He was supposed to be strong. Others counted on him.

'How often have you had this dream? Is this what keeps you up at night?' Pavia placed another cool towel on his brow, this one scented with lavender. 'Don't deny it. I see you pacing at the window, Cam,' she censured him when he said nothing.

'I didn't mean to wake you.' Cam deflected a direct answer. He felt exposed, ashamed. He hadn't wanted her to know. This was his private burden, his private guilt to bear.

'I wasn't bothered. I want to help. I can mix you something that will help you sleep, some herbs perhaps.' Pavia reached for another cloth. He pushed her hand away.

'I don't want another cold cloth.' He wanted to be strong.

He wanted things to be different that day at Balaclava.

'Lie still, then. Just for a moment and let yourself settle,' Pavia instructed. 'You are a terrible patient, Cam. I hope you never get truly sick.' She laughed softly to put him at ease. 'Do you want to talk about it? My mother used to tell me that bad dreams can't come true if you tell someone about them.'

How he wished that was the case. 'It's no use. This one already has.' Why hadn't he stayed closer to Fortis that day? Surely, he could have done something. At the very least, he could have taken him up on his own horse and carried him to safety. He tried to sit up, but Pavia pushed him back on his pillows.

'I see I'll have to come up with a more creative way of keeping you down.' She straddled him and pulled loose the ribbon of her chemise.

'What time is it?' Not that it mattered. His body couldn't care less. It had other things on its mind, like making love to his wife.

'Nearly seven. You slept the afternoon away.' And she had, too. Cam remembered her taking off her dress and lying down beside him, whispering herbal remedies to soothe his headache. She pulled the chemise over her head, her breasts lifting with the motion. He took them in his hands, revelling in the feel of them, their fullness, as they filled his palms. He ran his thumbs over the dusky peaks, watching them pebble. Pavia moved against him, teasing him with her hips until he thought his trousers would burst. When she released him from their confines, he was more than ready for her. But she was not done. She reached for the vial beside the bed and pulled the stopper. The room filled with the scent of sandalwood. She poured some into the cup of her hand and blew on it. 'To warm it, for you,' she explained in a husky voice. Oh, sweet heavens, she meant to put that on him.

She scooted back and reached between his legs, stroking him with her oil-slick hands until he was slick, too. 'Is this another of your remedies?' It was almost impossible to complete the sentence, so delightful did her hand feel on him.

'Yes.' She leaned forward to kiss him, her hips, her bottom, rising above his straining phallus. 'The ladies in my uncle's zenana said it was good for a man's arousal.' She paused wickedly. 'You'll have to tell me if that's true.' She slid down upon his shaft, as if to prove her point, and began to move, slowly at first, as if she alone controlled the tempo of their lovemaking. Cam let her believe it for a while. He loved watching her move, watching her pull up the skeins of her hair and let them sift through her fingers, watching her breasts rise with the motion. His wife was intoxicating like this. A thought crossing his mind. 'Are there concoctions to enhance your arousal? I'd like that. Perhaps we could experiment with that as well.'

'There might be. I could look them up.' Pavia reached a hand between his thighs and he shuddered. All potions and herbs aside, her touch was the best aphrodisiac he knew. Cam could only withstand so much temptation before he wanted control. He took her firmly by the hips and flipped her beneath him, taking her at the last.

* * *

'I was supposed to be seducing you,' she scolded with a breathless laugh, making it clear in the aftermath that she hadn't minded.

'Oh, trust me, you did.' Cam stretched beside her, his head propped in one hand. He was coming to love these moments afterwards as much as the pleasure itself. Here in bed, they were entirely themselves in a place the world could not touch. The darkness of his world was at bay when they made love. The newness of that was still heady even after a week. Would it wear off eventually? How long would this last? Cam traced a circle on her belly. He would miss it when it was gone. 'I think the baby's growing.' He was fascinated with her body. He put his palm over her stomach. 'When do you think we'll be able to really tell he's in there?'

'Another month. But even then, if I dress carefully, I can probably hide it for another two months. Most women don't get obviously big until their sixth month.'

'Why hide it?' Cam made a mock frown. 'I am looking forward to that, to seeing the child grow. I fear I am an impatient father.' He grinned.

Pavia laced her hand over his. 'We have much to do between then and now. Time will fly.'

Cam kissed her brow. 'We'll make the world perfect for our little one.' It was a heartfelt, if idle, promise. He couldn't make the world outside perfect. He'd seen that imperfection on display today. Some people had not liked his choice of a bride. Some had simply edged away, while others had chosen to voice their disapproval bluntly. They had a house to prepare and a world to prepare. He could only control the former. 'Don't worry, the house will be ready.' He would have their finances sorted out by then, too. His child, and the mother of his child, would want for nothing. He would see to it, even as his shoulders felt the weight of additional responsibility settle on them.

'Cam, what are you thinking? You're suddenly miles from here.' Pavia reached up a hand to stroke his cheek.

'That I should get headaches more often if this is the cure.'

'Cam, wake up!' For the second time in twelve hours, he awoke to those words with a jolt and a wave of panic, only this time there was no nightmare. Pavia was out of bed, hurrying into her dressing gown.

'What is it? Are you well? Is it the baby?' Cam shook off his grogginess, his mind discarding options at high speed.

'We have company!'

Cam shook his head. Perhaps he was still muddled. 'At eight in the morning?' Then he heard it—the sound of singing: male voices, female voices, a lot of them, joined in a folk tune, coming nearer. He laid back on his pillows and smiled. 'Yes, we do have company. Get dressed, my dear Pavia, and prepare to work. We are being treated to a house-warming.'

Pavia's eyes went wide. 'We can't possibly entertain. We haven't any food and we have barely any house to warm, whatever that means.'

Cam was out of bed, reaching for his trousers. 'That's the whole point. We do this for newlyweds, to help them set up house. The women will see to the house and the men will see to the other buildings.

'But the food?' Pavia protested again.

Cam winked, pulling his shirt on. 'Don't worry, there will be plenty of food, you'll see. Today will be a lot of work, but it's also a party.' He gave her a quick kiss on his way downstairs to greet the oncoming guests, 'Welcome to Little Trull, Pavia Lithgow.'

* * *

She'd never seen anything like it. It seemed as if the whole village had turned out. Of course, that wasn't true. There were notable exceptions missing from the work party. By the time she was dressed, the front lawn had been transformed with trestle tables while Betty Danson, the Vicar's efficient wife, oversaw the laying out of breakfast for fifty. There were stone crocks of hot porridge, loaves of fresh bread with butter and urns of steaming coffee. There was even a tray of sweet buns, baked that morning courtesy of the baker.

'You are too generous!' Pavia exclaimed to the baker, who beamed at her praise.

Letty Weldon laughed, tossing Pavia an apron. 'It's good business to be neighbourly. Now you'll know where to go the next time you want sweet buns.' She linked her arm through Pavia's. 'You and I are off to the kitchen to work with Mrs Bran this morning.'

Pavia looked around the yard in a panic. 'But what about everything out here? I can't just disappear.'

'Yes, you can. Betty Danson has it all in hand,' Letty assured her.

Pavia took another glance and saw that it was true. What had looked like chaos had some method to it. Women were grouped in teams and armed with mops, buckets and rags, ready to scrub the inside of the house, while men were busy turning the breakfast tables into work benches. Other men were already carrying out pieces of old furniture from the attic.

'By the time the rooms are ready, what can be saved of the furniture will be ready, too. Now, come on, we don't want the kitchen to fall behind.' Letty ushered her inside.

'Letty, the kitchen…' Pavia began to explain the kitchen would be a disappointment. It consisted of a skillet and two knives at present. But the sight before her when they stepped inside made her a liar. Crates of supplies, pots and pans, utensils and plates, were piled on the butcher block, Mrs Bran barking orders to two adolescent boys in the middle of it all.

'Ah, Mrs Lithgow, there you are!' Mrs Bran broke from her orders about hanging pots and bustled over to her. Mrs Bran was a large-boned woman with fading red hair and a kindly face. Pavia liked her immediately. 'It's almost like being home again, being back here in this kitchen. I was so thrilled when Vicar Danson told me Lady Lillian and Mr Elmsworth's great-nephew was in residence.' She barely drew a breath before she was disclosing her history. 'I was their cook, you know, for years. I remember the Major coming in the summers. He was a big eater then.' She slid Pavia a sly, womanly glance. 'He's grown up well. Looks like he's still a big eater.'

'Well, yes,' Pavia began to say, but Mrs Bran was ready to move on. She cleared a section of the butcher block and set down paper and pen.

'We must keep feeding him. A newlywed man needs to keep his strength up. I need you to write down the menus, with all of his favourites.'

Menus she could do. At last, here was a task she'd been trained for. But Cam's favourites? That was something else. She hadn't a clue what he liked beyond scrambled eggs and ham sandwiches, a reminder that for all they'd shared this past week, there was still so much to learn about each other. There'd been no long courtship, no pre-existing agreement between two families who had known each other for ages. But here were these women expecting her to know her husband. She couldn't very well tell Mrs Bran they'd married in haste as strangers without a clue as to who the other person was. That wouldn't help cultivate the image Cam wanted them to project to the village. It certainly wouldn't help win over the Mrs Brownings and Stiltons of the world who were determined to think the worst of her.

She had to brazen this out. Pavia took up the pen and tamped down on those negative thoughts. She would not be daunted by the task. She would start with menus she knew, menus she'd practised constructing at Mrs Finlay's. It wasn't as if she was expected to have a seven-course meal on the table every night. She would figure out Cam's likes and dislikes by trial and error.

Around her, the kitchen took shape: gleaming copper pots hung from overhead racks, dishes lined the shelves, foodstuffs filled the pantry and Mrs Bran had a giant kettle of soup on for lunch. Pavia handed Mrs Bran her menus, her stomach grumbling that it had been a while since breakfast.

Mrs Bran scanned them, nodding here and there. 'Very nice, Mrs Lithgow, these should be no trouble, but I see there isn't any Indian food on these menus.'

The observation took her aback and Pavia hesitated. Was Mrs Bran disappointed by that? 'I wasn't sure…' she said, but in true Mrs Bran fashion, the woman continued on.

'I was hoping to learn some new recipes.'

Pavia took back her menus and wrote at the bottom. 'We could make *chapatis* instead of bread and we could do *aloo gobi*—it's a stew dish made with potatoes and cauliflower.'

Mrs Bran nodded encouragingly, surprising Pavia with her excitement over the prospect of new dishes. 'We have plenty of potatoes. The English like potatoes.' She slowed down for the first time since Pavia entered the kitchen and fixed Pavia with a smile. 'My dear, just because most of us never leave the village we're born in doesn't mean we aren't curious about the rest of the world. We might never leave Little Trull, but now that you're here, some of the world has come to us. For many of us, it is more exciting than frightening.' She puckered her mouth in a disapproving frown. 'Mrs Browning and Mrs Stilton might not welcome you, but plenty of us do. It's good to see the Major settling down.' She patted Pavia's hand in motherly solidarity. 'It's a person's heart that matters and I can tell you have good one.'

'Thank you, Mrs Bran. That's very kind.' Pavia was touched by the older woman's words. She had expected far more Mrs Brownings than Mrs Brans when she'd started this adventure. She cleared her throat, struggling with a moment of emotion. 'If you'll excuse me, I should probably go and check on the others.'

Pavia stepped out of the kitchen, swiping at sudden tears brought on by Mrs Bran's kindness, and nearly ran into Cam. 'There you are!' Cam grabbed her by the forearms. His hair was a mess and he had what looked like paint stains on his shirt. His sleeves were rolled up and his breeches were dusty. Whatever he'd been up to, he'd been at it hard and enjoying it. She thought he'd never looked handsomer.

'I've been looking for you all over, Pavia. I want to show you something.' He was boyishly charming in his excitement and she let him tug her outside. 'Now, close your eyes,' Cam ordered playfully. 'Don't look until I tell you to, I won't let you trip.' She took a few tentative steps, letting him manoeuvre her into place. 'All right, now, look!'

Before her on the lawn was a set of four narrow straight-backed chairs, glistening with a rosewood stain. One chair had a scratch on its back, another had a gouge on the right leg, but they were a set and she had an inkling of how Cam's shirt might have got dirty. 'We found them in the attic and I stained them myself,' Cam announced proudly. 'Do you like them?'

'Are these the chairs you were telling me

about?' She trailed a hand over the surface of one, feeling more tears sting her eyes at this memory come to life. 'I love them.' She would have loved them if they'd been scarred and three-legged, because they were a product of his effort. In that moment, she felt a kinship with her new husband. She wasn't the only one trying to learn a new role. While she'd been in the kitchen, trying to guess menus he'd like, he'd been out here, the grandson of an earl, trying his hand at a little carpentry and painting. She reached up on tiptoe and kissed the corner of his mouth. 'Truly, they are wonderful.'

'I was able to sand out most of the scratches,' Cam said, a little more modestly now. 'There were some I couldn't get, like the one on the back here.' His voice dropped and he took her hand. 'If you don't like them, we can still get new. We can find a way to afford it.'

Pavia shook her head, not letting him finish. 'No, I wouldn't think of ordering new when we have these chairs to hand. I would much rather have something my husband made, something our neighbours did for us, than something impersonal from a factory.' In any case, it would be rude to refuse all that was being so generously offered today. They had a lifetime to redecorate. She beamed up at him. 'Would you like to know how I spent my morning? I made menus for Mrs Bran and she wants to try *aloo gobi*.' It was such a simple statement, but it carried a wealth of meaning and it warmed her inexplicably that the one person who understood it all was her husband. He knew how momentous it was. He shared her joy in the little victory. Not for the first time, she thought there was hope for them, hope that they would make something of this marriage.

Cam grinned. 'See, not everyone is as close-minded as the Brownings.' He nodded towards a pair of men bringing out a table. 'I suppose if you have menus ready, I'd better see to making sure you have a table to serve them on.'

Pavia gasped. 'Is that *the* table? The one where you ate *two* servings of green beans in one night?'

Cam's eyes danced. 'The very same.'

'Did I hear the words "dining table"?' Mrs Danson bustled up. 'Perfect timing! We have a box of table linens for you to go through, my dear, enough to get you started at least.'

'Yes, you did, the table's right over there.' Pavia beamed at the Vicar's wife. 'Have you seen these chairs yet? My husband re-did them. Aren't they lovely?' Out of the corner of her eye, she saw Cam stand a little straighter. The compliment pleased him, as she wanted it to. If this week of honeymooning had taught her anything it was that they had a lot to learn about each other if this marriage was going to be as much of a success out of bed as it was in. It would be up to the two them to work on it together. Today, for the first time since the wedding, she understood how much she wanted this marriage to work, not just for her child but for *her*.

Chapter Fourteen

Cam didn't have a chance to speak to his wife again until nearly dusk. But he was aware of her, keeping her in his sightline as he repaired a leg on the otherwise perfectly good dining table, and helped replace a wheel on the gig in the barn. It would be good to have something to drive to church on Sundays and into town. He didn't like the idea of Pavia walking too far, or having to carry packages on the return as her pregnancy progressed.

He leaned against the gig, watching her with the other women for a moment as they sorted quilts. He couldn't hear what she said, but occasionally her laughter floated back to him as she chatted. She was doing splendidly and the sight of her brought a proud tightness to his chest. She was his wife. His to cherish, his to protect for all his days. He'd not thought to feel this way about his marriage of convenience. He'd expected to love his child. He'd expected to grow a fondness for the woman who gave him that child. He'd not expected to fall for her. *Fall?* What did that mean? Surely not love. He was too worldly, too honest for that. Theirs was not a love match. But there were feelings, strong feelings growing within him for her that far outpaced the fondness and respect he'd expected. What he felt for her was more than esteem, but he had no name for it and it left him feeling emotionally at sea where Pavia was concerned. For a decisive man, the feeling was unnerving.

Despite the trials of yesterday, it was right to have brought her here, to the village where he'd known some happiness in his rigid childhood. This place was unlike London, where they would be questioned and ridiculed, where every step forward would be a fight, where every visit and friendship would be evaluated as a power play or an alliance. Here in Little Trull, they would be surrounded by people who would become their friends as he and Pavia made a place for themselves in the community, helping others in turn as those neighbours had helped them today. That's how small villages worked; neighbours cared for neighbours. Neighbours set aside their differences when the village had needs.

Today had been a significant start. The villagers had outdone themselves with their time and generosity, although he was aware there were those who'd chosen not to come. Still, Cam had every hope that, eventually, opposition would be overcome as he and Pavia bonded with the community through daily tasks: helping with harvests, building barns, bringing baskets to the sick. Whatever was needed, Cam would make sure they contributed.

The manse was already looking more like a home. Cam could see women in the windows hanging the last of the curtains. He could smell Mrs Bran's dinner drifting out into the evening air. He heard the laughter of the women upstairs finishing the last of the beds. Soon, all the villagers would go home and it would just be the two of them and that was fine, too.

Cam smiled. He could hardly wait to enjoy the house with her, to sit with her at the table. She was easy to talk with, a good listener. She'd enjoyed his stories and laughed with him. She'd nursed his headache, shown him compassion when it would have been easy to withdraw, embarrassed by his nightmares. She would be a good mother. Not only a mother. She would be a good *wife*.

Pavia had been a revelation today. Watching her with the other women had done something for his heart. He knew how difficult this was for her, how overwhelming. She worried about being accepted. And yet, today, she'd given her all, knowing how important this was for them, but especially for *him*. He would need to thank her for that tonight. This was a homecoming of sorts for him. But it was a proving ground for her. Pavia was among strangers, many of whom she felt would judge her suitability as a wife for him. At least this morning that had been true. Something had happened throughout the day as everyone had worked together. He'd seen her relax, seen her confidence come to the fore. As the day progressed, she was not among strangers any more, but friends.

'Major, might I have a moment?' An older man, Martin Kinsley, approached. He gestured towards his wagon. 'I brought something over for you and your wife. My Alma told me you're expecting already.' He winked. 'You didn't waste much time.'

'I've already wasted too much, some would say.' Cam laughed and clapped the man on

the shoulder, gesturing for Pavia to join him
at the wagon.

'Mrs Lithgow, I was just telling your husband, Alma and I have a little something for
your little something.' He drew back the tarp
covering the item in the wagon bed, revealing
a hand-carved oak cradle. Pavia gasped and
Cam could see tears welling up in her eyes
over the gift.

'It's too lovely, it's too much,' Pavia said.
They'd drawn a crowd as people finished their
final tasks.

'It's not too much,' Martin insisted. 'Our
children are grown and have half-grown children of their own. This cradle is just sitting up
in the hayloft getting old when it might be sitting in your nursery getting used. I polished it
up today myself while everyone was working.'

'We would be honoured, Martin.' Cam
shook the man's hand. 'Would you help me
take it inside? Vicar, would you bless it?'

Vicar Danson cleared his throat and the
neighbours bowed their heads around the
wagon. Cam slipped his hand around Pavia's.
This was a 'for ever' moment, a moment he
never wanted to forget: the Vicar's voice in the
twilight, his neighbours gathered about him,

his wife beside him, his child growing in her belly, as they celebrated the gift of a cradle.

For the first time in months there was peace in his heart, a voice inside him that whispered, *This is why you lived; so you could come home and have a family.* Cam smiled quietly to himself, his head bowed. *Can you see me, Fortis? Can you forgive me if I don't come back? I am family man now. I am going to have a child. I don't know how I can be both soldier and father.* It was a dilemma he was going to have to resolve soon. But not tonight.

The cradle was delivered with much fuss, the women already talking about soft blankets of local alpaca wool for the baby, while the men heaved it upstairs. Then it was time for the neighbours to find their own homes. Pavia stood beside him as they thanked each of those who'd come to work.

Mrs Bran was the last to leave. 'Don't wait too long to eat—dinner's on the table. I'll be here early in the morning.' She paused and patted Cam's cheek. 'It's good to have you home, dear boy.'

Cam saw Mrs Bran off and returned to where Pavia waited for him out front. It was late, stars pushing through the dark sky in brilliant pinpoints. They stood for a moment, looking at the manse. Someone had left a lamp burning in an upstairs window. It looked homely. It looked like place for a family, a real family, a family that loved and perhaps sometimes even fought, a family that was nothing like the one he'd had. 'Mrs Lithgow, may I carry you over the threshold?'

Pavia laughed up at him. 'I thought you already did that?'

'This time I have it on good authority the door won't stick. Besides, I want to do it once more before you get too heavy to carry.' Cam swung his wife up into his arms and they both laughed. His heart swelled. Life was good, which was something he hadn't been able to say for a very long time.

Life was not perfect, but it was good. Perhaps good was enough, Pavia reflected as she glanced around the sewing circle at the blanket committee meeting. These women were becoming her friends. They laughed and chatted with her. They sought advice on needlework from her after admiring her own embroidery. Pavia smiled privately to herself as she pushed a needle through the cloth. Who would have thought needlecraft could be a diplomatic tool, bringing people together? But it had.

'You're smiling, Pavia.' Next to her, Letty Weldon gave her elbow a friendly bump as she teased, 'You must be thinking of your handsome husband.' The circle around her laughed. 'I remember what it was like, so many years ago.' Letty gave a melodramatic sigh, her eyes twinkling. 'I couldn't stop thinking about my man either. He was handsome back then, too.' She chuckled and shook her head. 'But now he's had too many of his own baked goods.' She pouted good-naturedly. Anyone could see that Letty Weldon was still madly in love with her baker husband. 'Enjoy it while it lasts, my dear.'

The others joined in with their stories and advice, reliving their own early days of marriage with much laughter. It was a good way to pass the time as they sewed and their morning went quickly. Too soon, it was time to pack up sewing baskets. The other women had lunches to prepare and children to take care of. Afternoons were hardest for Pavia, though. Most days, Cam wasn't home until dinner and Mrs Bran was sometimes too efficient. There was little for her to do other than nap and sew. That would change when the baby came, of course. But for now, it was a lonely time.

'We seem to have lost some of our initial

closeness,' Pavia lamented to Letty on their walk home. It had become their habit over the weeks to walk and talk as far as the fork in the road and Pavia was grateful for the private time with her new friend. 'Cam has his own routine during the day and I have mine. I seem to only see him at night.' After breakfast, Cam spent mornings in the little office, taking care of correspondence and who knew what else? Then, he'd ride out for who knew where and come back in the evening, sometimes sweaty with dirt and dust, both he and his horse lathered. When she enquired about his day, he said very little, choosing instead to focus on her day.

'It's all part of learning to live together,' Letty assured her. 'The early days aren't all fun and games.' She laughed. 'Even though it seems like that when we remember them. We might tell tales of hot romance, but there are practical issues, too. I remember getting used to a baker's schedule. My husband got up well before dawn to start the bread and then he went to bed early. I wasn't used to that. It was hard to adjust my schedule to his, otherwise we'd have had no time together.' Letty winked. 'We certainly wouldn't have had four strapping sons.' They laughed together and then Letty sobered. 'It will come, though. You will both find your rhythm together. Give it time.'

Pavia hoped that was the truth. She wasn't sure her situation with Cam was only about finding a rhythm. She was glad when they reached the fork and parted ways. There was more on her mind, but she felt she couldn't discuss it without sharing too much, without betraying Cam. Letty's husband didn't wake in the middle of the night and pace the floor until dawn. Letty's husband didn't cry out with nightmares he refused to discuss beyond the basics. Letty's husband wasn't consumed with a secret life she knew nothing about. She might be exaggerating there, but Cam sent so many letters it seemed there must be a whole other life he was living.

Letty said to give it all time, but Pavia wasn't sure she had the time to give. Bakers didn't share their time with the army. Cam's leave would be over in a month and they still hadn't discussed what happened then. Would she go with him? Would he stay here? Would he leave her here? Would he be home when the baby was born? Would he even come back? Those questions could no longer be set aside. They needed to be answered, soon.

At the house, Mrs Bran had left the post

on the front console. Pavia sifted through it, a sinking feeling in her stomach. Cam wrote letters and people wrote back, people she didn't know, people he didn't discuss with her. No one wrote to her. She set the post down. She would take it into Cam's office after lunch.

It was silly to be dismal about the post, she told herself as she sat down to the meal Mrs Bran had prepared for her. She didn't have a lot of correspondence in general. No one but family wrote to her when she'd been at Mrs Finlay's. Her mother had written once a week, her letters full of encouragement, to keep her chin up, to study hard, to not let the other girls make her disheartened. Pavia missed those letters now. Those letters reminded her she was connected to someone, somewhere. These days, her only connection was to Little Trull and that was a new, fragile bridge. She couldn't pour her heart out to Letty Weldon and the sewing circle. She didn't know them well enough. She didn't want to become fodder for gossip and she certainly didn't want to give Mrs Browning anything to nod her head over and say, 'I told you so, those foreign types...'

Pavia buttered a slice of bread. Being alone shouldn't be that hard. She'd been alone before at Mrs Finlay's. The girls had been far more reticent to befriend her than the ladies of Little Trull. The women of Little Trull were not bothered by what society thought and that had opened a great window of opportunity for her here. Mrs Finlay's girls felt they had more to lose by associating with her, that society would judge them and they were right. Society wasn't ready for a mixed-blood heiress in its midst.

Oh, how those girls would be laughing now. Her life had turned out far differently from the one even she'd imagined for herself. Mrs Finlay's Academy had prepared her for the life of a peer's wife. Her own dreams had been to travel, to return to India. Neither were anywhere near the life she was living in Little Trull: church on Sunday, sewing circles on Wednesday and a husband she only saw at night, a husband she was desperate to know.

Pavia pushed her lunch plate away, her appetite gone. She was being maudlin *and* unappreciative. So what if things had turned out differently? She'd have a baby to love. Pavia put a hand to her mostly flat stomach. Would it kick soon? That was something else she missed. Who could she turn to with her worries and questions? The ladies in the village were eager to advise her, but they were new friends, women she didn't know well just yet, not even Letty. It was hard to confide in them about something so personal and it was another reminder just how alone she was even when she was surrounded by people. These days, even when she was with her own husband, the one person she ought to feel closest to.

She was back to that. The estrangement she felt with Cam. Therein lay the one crack in the foundation of their marriage. The base they'd laid during their honeymoon had failed to progress. As soon as she thought such traitorous things, Pavia felt selfish wishing for them. Cam had been good to her. She expected too much because of that goodness. But in truth, he'd already exceeded expectation. He'd offered her a marriage of convenience, not one of romance. Many would argue it was more than she deserved and here she was wanting more, wanting her husband to love *her*. It was an unseemly want when, if not for her escapade at the Tiger's Tooth, they never would have met. They'd been meant for other people, for other lives. For him, other loves.

Pavia gathered up the post and delivered it to Cam's office. She set the packet of letters down on the desk, as she usually did. Normally, she did not linger. This was his domain and she respected his privacy. She had the little sitting room at the back and he had this office. But today, his desk wasn't cleaned off as it normally was. An opened letter remained on top.

She should walk away. But in her current mood, she found she couldn't resist. Her curiosity would not be swayed. It was just one letter. It wasn't as if she was going to rifle through the drawers, deliberately searching for things. This letter was open. It gave every appearance of already having been read. Why shouldn't she read it, too?

Pavia picked it up and froze, recognising the seal. Cam's grandfather had written. Her pulse sped as she read. She sank into the nearest chair, overwhelmed by the letter's contents. It was essentially a bribe. The Earl of Aylsbury was offering Cam a fortune and land to return to the city, to live apart from her and eventually divorce her, claiming the child wasn't his. He would be free to wed Caroline Beaufort this time next year. Caroline and the Beauforts were willing to wait. He could have his old life back if he was done with—how had the old man put it?—*'rusticating in the country with the Indian whore'.*

That had been bad enough, but the worst of the letter was the postscript Aylsbury had added.

I am told you met her dancing in a tavern. Blood will always tell, my boy. Cut your losses now before she drags your good name any further through the mud.

He knew. Of course he knew. He was a man with power who could command men and information. Moreover, Cam knew that his grandfather knew and Cam had said nothing to her. Pavia looked at the date on the letter. It had arrived over a week ago. For a week, Cam had possessed this information and let her go on with her life, thinking the worst she had to worry about was Mrs Browning's disapproval. In reality, her marriage was being tested by Aylsbury, who threatened to expose her if Cam didn't comply. He'd have Cam's obedience one way or another. Pavia folded the letter and put it back on the desk. It was time to confront Cam about this and much more. She drew a breath and smoothed her skirts. She would do it tonight, over a supper she cooked herself.

Cam was late. She knew because the tapers had burnt down an inch since she'd lit them an hour ago. Pavia paced the entrance hall. Dinner was going to be cold at this rate. She peered in at the dining room, the table she'd set so carefully with fresh flowers and candles. The room had been beautiful at summer twilight. It was darker now. How dare he be late, tonight of all nights when she needed him home, when they had serious issues to discuss! He'd never been late before. Her anger warred with worry. Was he hurt? Had his horse thrown a shoe? Or worse, had his horse thrown *him*? It seemed unlikely, but even cavalry officers fell off once in a while.

By the time she heard hooves on the drive, she'd worked herself up with worry and her first words to him since breakfast came out more sharply than intended. 'Where have you been? Do you know what time it is?'

The smile on Cam's face faded. He stopped where he was, not coming forward and giving her the usual kiss. 'I apologise for my tardy arrival. Business took longer than anticipated.'

'And what business is that?' Pavia snapped. They might as well get to the heart of it. There was no sense putting it off.

'Alpaca wool. I can tell you over dinner.' Cam offered an olive branch, his brow furrowed in genuine concern and Pavia immediately regretted her shrewish offensive. 'Are you well, Pavia? Did something happen today?'

'Yes, everything happened today.' The dam

of her restraint broke entirely. 'I made you dinner, but it's cold now, ruined because I didn't know when you'd be home. I don't know where you go, or what you do. I only know that I don't see you any more, I don't know you any more. Maybe I never did. I know this marriage was not what you'd planned, but I thought I knew you, at least a little. But now you get letters from people I don't know. You spend the day out somewhere. You're planning things, but I don't know what.'

'For you and the baby. I am planning things for you and the baby, for us.' Cam strode forward, taking her hands. 'Look, I am sorry I am late. Might we sit down for that dinner you made and talk about it?'

Chapter Fifteen

He'd eaten worse in the military on campaign. Cam scooped a glob on to an edge of a round *chapati* and choked it down. The bread cold was one thing. Cold potato-and-cauliflower curry was another. But he was going to eat cold *aloo gobi* even if it killed him, as long as it brought a smile back to Pavia's face. Cam reached for his mug of ale and took a big swallow to wash it down. He wasn't certain her upset was entirely due to his being late for dinner, but if eating was a way back into her good graces, he'd do it.

'As I said, I was discussing alpacas with a friend, actually.' Cam took a smaller bite this time, hoping the *chapatis* wouldn't run out before his serving of *aloo gobi* did. 'My friend, Viscount Taunton, has an alpaca farm and a mill where he turns the fleece into wool. From there, they sell the fleece abroad to all the great weaving capitals. They also make their own alpaca products—blankets, shawls and such.' He took another long drink of his ale. 'He is starting a syndicate of investors and I thought it might be a good opportunity for us.'

Pavia stopped pushing her food around her plate. 'In what way? You want to farm alpacas here?'

'I suppose we could, eventually.' Cam shook his head. 'I meant for investing. He needs capital and we need an income. He's invited me to visit tomorrow to go over his books. He turned a decent profit with his first shearing last summer.' Cam paused. 'Would you like to come? You could meet his wife, Sofia. She just had a baby in March and apparently she's the mastermind behind the business end of their venture.'

Pavia nodded. 'It would be nice to spend some time with you, just you.'

Cam fixed his wife with a penetrating stare. 'We do spend time together. We have breakfast every morning, dinner every night. We go to church on Sunday.' He tried for a charming smile. 'We go to bed together every night.'

'To sleep.'

'We do other things besides sleep,' Cam reminded her.

'I am talking about our waking hours. You're gone every day until dusk. I don't know where you go or what you do. And now you've shown up with this idea to invest in alpaca. But I don't have any idea what kind of money we're talking about or where it would come from. I was under the impression we had a comfortable but limited income.'

Even more limited now that his grandfather's allowance, which had supplemented his military income, had been cut off. He earned three hundred pounds annually as a major, but his grandfather had paid out over six hundred pounds to offset the need for uniforms and other expenses of military life. 'I've saved some money over the years.' Cam explained. 'And there's been a few small investments I've been able to take advantage of. There's enough.'

But Pavia had gone very still, her face paling. 'You have not taken money from your grandfather, have you?'

'He's cut me off entirely,' Cam replied.

'Has he, though?' Pavia was watching him carefully. 'You've had no contact with him since we married? Tell me the truth, Cam. Have you had contact with your grandfather? Please, don't lie to me.'

She knew about the letter. There was no reason for her to push this hard otherwise. His gut tightened. He could only imagine what she was thinking, feeling. None of it good. 'Let me be clear, Pavia. He has cut off financial support. That is not the same as cutting off contact, as I think you well know.' Cam met her gaze sternly. 'I have taken no money from him. However, he has written, as I think you also know. Now it's time for your truths. You've seen the letter? On my desk? You went through my things?'

'Yes. I saw it today when I took the post in. It was just lying there. I did not ransack your desk as you imply.' She was not penitent. A quarrel was brewing. Their first. He ought to head it off and make a judicious response, but his patience failed him. He did not like being accused.

'My wife has a healthy dose of curiosity.' That letter would have hurt her. He remembered every vile word of it: the assumption that he could be bought, that he would not honour his commitment to his child in exchange for money; the assumption that Pavia was not worthy of him. There was the postscript, too, the subtle threat to expose her if Cam didn't come to heel. Cam understood the deeper root of her anger tonight. She'd had to stew on this, to worry on this latest development, all afternoon with no one to share it with while he'd been out riding with Conall and talking about alpaca. 'Did you think about why I hadn't shown you the letter?' He should have burned it. This conversation wouldn't exist if he had.

'Why? Because you hadn't made up your mind?' Pavia was defensive. Good lord, did she actually think he was considering his grandfather's offer? After all these weeks, did she not know him better than that?

'Is that what you think of me? That I would walk away from my responsibilities to the mother of my child? That I would denounce my own blood? Force my child to live as a bastard?'

'Cam, you know how hard it is for children without fathers, without names. Without you, your child will be nothing, have no chance. He needs you.' Pavia held nothing back. 'As for the rest, how can I think *anything* of you? I don't know you. We married a month ago, entirely strangers to one another. And we are strangers still.' Her voice broke and she needed a moment to regain her composure. 'If we were more than that, you would have told me about the letter when it came over a week ago. You never meant for me to know about it.'

'I was protecting you. That letter was hurtful and it means nothing to me. Why would I show it to you if means nothing? There was nothing to discuss. It changes nothing. We are having a baby together and it will have a mother and father. It will have a loving home.' Cam's fist banged down on the table, rattling the mugs. 'It will not grow up like we did, two children raised to be the pawns of our fathers.'

Cam put his head in his hands. This was not the homecoming he'd been expecting tonight. All the way home, he'd imagined telling Pavia about the alpaca, Pavia being excited about his news. They would eat dinner, they'd go upstairs and make love and afterwards she would lie in his arms and they would weave alpaca dreams. Instead, he'd ruined her dinner with his tardiness. She'd found his grandfather's letter and spent an afternoon worrying that he would leave her until that worry had erupted into this mess of accusations and uncertainties they weren't prepared to weather in their short time together.

'We're having our first fight.' Cam looked up, remorsefully.

'It was bound to happen.' Pavia sighed.

The angry fire in her dark eyes had banked to sadness.

'I didn't want it to, though. I liked things the way they were,' Cam confessed. He wanted the honeymoon. How had they lost that? How had all that happiness slipped away?

'Fairy tales aren't real, Cam. In real life, people quarrel. I suppose having a "first" fight implies there will be others.' Pavia rose and began to collect the dishes of their half-eaten dinner.

Cam rose with her, putting a hand on her wrist to stall her departure. 'I am sorry I didn't tell you about the letter. I wanted to protect you. I am sorry I haven't discussed business with you. I didn't want you to worry about money. I didn't want you to feel responsible.' That wasn't the right word and Pavia knew it.

She cut in. 'Responsible? For what? For stealing your old life from you? For getting you cut off? For costing you the perfect Caroline Beaufort and all the money you could imagine?'

'No! I don't want Caroline Beaufort, I don't want any of it. I never have. I told you as much before.' This life was different than the one he'd been bred for, but that didn't mean it was bad or wrong. Cam rose, his own temper overcoming his regret. 'I want *you*. You captivate me. You are giving me a child. I want the life we will make together, whatever that looks like. But if we're going to succeed, you must stop thinking the worst of me. I did not ask my grandfather to write. I cannot stop what comes in the post.'

'Me? This is all *my* fault?' Pavia glared at him. She wrenched her hand free and set the dishes down with a clang that nearly shattered them. 'You're the one with secrets! You can't stop what comes in the post, but you invite it, with all your letters. You have to let me in, Camden. You have to let me know you. You have to tell me about Fortis, about your night-mares, why I wake at night to find you gone from our bed and why you don't return until dawn. You have to tell me about what comes in the post, who you write to with such regularity that it requires hours of your morning every day. You have to tell me about your grand-father's shenanigans. We are all each other has. You have to let me in, but you don't. Every day you choose to shut me out. Well, tonight, I shut you out. You can sleep in your dratted office.' Pavia stormed from the room.

Dear God, all of that had been beneath the surface and he'd missed it. He hadn't known.

Cam slumped in his chair and ran a hand through his hair. There would be no reasoning with her now. He'd best wait until morning and try again. But what a hash he'd made of it. He had commanded troops of men and yet he couldn't command his wife. Not that Pavia would ever tolerate being commanded, even when it was done subtly. Perhaps that was the problem. He'd tried to run his marriage like he ran his troops—making decisions, issuing orders and expecting Pavia to abide by them. But he hadn't understood what it was like for her at all here. He'd thought she was happy. He'd been wrong and now, for the first time since his marriage, he would be sleeping alone.

Sleeping alone did not recommend itself. There were several times in the night when Pavia almost gave up and went downstairs. Having Cam beside her would be far better than tossing and turning, only to wake tired and disgruntled in the morning. But going to him was tantamount to admitting she was wrong. She was not ready to do that.

Regardless of how this marriage had come about, she was not willing to be treated as anything less than equal in it. She felt she had a right to know her husband's thoughts, his business, to be a part of the decisions he made about their finances. She would not make her mother's mistakes and be rendered powerless. They were both products of a convenient marriage, but that's where Pavia promised herself the similarities would end. Her mother had given up her power when she'd let her husband shut her out of his business dealings. Now her mother sat quietly by, letting her husband decide everything, even who her daughter would marry. Her mother had allowed her husband to send her daughter away, cut her off entirely. Pavia put a hand over her stomach. She would not make that mistake either. When a mother ceded her power, she ceded her children's power by proxy. Who would fight for a child if not their mother?

She was going to be a mother.

Pavia turned on her side and tucked the pillow under her head. Every day it became more real as June marched towards the beginning of July. She was three months gone, by her count. Maybe she could feel a bit of a belly starting to form, after all. This week, her dresses had got tighter. Up until now, it had been hard to think of the baby as growing inside her when there was no visible, physical proof yet. But it was coming. She would love this baby. She would protect this baby. To do that, she needed a strong marriage. She and Cam would need to find a way to be more than bed partners.

She saw now that the bliss of their honeymoon had been an illusion. It took more than pleasure to make a marriage. Theirs had cracked at the first challenge. Cracked, not broken. But she wasn't sure how to mend the crack. Cam simply had to choose to let her in. If not, the rift tonight would not be healed. This had to be his choice. There was nothing she could do. She didn't like to feel powerless, didn't like the thought of her husband *deliberately* rendering her powerless with his choices.

Neither of them had slept. Cam was already at the breakfast table, drinking coffee and perusing newspapers with dark circles beneath his eyes. Pavia was sure she looked no better. Breakfast was a terse affair, at odds with the usual, easy atmosphere that accompanied their mornings. Even Mrs Bran was taciturn when she brought Pavia's toast. Mrs Bran did not linger, as if she knew what had happened last night.

'Would you like jam?' Cam offered her the pot.

'Yes, thank you,' Pavia replied and went

back to buttering her toast. She tried not to re-member other times he'd offered her jam, other things they'd smeared it on and licked it off. Those had been more pleasurable mornings.

'Is your tea warm enough? The pot was out for a while before you came down,' Cam enquired again when it was clear she wasn't going to start a conversation.

Pavia set down her knife. 'It's not going to work, Cam.'

'What's not going to work?' He looked up from his eggs, eyebrows arched.

'Pretending last night didn't happen.' Pavia took a succinct bite of her toast, her gaze steady on him although it took all her strength. Her husband was hurting. She wanted to go to him, to soothe him. Had he slept at all? If he had slept, had he dreamed those terrible nightmares again? And she hadn't been there to wake him, to make him a scented compress. That was a choice she'd made for both of them when she'd stormed upstairs last night. She hadn't wanted to hurt him, but these issues had to be dealt with. 'Avoidance isn't resolution, Cam. If we don't settle this, it will settle us.'

'What do you think there is to settle?' Cam's gaze was blue steel. It would intimidate many a soldier, but she could not let it intimidate her.

'My place at your side. I want to be a partner in this marriage. I want to make decisions with you. I do not want to be told about them post facto, as if my opinion is of no consequence. I want to know what is on your mind. I want to know about the war and your friend. You don't have to hide these things from me.' Pavia paused. 'Acting as if last night didn't happen is not acceptable to me. If we decide it didn't happen, we are also deciding it didn't matter. My mother tried such a tactic with my father. It only served to validate that her opinions were of no regard. She could voice them and my father was free to ignore them. So he did. By the time we returned to London, he was spending most of the year away building his business and his fortune on his own. My mother and I became of little consequence to him. That will *not* happen here, Cam. I will not be relegated to being a pretty plaything you take to bed when the mood strikes you.'

'You are not that. Do not ever classify yourself as nothing more than a whore. You are the mother of my child.' Cam's voice was rough, gravelly with emotion.

'It's not me doing the classifying. You do it every time you choose not to involve me,' Pavia replied evenly. 'I have a right to be more than a doll, a right to be more than a vessel for carrying your children. I have a right to be my own person.'

'I have a right, *a duty*, as your husband to protect you,' Cam growled. 'Why can't you understand that?'

And so the stalemate continued. The drive to Conall and Sofia's was accomplished, not surprisingly, in taut silence.

Chapter Sixteen

'Your son is beautiful. Congratulations, Conall. I am happy for you.' Cam gave his friend a warm smile as they settled into big leather chairs in the bay window of the Everard estate office. Beyond them, in the garden, Pavia and Conall's wife strolled the garden, the new baby in Sofia's arms as the two cooed over it. The two women, one dark haired, the other blonde, made a fetching picture in their white summer dresses, the baby between them. Sofia passed the baby to Pavia and a vice of emotion tightened around Cam's heart at the sight of his wife with the infant, a preview of what the future held for him. How many times would he look out his window and see Pavia with his child in her arms? Or hear her laughter as she played with a toddler in their gardens? The gardens should be in shape by the time his son was walking. It was hard to imagine, given the conditions of the gardens currently. Perhaps he'd help that along when they got back. He could make a bench for that patch of shade behind the house, where Pavia could sit and enjoy a cool afternoon on a hot summer day. He could almost see the image in his mind: Pavia with her needlework, the baby playing on a quilt at her feet.

'My son is beautiful and something of a surprise.' Conall's gaze, too, was locked on the scene outdoors. 'We weren't sure Sofia could have children. There'd been none with her first husband,' he added with a hint of hesitation. 'Your wife is beautiful and something of a surprise as well, I think.' Conall's gaze turned from the window to Cam. 'I thought your grandfather was set on Caroline Beaufort?' he asked carefully.

'We are to trade confidences, then?' Cam smiled at Conall, understanding his disclosure about Sofia better now.

'I want to understand what brings you here, Cam, after years of wandering.'

'It's not wandering, it's military service,' Cam corrected. 'And I am here for the alpaca.'

Conall laughed. 'The question is why, old friend? You have a story to tell. What happened to Caroline Beaufort? Not that I'm sorry to see her go.'

'I had different ideas.' Those were looking like bad ideas this morning with the cloud of the quarrel hanging over him and Pavia. The bubble was definitely off the wine.

'You stood up to the Old Man, finally. Good for you. It's a love match, then?' Conall's audacity had no limits, it seemed. And yet, Cam found himself wanting to tell Conall everything. Conall could just *look* at someone and persuade them to spill their secrets.

'She's pregnant, Conall.' Both of their gazes drifted out to the garden once more. 'It's a marriage of convenience.' The words felt hollow. He'd finally recognised that during his sleepless night on the sofa. 'Seems I was fated for one, after all. Just not one to Caroline Beaufort.' The irony of it had struck him somewhere around three in the morning. He'd not escaped anything when he'd married Pavia, merely traded one convenience for another, only that convenience seemed rather inconvenient at the moment. No, that wasn't fair. Pavia wasn't inconvenient. It was the feelings his marriage roused in him, the frustrations of being wed to a stranger who wanted him to pour out his heart. *That* was the inconvenience.

'Pregnant? I thought so. A woman has a certain look to her when she's expecting.' Conall paused. 'But it's not a love match?'

After last night, the words were laughable. 'My wife thinks I am an ogre.'

'Oh? First fight?' Conall chuckled. 'Ours nearly broke us. That's the problem with first fights. They're intense and they're about real issues your marriage has to deal with, but you haven't the tools, the trust, the knowledge, to cope with them effectively.'

Cam knit his brow. Conall's world was perfect. He had a title, a beautiful wife, a child, the support of a loving family. The Everards had always been that. Cam had envied Conall his parents growing up. 'But not you and Sofia.' Conall was also extraordinarily level-headed. He couldn't imagine his friend yelling at anyone or making irrational demands.

'Oh, yes, old friend. I kept a rather large secret from Sofia and she found out. After she married me, thank goodness. She might not have gone through with it otherwise. I never meant for her to find out at all, but she did.' He wagged an instructive finger at Cam. 'Lesson one for today: they *always* find out.'

'But it was different for you,' Cam argued. 'You and Sofia were in love.' Love was not something he and Pavia had ever discussed. What affection existed between them had never been named. It made him doubt the early days of his optimism. Had there ever been a chance for love? For passion, certainly. Their nights, their honeymoon were proof of that. But passion was different than love.

'We weren't always in love,' Conall confessed. 'I think we always had "respect" but not love. I think someone's been filling your head with tales. Frederick Tresham, maybe? He thinks everyone needs a grand romance simply because he had one.' A brief smile flickered across Conall's mouth before he leaned forward with a comforting hand on Cam's leg. 'I am sorry about Fortis. Frederick wrote to tell me you'd called on them with the news.'

Conall rose and glanced at the clock. 'It's five past noon, perhaps we can a manage a drink now? I think a brandy is in order.' He poured two glasses and returned to their chairs. Cam took the glass gratefully.

'A toast.' Conall raised his glass. 'To weddings, to children born and unborn, to friends returned and those who remained behind.'

They drank in silence, each letting the other reflect on his friendship with Fortis, Conall letting him decide how much was said. 'I should have been able to save him. He was only feet away. I was there.' The words tumbled out. He'd thought of those moments so often in the past ten months.

'That's a hell of a monkey to carry on your back. But you always did want to save the world. It's in your blood, Cam. You're a born protector.' He paused and Cam felt the weight of his stare. 'Is that what you and Pavia fought about? You want to protect her, but she sees it as a challenge to her freedom?'

'A challenge to our marriage,' Cam amended, surprised by his friend's insight. 'How did you know?'

Conall laughed. 'You're not the only one with a headstrong wife.'

Cam set aside his glass and leaned forward. 'Pavia wants to be a partner, an equal. She wants to make decisions with me. She wants to know my thoughts, my past.'

'Then let her,' Conall broke in. 'The marriages our parents had, even the good ones, are a thing of the past. The world is changing and the relationships between men and women will change with it.'

'It's not that,' Cam said defensively. 'I've always been a proponent for change, you know that.' It was one of the things that had brought the four of them together—he and Conall, Fortis and Sutton, these modern beliefs in equality between the sexes, the races, beliefs that weren't always championed in their exalted circles. Men like Cam's grandfather were eager to hold on to the old order.

'Then what is it?' Conall prodded.

'If she knew who she'd really married she might not care for her husband,' Cam confessed. 'There are things that happened after Balaclava, things I don't want to talk about today.'

'Good. I'm not the one you should tell, at least not first,' Conall encouraged. 'Tell her. Her response may surprise you. She is your wife. She deserves to know her husband in all his glory, weaknesses and strengths together.'

'Easier said than done,' Cam argued. Conall was right, but Conall didn't have to confess he'd nearly killed himself out of grief.

Conall laughed. 'If it was easy, Cam, everyone would do it.' He smiled. 'What are your plans? Are you going to go back when your leave is over?'

'That depends on you. Do you want a partner of sorts in your alpaca syndicate?' Cam held his breath. He hadn't realised how much hinged on this decision until now; his military career, his ability to support a family through gentlemanly pursuits like quiet investments with viscounts. 'I can't be a full partner, don't have the blunt for it,' Cam confessed awkwardly. The tables were turned now. He used to be the one with full pockets back in their early days on the town. 'Perhaps an eighth of a share?'

'With your connections to the military? I'd be crazy not to take you on. We'll have contracts for blankets in no time.' Conall nodded out the window. 'But don't you think we should discuss it with them first?'

Cam laughed for the first time since he'd come home late and ruined Pavia's dinner. Outside, the women were still chatting and playing with the baby. 'What do you suppose they're talking about?'

Conall clapped him on the shoulder. 'That's easy—they're talking about us.'

Cam grimaced. 'And the fight?' Conall was enjoying his discomfort too much.

'Most definitely your fight. This is your Waterloo, man.'

Cam grumbled. 'As long as I am not Napoleon.'

* * *

'Don't look, but the men are watching us.' Sofia slid a knowing smile Pavia's way. 'Your husband is quite enchanted with the sight of you and the baby.'

'Just the baby, I think.' Pavia smiled down at the little bundle in her arms with its perfect, tiny features. Would her own child look as perfect? She would hold her child all day. She'd get nothing else done but look at it. 'My husband's not enchanted with me at the moment. I challenged his authority.'

'I thought so. You hardly looked at one another when you arrived.' Sofia put a consoling hand on her arm. 'The sooner you find your way through it, the sooner you can get back to loving each other. Not that you ever stop loving, not even when you fight. I think that's what makes the fighting hurt so much.'

'We're not in love,' Pavia interrupted with the horrible words. 'We never were. We were never supposed to meet, let alone marry. But we did and now I fear he will resent me long before he has an opportunity to love me.' She used to think they had a chance at love.

Sofia took the baby from her and smiled with maternal confidence. 'Whatever struggles you have now will seem meaningless once he holds his child. Perhaps even sooner. Has the baby kicked yet?'

'No.' Instinctively Pavia put her hand over her stomach. 'But I'm only three months along. A woman in the village said first babies often don't kick until the fifth month.'

'Cam will be over the moon once that happens.' Her voice dropped confidentially. 'But once that child kicks, it changes a man. Conall couldn't keep his hands off my belly.' She laughed, her eyes soft with love. 'I had to swat them away at one point.' She was quiet for a moment, lost in recent memory. 'The baby will bring you closer together. Cam could never resent the mother of his child. You will see.'

'And what of his wife? Shall I be nothing more than a mother for his children?' Pavia wished she shared the other woman's confidence. Perhaps she simply wanted too much, hoped for too much from a man she'd essentially cornered into marriage.

'Pavia, you can't bend a man like Cam Lithgow to your will overnight.' Sofia gave a coy smile. 'Maybe that's what you're really upset about. You want him to pour himself out for you, mind and soul. You want to know him instantly. These things take time. Marriages are built piece by piece over years and experiences until one day you look back and see a glorious patchwork quilt that has been your life together.' Sofia gave a soft laugh. 'Conall's mother told me that.'

'You are lucky to have her.' Pavia swallowed around the lump in her throat. She was missing her mother sorely these days. She needed someone to confide in. 'We are very much alone. The day we left London, we were so defiant, marching out of my father's house with nothing but a trunk I'd packed and our pride. I worry every day that Cam will regret that decision.'

'Do you regret it?'

'No, except for what I've cost him. He gave up so much more than I did.' She feared now, that despite whatever protestations he'd made to the contrary, that imbalance would hang between them for ever.

'Perhaps you'd be surprised to know your husband worries about the same things, that maybe he doesn't see it in that light, that he's the one who has cost you. You need to tell him you have no regrets.' Sofia rose. 'The men are staring again. I think they've concluded their business.' She gave Pavia an encouraging look. 'We'd invite you to stay for tea, but it looks to me as if your husband is eager to get home.'

Cam *was* eager to get home. Sofia's prediction proved true. They left shortly after the men emerged from the office. But silence pervaded the drive back, neither of them sure how to begin. 'I'm sorry we quarrelled, Cam,' Pavia began tentatively. She'd started the fight, she had to mend this. 'I never meant to hurt you, but I am not sorry for what I said.'

Cam nodded. 'Agreed. So, where does that leave us?' Already, she could feel the tension ebbing and the part of her that had been in knots since last night began to unwind.

'Two people trying to get to know one another?' Pavia ventured.

Cam didn't look at her, but he smiled, just the faintest crook of his mouth. 'Do you want to know something about me?'

'Anything you want to tell me,' Pavia answered. They were nearly home. She could see the outline of the manse in the distance.

'I like to put the phrase "in bed" at the end of my sentences to make them more interesting.'

He was teasing her. Pavia laughed. 'Such as "two people getting to know one another *in bed*"?'

'Yes.'

Pavia was laughing hard now and it felt good. 'I see the merits of your game.'

'In bed,' Cam added, pulling into the drive. He helped her down from the gig, his hands lingering at her waist, his eyes smoky dark. 'I need to put the horse away, so why don't you go upstairs and wait for me.'

'In bed?' she whispered.

'Most definitely in bed. I'll just be a moment.'

'Not in bed, I hope?' she asked in mock horror.

'Oh, no, my dear. I intend to take my time there.'

He would, too. Pavia knew that unequivocally. She let a delicious rill of anticipation run through her as she undressed. Bed was their safe place, the one place where they could find each other, find themselves, together. This bed, this time, would be more important than ever. Tonight, they would find their way back to a place, if not of happiness, of security, where their relationship wasn't threatened by doubts and secrets. But first, she had a surprise or two for Cam. There were things that needed to be sorted out. *In bed.*

Chapter Seventeen

Pavia was waiting for him. Cam took the steps one at a time, curbing his impatience. This would not be a rowdy, hasty coupling. This needed to be a seduction, a persuasion of the body from which persuasion of the mind might follow: to forgive, to remember the possibility of how it could be between them.

That's up to you, his conscience prompted. *Giving yourself to her is more than the giving of your body and your worldly goods.*

Cam opened the bedroom door and nearly forgot his strategy. The air was filled with the sophisticated scent of basil and rosemary. Pavia lay curled on the bed, wearing only her hair, the long skeins of it draped over her breasts, her nipples playing peek-a-boo between heavy, silken strands, candlelight wandering over her skin creating shadows, valleys, secrets, seductions. She rolled on to the pillows and spread her legs in provocative invitation. Cam liked boldness, liked to see her experimenting with her passion and his, and it worked.

'I see I have your attention.'

More than his attention. His mouth was dry, his pulse was racing. 'You don't play fair, Pavia Lithgow.' Cam advanced on the bed, already ripping his cravat loose, already pulling off his boots, pulling the tails of his shirt from the waistband of his trousers, clothes littering the floor in the wake of his progress. He was naked by the time he reached the bed, his body on fire for her by the time he raised himself up over her, his arms bracketing her head, their corded muscles taut. 'I meant to seduce *you*, but you have quite undone me.'

'I play hard for what I want, fair or otherwise, and tonight that's you.' Pavia licked her lips in sensual invitation. 'In bed,' she whispered, the husk of her voice transforming the words they'd laughed over in the gig to something more seductive, more powerful.

Gone were any thoughts of a slow seduction. He wanted her *now*. He moved to take her and her legs snapped shut, barring him entrance. 'Pavia.' His voice was a frustrated rasp of confusion. He groaned—too late he saw the price for pleasure tonight.

She soothed him, a finger at his lips, her eyes hot on him. 'I want nothing between us, Cam. Not secrets, not people. Promise me that.'

He would promise her anything in those moments in order to have what *she* promised with her body, her touch. Her fingers caressed his jaw. 'Let tonight be a new start for us, Cam, with nothing between us.'

'Yes.' He breathed, at the end of his leash. Wasn't this what Conall had told him to pursue, wasn't this the way to happiness? Why hold back? Why not give her all she asked for? He kissed her hard, trapping her wrists in his grasp, stretching her arms over her head until she wriggled beneath him, wet and hot and eager. Only then did he come into her, giving them both the release they sought: release from want, from need, from the pressures of the world around them and the pressures they created. As she climaxed beneath him, Cam's one thought was 'it's over, the fight is behind us'. They'd found their way back, or perhaps down a new path altogether.

Cam kissed her hair, drawing her close. 'I missed this last night. You don't know how many times I nearly climbed those stairs, ready to beg, ready to do anything to have you beside me again.'

She laughed softly, her breath feathering across his skin. 'I might have met you on those steps. I nearly came down. Once I even got to the door. But each time, I turned back. What would I say when I got there? I didn't want to say I was sorry. I didn't want to say I was wrong.'

'Yes, you made that clear in the gig on the way home.' Cam chuckled. 'We will learn how to deal with one another and we will find our way, Pavia.'

She sighed against him. 'That's what Sofia said today. She said marriages were built year by year, that we couldn't expect perfection all at once.' He heard her hesitate. 'I was thinking today, if the baby was a boy, perhaps you'd like to name him Fortis?'

The offer touched him. His hand stilled where it played with her hair. This was her olive branch, her request to be let in to the things that were important to him. This was his chance to keep the promise he'd made her a half an hour ago. He had not thought to have his word tested so soon. Perhaps he'd even hoped that promise would be forgotten or that it would manifest in a different way. 'Perhaps as a second name.'

Pavia raised herself up on an elbow beside him. 'Did you have something else in mind for a first name?' She traced a light circle around his nipple, made it stiffen excitedly. He would want her again soon at this rate. And then he'd be at her mercy once more. His temptress would extract another impossible promise from him. Cam sighed. An insatiable wife was not an onerous problem to have.

'No, I hadn't thought of names yet. I thought it was bad luck to think about names too soon. Besides, it might be a girl,' he teased.

'Why not Fortis for a boy?' His wife was not only insatiable, but relentless, too. 'He would love the story of his name and how he was named for his father's best friend, a brave man who died in service for his country. A boy needs heroes.'

He could hear Conall's voice in his head. This was the moment of truth. If he meant to commit to this marriage, to this woman, he had to let her in. Secrets would beget more secrets, more fights, until the path back to who they wanted to be was choked with thorns of resentment. 'It would hurt too much. It would be too vibrant a reminder.'

'You can't forget your friendship. You can't pretend it never existed just because he's gone.' Pavia's brow furrowed, misunderstanding.

'That's not it. Every time I looked at the boy, I would have to acknowledge how I failed to save my friend.'

'Oh.' Pavia sat up, her hair falling forward, shielding her face from him. 'Were you supposed to save him?'

'Conall and I have always been the level-headed ones in our foursome. Fortis and Sutton, they've always been adventurous, shall we say, in their own ways.' Cam sighed and put his hands behind his head, looking straight up at the ceiling as if he could see through it right into the past. 'Fortis was a grand soldier, a brave one, that's all true. But he was a reckless one and he was reckless that day at Balaclava.' He'd not told anyone this. Not Cowden, not Conall. He'd not wanted to pollute their memories. They should remember Fortis at his best.

'He'd ridden past the Russian lines. We were deep in enemy territory, far too deep for good sense, but Fortis would not turn back. By the time it became imperative, it also became impossible. The Russians turned the cannons on friend and foe alike. We were slaughtered, cut down.' Pavia's fingers laced through his own and he knew he had to finish it. 'I saw him fall, but we never found his body.'

This was the hard part. He recounted for her in halting half-sentences, the dark horrors of combing a battlefield after fighting. 'You want to find the body because it completes your task. You can go back to your tent, eat your dinner, sleep knowing your mission is accomplished. And yet, it's a task that you don't want to complete. Each body you turn over you hope it's not your friend. Too often it is. I was looking for Fortis, but to find him I had to find too many of our brigade, all of them slaughtered.' Cam felt his throat close up, the words choking his throat as images of those bodies choked his mind. 'Men I drank with the night before, men who had saddled up next to me hours before, laughing and joking. We had wagers on as to whether or not we'd see any action. The Commander, Lord Raglan, had not used the cavalry in previous engagements. One man remarked that we were in the safest position the British army could offer. That turned out to be far from the truth.'

'Did you find him?' Pavia's question brought him back from those memories. Too many friends had fallen that day.

'No.' He heard Pavia's breath catch in anticipation. 'I did not find him that day, or the days after, or the months after. I searched all the British field hospitals, I asked for permission to search the Russian hospitals. I made enquires at the Russian forts, thinking he'd been taken prisoner. Officers make for good ransom and his father is a duke even if he is, *was*, a third son. But there was nothing. I searched the countryside, I made forays on my own. Nothing but a few false leads and oh, how my hope would surge in those days only to plummet again when the trail proved cold. He was gone and I couldn't even mourn him, couldn't even bring his body back to England for a family burial.'

'Oh, Cam. How horrible for you.'

He drew a deep breath, for the rest of it, the worst of it. 'Yes, so horrible I nearly killed myself.' He saw her thoughts so clearly on her face. She thought he'd exhausted himself with his efforts. The only thing he'd exhausted was his sanity. 'On purpose. With my service revolver,' he added bluntly. 'I was an embarrassment to the army so they sent me home under the guise of telling Fortis's family the news.' He waited for her to withdraw her hand. When she did not, he pressed for a verdict. 'Are you horrified beyond words? Your husband tried to commit suicide.' He was supposed to be strong, but he'd been so very weak when it came to his grief.

'No—oh, no. If I am silent it's because I am horrified you were forced to bear that burden alone. But it's not just that.' She squeezed his hand, refusing to let go. 'The hopelessness and despair you must have felt is the true horror. I cannot imagine the darkness of that pit, Cam. I don't think many men could survive it—that you did is nothing short of miraculous.'

Something akin to relief swamped him. At last, someone understood, someone could give words to what he'd felt, feelings even he hadn't been able to accurately name. But Pavia had. That this someone was his wife nearly moved him to tears. But Pavia wasn't done. He could hear her thinking, breathing in the darkness. Her hand was cool on his brow. 'You haven't stopped looking, have you? Those letters you send, they're to contacts in the military.'

'Some are about Fortis, yes. But there's been no news and news is slow this far away from the Crimea.' He hated his weakness. He could hear the ridiculous hope in his voice.

'It is all right to hope, Cam.' She kissed him softly. 'You never have to be alone again. I need you to know that. I am here. I am beside you in all ways and through all things. You can believe in me.'

Her words undid him. When had anyone ever offered to be his partner? Emotionally? Physically? Not even Fortis had offered that. He and Fortis, like most men, kept their emotions hidden even from each other, best friends. Once again, she overwhelmed him, this woman whom he had not meant to love. His throat tightened, his own words failed him, but his body answered, rousing past his sorrow and fears. He took his wife beneath him, his gaze holding hers, as if he could see into the very goodness of her soul. What had he done to earn such an incredible woman?

'What are you thinking, Cam?'

'I'm thinking I should tell you my secrets more often.'

'Yes.' She pulled him close for a kiss. 'You definitely should.'

Cam surprised her at breakfast by announcing he was staying home for the day. 'I thought you might want to have a garden space like Sofia's, a place where you could sew and the baby could play on hot days. There's a patch of shade beneath the tree in the back that would work. There's an old bench in the hayloft I could repair.'

Pavia smiled, not only because of the offer, but because the man making it wanted so desperately to please her. 'That would be lovely. I can help you weed.' They could spend the day together, working on a project like they had during their honeymoon. She would have raked muck if it meant they were together.

Cam gave her a questioning look. 'Should you be doing such work in your condition? Promise me you'll stop if you get tired.'

'I promise. I'll sit in the sun and watch you slave away.' Pavia laughed. Life was good this morning. She felt as if she and Cam had turned a corner. Their quarrel had passed, but that wasn't truly it. Her real joy came from knowing he had shared with her, opened himself to her in a way he had not before. She understood who he wrote to and why. It was not just facts he'd shared with her last night, but his heart. She understood, as well, the dilemma facing him as August loomed on the calendar, one final hurdle for them to overcome. Would Cam choose her and the baby over the military, his career, his men and the search for his friend? If he chose the latter, how could she begrudge him that choice after all he'd endured?

She didn't envy him the decision. She knew how she wanted him to decide. She wanted him to stay. She wanted him safe, with her. But the cost would be high for them both. She might resent that decision some day and so would he. He would hate her for taking him away from his friend. What if Fortis was still out there? Lost? Hurt? Needing Cam? But she needed Cam, too.

Pavia pushed back from the dining table and stood. Perhaps too fast. A sharp twinge caused her to flinch. She put a hand to her back and stretched to alleviate it.

'Are you all right?' Cam shot her a worried glance.

'I'm fine. I think I slept wrong on my back last night. It feels a little tight. Let me get an apron and I'll meet you by the tree.' She smiled, this time to assure him.

They spent a pleasant morning weeding the patch of grass and clearing away stones. Cam used the stones to make a border around their little space. Mrs Bran brought out lunch and they made a picnic of it on an old blanket, Cam's head in her lap as she fed him apple slices. 'This reminds me of our picnic in the fairy glen.' Pavia held an apple slice for him to bite. 'It seems like ages ago.'

'We should go back, then,' Cam offered, taking a chomp from the slice. 'Maybe the day after tomorrow? The garden will be done and the weather's fair. Meanwhile, you can take the afternoon off. There's not much more you can do. I'm going to drag out the bench and work on it.'

Usually, she would have protested but she did feel tired. A rest sounded refreshing. 'If my back wasn't bothering me, I'd nap out here on the blanket while you worked.' Pavia stifled a yawn and fed Cam the last piece of apple before he insisted on seeing her upstairs. He helped her out of her skirts and saw her settled on the bed.

'Sleep well, Wife.' He left her with a kiss and a promise to wake her in two hours. But her nap didn't last that long.

Mrs Bran knocked on the bedroom door an hour later, dragging her out of sound sleep.

'Mrs Lithgow, you have a guest.'

A guest? Pavia sat up, thinking quickly. She wasn't expecting anyone today. Cam would be in the back garden, sweating, perhaps shirtless, and in no condition to receive anyone.

Mrs Bran must have deduced that as well. She tried to clear her mind and put her thoughts in order. 'Put them in the front parlour, I'll be right there,' she called out, already rolling out of the bed, her back twinging sharply from the sudden movement. 'And put on a pot of tea!'

Pavia dressed in a loose, clean dress of white muslin and hastily repinned her hair. A glance in the mirror confirmed, though, that she still looked as if she'd come straight from bed. Well, so be it. That's what happened when someone called unannounced. It served them right if she looked abruptly awakened.

Pavia pasted on a smile and headed downstairs. She could be civil. After all, this was her first guest. She tried to guess who it might be. Letty? One of the ladies from the sewing circle? Betty Danson, perhaps? She was wrong on all accounts. Pavia reached the front parlour and froze. Her guest was not a woman, but a man. A tall, dark-haired man. He rose from the sofa and turned to her; hat in hand, clothes of the first stare of fashion, eyes hard as black diamonds. Dear God, her father was here. For a moment there was elation. If Father was here, Mother would be, too. But she wasn't. There was only him and that filled Pavia with fear.

'Father, what are you doing here? Where's

Mother?' An awful thought came to her. 'Is
Mother all right?' Surely, he hadn't come to
tell her bad news, news so bad it couldn't be
sent in a telegram or so urgent it couldn't be
sent in a letter.

'Your mother's fine.' He looked about the
little room, refusing to hide his disdain, and
she saw the place for the first time through his
eyes, the eyes of a man who commanded more
wealth than he could spend, a man who never
thought twice about waiting for something. He
could have it all, the very best, at the snap of
his fingers. He would not think much of her
faded sofa or the thin carpet, or the worn, but
polished, oak chair rail. 'I came to see if you
were fine, if you had tired of playing house in
the middle of nowhere with your misbegotten
husband. You've survived months of this—
I'm surprised. It's nowhere near the opulence
you're used to at your uncle's court or at home
in London.' His disapproval for her house, for
her husband, were evident in his voice.

'*We* are very happy here,' Pavia answered
tersely. 'This is our home. It was his great-
aunt's. He has good memories here and we
hope to make even more.'

'It's a cottage,' he scoffed. Her father
stepped out into the hall and snapped his fin-

gers at a woman hovering by the kitchen. 'Margaret, make yourself useful and go upstairs. Hurry now.'

'Margaret?' Pavia followed him out. 'What's my maid doing here?'

'I've brought her to pack your things, my dear girl. I am taking you home and not a moment too soon from the looks of it.'

'I am married, Father. I belong with my husband. What about the baby?' She rested her hand on the tiny swell at her waist, wishing it was larger. 'I need my husband. There will be talk if we're living apart.' Her father hated scandal more than anything, except perhaps a woman with an opinion.

'No one will notice, least of all your husband. I think he'll be glad enough to forget you. We have it all worked out, the Earl and I.'

'The Earl?' Pavia gripped the door frame for support against the words and against the pain in her back. It was worse now and on the move, to her hips, her waist.

'Yes. You will go to India and have the baby there. You can spend a few years in your uncle's court, just as you like. You've talked of nothing but going back there since we left it. You've never made any secret about preferring your uncle's palace to London. Then you can come back and we'll try again. You'll only be twenty-two at most, still young enough to attract the title we want.'

'The title *you* want. I already have a husband.' She didn't like where this was going.

'The Earl and I will have the marriage annulled, declared invalid.'

He must love saying that—'the Earl and I'. How long had her father coveted such a relationship with a peer of the realm? And now she'd provided him one, albeit under very different circumstances than either of them had imagined.

'The Earl,' her father went on, 'is prepared to offer Lithgow money, land, a seat in Parliament and a pretty debutante wife if he'll end the marriage, which he will. He's no more used to living in hovels like this than you are and no more suited to it. Whatever money the Major has will run out and then what will he do? He will be desperate for his grandfather's help.'

He pulled out a gold pocket watch and studied it, clapping it shut with satisfaction. 'We'll be able to catch the five o'clock back to London. You'll sleep in your own bed tonight.' The last was said with an unbelievable amount of good humour, as if she would also find that prospect welcome.

Emotions roiled through Pavia: anger and no small amount of fear. In all her life, she'd known her father to be a man who got what he wanted. What would he do? How far would he go to get what he wanted now? How far had he already gone? He must be very sure of himself indeed if he'd ordered her trunk packed. 'No, I will not. You may take my clothes, but I am going nowhere with you.' Pavia folded her arms and stood her ground. 'My place is here.'

Her father grabbed her arm. 'It is not. You embarrass us by lowering yourself to this station. Now, be a good girl and come with me. I do not want to have to force you.'

Her back spasmed, followed by a sharp pain to her stomach. She wanted to sit down, but she couldn't show weakness, not now when so much was at stake. 'No, Father. I am not your little girl to order around any more. My place is here.' She hoped Mrs Bran had the good sense to find Cam. She needed him.

Boots clomped in the kitchen door in welcome relief as Cam filled the hall, sweaty and dirt streaked, his eyes narrowing as he took in the scene, divining the situation immediately. Cam fairly bristled with protectiveness. She'd never seen a more handsome sight. Cam wiped his hands on a towel and tossed it aside. 'We were unaware you planned to visit, Honeysett, or we would have made preparations.' A sweet sense of peace swept her. Cam would put a stop to this nonsense. Just his presence brought a swell of easement to her. She could see anything through as long as he was beside her. It was a stunning revelation made at a most difficult juncture. Slowly, steadily, he had become an integral part of her world.

'I just came to collect my daughter,' her father announced, his eyes challenging Cam. It was a bold move. No one would miss the tension of Cam's body, a soldier's body wound tight for a fight.

'Is that so? It doesn't seem to me that she is interested in leaving. She's made it clear her place is here, with me.' Cam moved to stand beside her, his very presence lending her strength. 'Yours, however, is not. I must ask you to leave. I don't tolerate uninvited guests bothering my wife.' He locked eyes with her father, answering her father's challenge with a stare that sent corporals to do his bidding. 'I do not want to force your departure, Honeysett. But I will. I am sure you understand.'

Her father held Cam's gaze a moment longer, then picked up his walking stick from the corner where it leaned and levelled it at

Cam. For a moment, Pavia thought he meant to strike him. 'Do not mistake this for a surrender, Lithgow. This is merely a retreat. The field is yours. Today. But you cannot hope to sustain the advantage.' He strode past Cam with a snap of his fingers. He called up the stairs, 'Margaret, come. Leave the trunk.' And Margaret came, like the servant she was.

Chapter Eighteen

The peace so carefully restored in the night hadn't lasted long. One look at his wife's pale face was enough to tell him that. The sight of Pavia's trunk at the bottom of the stairs, and the snatch of conversation he'd caught, was enough to tell him the rest. Her father had threatened her. The man should be called out for such an action. 'Are you all right, Pavia?' He kept his temper in check and focused instead on her. He helped her to the sofa.

'How dare he come in here and attempt to abscond with my wife!'

Pavia leaned on the arm of the sofa. She looked frighteningly unwell, but there was still fire in her voice. 'He dares because he has the support of your grandfather, the Earl.'

'What?' Cam furrowed his brow. 'That makes no sense. No offence, but my grandfather would not lower himself to do business with a Cit like your father. That's his objection to the whole marriage.'

'Not entirely his only objection, Cam. But dislike of our marriage is the one thing the two of them have in common.' Pavia drew a sharp breath.

'The enemy of my enemy is my friend?' Cam mused with a cynical chuckle. 'So the two of them are in bed together now. But what for? Neither of them needs money.' A rather humorous picture came to mind of Oliver Honeysett and his grandfather trying to buy each other off with money neither was interested in.

'We are, apparently, more valuable to them than money. We are their keys to advancing their influence, but not when we're together.' Pavia outlined her father's offer. 'It's not that much different than your grandfather's letter. I go to India, have the baby, come back in a few years and try to marry for a title once more. Meanwhile, you go back to London, run for Parliament, have your grandfather settle an impressive estate and allowance on you, and pick up where you left off with Caroline Beaufort.'

'And our marriage?' The plan sickened Cam. His grandfather and Oliver Honeysett were attempting to dismantle his life: his career, his wife, his child.

'Annulled at worst, forgotten at best.' Pavia shifted on the sofa, trying to find a comfortable position.

'And our child?' A child could not be dismissed as easily as a marriage. A child was flesh and blood, a marriage was just paper.

'The child would be passed off as the product of a fictional marriage in India where I was widowed. With my father's money, no one will look closely at that claim. At any rate, record keeping in India is not as accurate as records are here. There are a hundred reasons there might not be record of anything: water damage, fire, monsoons.'

A knot of primal possession tightened in his stomach. 'My child will *not* be passed off as the child of another, fictional or not.' Rage simmered. His grandfather and Honeysett not only sought to erase his marriage, they sought to separate him from his child, to make arrangements that did not allow him to claim his child, to raise his child. Cam leaned forward and reached for Pavia's hand, his eyes steady on her. 'There is no amount of money, of land, of position in this world that would ever tempt me away from my child. They are not men who can understand that. If they did, they wouldn't bother asking.'

Pavia gasped. For a moment, Cam thought it was in reaction to his vow, but the shock on her face disabused him. She gripped his hand tightly, her other hand cradling her belly as another cry escaped her.

'Pavia, what is it?' Her sudden fear fed his. He followed her gaze down to the floor where blood dripped from her leg. 'You're hurt!' If that bastard father of hers had harmed her, Cam would chase down the train and call him out.

'No, Cam. Get Mrs Bran. I'm afraid I am losing the baby.' He rose to fetch the house-keeper, but Pavia held his hand, giving a con-tradiction of commands. 'Don't leave me, Cam. Oh!' A sharp pang took her. The sight of Pavia in distress galvanised him into action.

Cam lifted her into his arms, calling for Mrs Bran as he took the stairs to their bedroom. 'Send for the doctor, Mrs Bran! We need hot water and towels, as fast as you can!' He el-evated Pavia's legs on pillows, as if he were treating a battlefield wound, and talking all the while. Voice contact kept the wounded calm, kept them focused on the next step and the next step after that—it gave them hope. That's what he wanted to give Pavia and, in truth, himself in the long minutes before the doctor arrived. How many soldiers had he done this for?

'Here, have some water, it will ease the pain...once we get a bandage on this, the bleeding will stop, we'll get you to the field hospital. It's not as bad as it looks. You will be fine.'

He hoped Pavia would be fine. He had never expected to use those skills with his own wife.

Cam sat on the edge of the bed beside her, Pavia's hand in his. 'Mrs Bran says babies shift positions and that can cause bleeding. Perhaps there's nothing to worry about and this is quite normal.' He tried to soothe her, tried to reason with himself. The doctor would fix this and they would move on.

'No, Cam. It's too soon for that kind of shifting. Letty says babies shift much later. Besides, there's not much of him to shift, certainly he's not of a size to cause any discomfort or stretching.'

'Aha! You do think it will be a boy. You called it "he".' Cam tried for levity to take her mind off the negative. He wished she wouldn't argue with him. His soldiers never did. If he told them to drink, they drank. If he told them the wound wasn't as bad as it appeared, they believed him. He wanted Pavia to believe him now. She looked so frightened and pale on their big bed and he felt helpless in a way he'd never felt before. On the battlefield there were plans to make, men to rally. He could do that. He'd turned defeats into victories countless times with strategies and quite often with nothing more than bravado. But here, he could do nothing. Pavia was suffering and he was helpless. Impotence curdled in his stomach.

Mrs Bran brought the doctor up the stairs at last. He shook Cam's hand, looked at Pavia with kindly eyes and patted her hand. 'It won't be long now, my dear, and it will be over.' Pavia sobbed and the dam of restraint in him began to crumble.

'What do you mean, over?' Cam challenged the doctor. 'Can't you save the baby? There has to be a way.'

The doctor fixed him with a pityingly stare. 'Major, leave us please. Your wife is in good hands.'

'That is not acceptable!' Cam grabbed the doctor's sleeve, but Mrs Bran's hand was on his arm, leading him out of the room.

'Vicar Danson is downstairs. Go and have a drink with him. Let the doctor do his work.'

'I don't want a drink, damn it, I want my wife, I want to be with her, with our child!' The old madness leeched into his blood. 'I have to save them!' He knew this madness— it was the madness of losing Fortis, of not finding him, only now it was Pavia he was losing, his child he was losing and the pain was so much worse.

'Your wife will be fine.' Mrs Bran ushered him downstairs. 'She is young and healthy. She's not the first young woman to lose a child, although I know that's little comfort to you at the moment,' Mrs Bran counselled. She handed him off to Vicar Danson, who waited at the foot of the stairs, a knowing look passing between them. More pity. It was the way Lord Cardigan and Raglan had looked at him before they sent him home, mad and helpless.

Cam drew a deep breath. He had to get a hold of himself. He would be of no use to Pavia if he gave in to the madness. 'Vicar, so good of you to come.'

'My son, come and sit. It's never easy.'

The words broke him. Cam felt his body begin to tremble, the sobs welling up from deep inside him, somewhere unknown, somewhere heretofore untapped and unexplored.

Lithgows never cried. Never grieved. Lithgows went on.

'That's right. It's best to get it out now.' The Vicar's fatherly arm was about him, drawing him close as if he were a beloved child, like Uncle Elliott used to do. 'You do your grieving here, so you can be strong for her later when she needs you.' It was all the permission Cam needed. There, in the front parlor, Cam Lithgow, who hadn't cried when Fortis had fallen, wept for all the things he'd ever lost. But most of all, for the child he'd never know, never raise. There would be others, perhaps, but not this one. The knowledge of that loss hurt like a knife to his gut. He'd built his future on the hope of that child. Now that future was gone. What did he and Pavia have without that child? Would she still *want* him if she didn't *need* him?

People respond to others' grief in different ways. Some want to give hope, some want to find justifications for it, others search for blame. The people of Little Trull did all three, Cam noted as villagers greeted them quietly after church on Sunday. He had argued to stay home, but Pavia had insisted they go and get it over with. It had been almost a week since the accident, as she referred to it, refusing to name it for what it was: a miscarriage. There was no reason to hide away in the manse. She didn't look any different, she'd argued. She'd hardly looked pregnant then and now she wasn't, so what did it matter?

The doctor had offered his medical opinion that it was far better to have lost the child now instead of later when Pavia would have been at greater risk, too. After all, the pregnancy was hardly out of its first trimester. Cam knew what that meant. That the baby was hardly a baby at all. Not true. Not to him, not to Pavia. That baby had been everything, the dream of a life full of love, a far better one than the one he'd lived amid the opulence of his grandfather's house.

The Vicar had called it God's will, confident that there was a purpose for this. Letty and the ladies offered the consolation that there would be other babies when they brought meals to the house. There were others who were less kind in their intentions. Mrs Browning had passed them in the churchyard with her head held high, a smug smile on her face as if to imply they'd got precisely what they'd deserved. In her mind, like should stay with like. Englishmen didn't wed half-breeds from India. Others offered their own stories of loss as proof that the Lithgows, too, would rise up from the ashes of this setback. Cam wasn't so sure.

Pavia was distant. She refused to discuss it, saying there was nothing *to* discuss. The first few nights, he'd slept elsewhere out of deference for her, but in hindsight, he thought that might have been a mistake. When he went to hold her, she moved away, always discreetly, always politely, never an overt rejection of his touch, but the rejection was there all the same. She allowed him only cursory, necessary touches. She found a reason to move out his reach and he had not gone back to their bed, feeling unwelcome.

'Do you think we are cursed? Is Mrs Browning right?' she asked as he ushered her into the house after the service.

'No, absolutely not,' Cam said firmly. 'That old besom doesn't know anything.' He followed her into the kitchen, where Mrs Bran had left cold meat and bread for their Sunday lunch.

'Maybe she doesn't, but have *you* ever thought maybe we don't belong together? We never would have met in that tavern if I had obeyed my father and married Wenderly. It's not the difference in our races. It's the difference in us. We were never supposed to meet.'

Pavia laid out the bread and Cam sliced the meat, choosing to ignore her remark. 'Ham, just like old times.' Old times that had happened not so long ago. A honeymoon, where they'd lived for a week on ham sandwiches and passion. How he wanted it back: the excitement, the uncertainty of being on their own, of looking forward to the future. Not just for the passion, but for the companionship they'd started to build. When she didn't respond to his jest, a thought came to him. Perhaps she wasn't interested in a male's companionship at this time, but maybe a female friend would help. 'Would you like me to send for Sofia? She could come and stay for a while.'

Pavia looked at him as if he'd just suggested they fly to the moon. 'No, I could not bear it, to see her with her son, so small and so perfect, while...' She drew a breath, unable to complete her sentence.

'While what?'

'While we're being punished for defying karma.' Pavia hacked viciously at the loaf of bread. 'Our baby died because of us, because we created an imbalance in the universe.'

Cam slammed down his knife. 'Enough of

that talk! Do you really think there's such a thing as karma? That the miscarriage happened because we did something wrong or evil? I can't believe you'd set such credence in the ideas of a woman like Mrs Browning, a woman full of hate and prejudice.'

Pavia's eyes snapped, some of their usual fire returning. 'I'm not talking about Mrs Browning. I'm talking about karma. My uncle's court believes it. Don't you dare make fun of it.'

'You've never mentioned any particular attachment to such beliefs until now.' Cam sliced the ham with a fierce stroke. At this rate, he was butchering the pig all over again in his frustration. He forgot too easily the differences in their backgrounds, their childhoods. They might have both been raised Protestant, but their experiences were very different. His was the experience of Anglican England, while hers was a Protestantism presented amid a backdrop of Hinduism and local Khasi religion, where it had to be flexible in order to be persuasive. And it hadn't been all that persuasive. He knew from his own experience in other parts of India that conversions to Christianity were slow in coming.

'Just because I was raised Anglican doesn't

mean I don't have those influences in my life. Did you know my name was chosen because of its association with the Hindu concept of completeness and perfection? It was a compromise between my mother and my father. He wanted to give me a good, strong European name. Pavia actually comes from northern Italy. It has a "respectable" medieval history to it, according to my father. But my mother wanted her heritage represented, too. The astrologer agreed to Pavia.' She spat out the information with a hint of pride as if it were an argument. It was a wedge, Cam thought. A reminder of all they didn't know about each other, of the walls that remained between them and were growing taller every day. 'I was born healthy and safe, perhaps because of that compromise, perhaps because of my father's concession. Maybe *we* should take karma more seriously after all that's happened. I defied my parents, you defied your family, we defied society and now our baby is gone.'

'Science has reasons for what happened,' Cam answered swiftly. 'And none of them are about the Mrs Brownings of the world or about karma.' He piled the meat on a plate and sighed. 'Pavia, we have to get past this.' But there was so much more they had to get past.

This was merely one more obstacle. Would it ever end?

'What if we don't? What if we can't?' Pavia asked softly, her earlier acerbity replaced with something akin to sadness. It was the first time she'd let her defences down in a week, just long enough for Cam to see a glimmer of hope. *We*. She'd said we. Once upon a time that word had meant so much to him. It meant even more, now that it had become elusive.

'As long as there's a "we", Pavia, there is something to fight for.' He covered her hand where it lay on the butcher block. This time she didn't pull away. 'We can get through anything. We just have to want what's on the other side.'

The words were meant to be encouraging; they were meant to let her know he was there for her, completely. Instead, the words raised questions. Did she want a we? Did she want him? She'd already confessed they would never have met if not for the tavern and her desperation. She didn't need his name any more—the one thing he had to give her that had any value. He felt the beginnings of ghosts gathering in the kitchen, doubts and fears, converging on the periphery of their hope, and he remembered a thought he'd had before. Their worst enemy wasn't what the outside world could do to them, but what they would do to themselves. If this marriage failed, it would be their faults.

Chapter Nineteen

It was all her fault. Every last scrap of it. Pavia bit off a length of thread and pushed it through the eye of her needle with determination to ward off such thoughts, but it was hard to escape the truth. It was her fault Cam was back to riding out every morning, purposely to avoid her. It was her fault she sat in this garden right now alone, this beautiful oasis at the back of the house that Cam had created for them, a place where they might escape the heat, together, spending long summer afternoons, lazing about here.

Tears pricked at her eyes and Pavia laid aside her needlepoint. She wished he was with her to share the garden he'd created. It was a simple space with the bench he'd repaired by hand, the shady trees, the fragrant rose bushes, the lush green grass, all designed with a summer afternoon in mind. The shade was cool, the grass soft, made for throwing down an old quilt so that a husband could nap while his wife stitched, or so that a baby could play, waving its fists and feet in the air with a coo. But she had neither baby or husband now. She was entirely alone and no one to blame but herself.

It was quite the litany of sins she'd accumulated. She had not thanked Cam for the garden when he'd shown it to her the first day she was out of bed. She had not invited Cam back to their bed even when the doctor had given permission. He'd ridden out the next morning and every morning after, coming home late until July was nearing its close and with each passing day it grew harder to bridge the expanding gap between them. What was the point?

The one thing that had rooted the marriage was the baby and it was gone. What did they have now? Nothing. Pavia swiped at her tears, staring at the half-completed stitchery, a little sampler with the words 'bless this house' surrounded with a profusion of wildflowers. There were no blessings here, only curses, and that was her fault, too. She'd interfered with her father's plans. She deserved an empty marriage to a man who honoured her out of duty, but didn't love her, a man whom she'd forced into a marriage he had not sought. She'd stolen him from his intended path. Oh, yes, the list of her sins was long indeed. She deserved her suffering because of the suffering she'd caused others. But Cam didn't. Why should he suffer?

She needed to make amends and soon or it would be too late. Cam's leave was up in August, less than a month away. They'd never talked of what happened then. There had been too many other things to talk about, easier things. To talk about his leave might expose the flaw in the fairy tale. If he left, it would prove this was only a matter of duty to him. He'd done that duty, given the child his name and was off to resume his regular life.

She had not wanted to face that reality. It was far nicer living in their ham sandwich, fairy-grove cocoon, pretending they were in love. And maybe they had been in love with the family they were making, if not each other. The latter seemed too much to expect for two strangers. It was a nice feeling, none the less, and it had led to other nice feelings, at least for her. That's where things got blurry. His feelings had been for the baby, always for the baby. He was in love with the idea of being a father more than being a husband. Being a husband was a means to the end. But not for her. Somewhere, somehow, she'd fallen in love with him. At some point, he'd stopped being a stranger and become her bulwark, her strength.

When had it happened? Had it been when he'd watched her walk down the aisle on their wedding day and he'd taken her hand and whispered how beautiful she looked even though she was in a simple travelling gown? Still, the words had given her confidence. Had it been when he'd donned his uniform that first day at church to project his status on to her so that others would see her not as foreigner, but the wife of an esteemed officer? Had it been the day of the house-warming and the myriad times she'd looked across the lawn or out a window and seen him with the other men, sweating and laughing as they laboured? The picnic in the fairy glade? Or was it simply every time she looked at the rosewood dining table and remembered the pride with which he'd presented the used table to her?

There were countless memories to choose from. Perhaps it didn't matter when it had happened, only that it had. *She* had fallen in love. And foolishly so. That love was a chasm between them and no way across it. The baby might have been their bridge. What would keep him here now without the baby to anticipate? She could think of nothing to keep him here past August, not when the lure of finding Fortis called. She could see it in his growing restlessness. She knew without being told that he didn't always ride out to see Conall. Some days, he rode out just to ride. Just to give vent to his wildness, his grief.

She was not enough to hold him. Once, she might have gambled that he'd stay and live the life of a minor country gentleman, investing in Conall's alpacas and his family. But on their own, the alpacas wouldn't be enough to keep him here and neither would she—a wife who'd pushed him away in her pain. The last weeks had proven her fears were justified all along. She was only the mother of his child, nothing more. Cam wanted to leave. She should let him go, back to the military, to a life he had chosen. But then what happened to her?

If he left, there would be nothing to keep her here either, except a misguided sense of hope that he'd come home to her some day. *Like Fortis Tresham's widow.* The thought came to her in a wave of truth so ferocious Pavia closed her eyes against it. Was that her fate? To be left behind? An unwanted wife with an unrequited love for a husband who didn't feel the same, but would not dishonour his wife with divorce?

But her suffering was not reason enough to make him stay and suffer, too, a married couple together but separate. She had no right to consign him to that hell for life.

Hooves pounded on the drive at the front of the house and a voice called out for the groom. Cam was home. The urgency in his voice called to her. Pavia rose and shook out her skirts, moving towards the house as she did so, a little ashamed she'd idled away the afternoon again. Cam never complained about it, never commented on it. Perhaps he didn't notice. Or perhaps he didn't care. He'd found other things to keep him busy these days outside the house. That was her fault, too, one more to add to the pile.

She heard the sound of the pump and she stopped at the front parlour window, keeping herself hidden behind the curtain. This was her guilty pleasure, watching him strip and wash in the pump before he came to her. He'd not been with Conall today. He'd been out riding. On those days, he came home in a sweat, his shirt and his body grim with dirt, his golden hair dulled with dust. And she'd watch. From inside, from behind a curtain. Did he know she watched? He never commented on it. Despite all that had happened, he still made her mouth go dry. Was there ever a man as beautiful as her husband with those sculpted biceps and that chiselled chest?

A pang of longing speared through her. She wanted him one more time before she let him go, one more time she wanted to feel what they'd once had. That's where today's ruminations had led, hadn't it? To a conclusion that would be difficult but necessary? That's what you did with things you loved, *people* you loved. You set them free. She'd kept him too long as it was. His duty to his child, to her, was fulfilled. She would let him go now, but maybe it was all right to kiss him goodbye first. Cam had reached out before and she'd rebuffed him. If there was any reaching out to do, it had to come from her. She moved out into the yard before she could rethink her actions.

'Pavia!' Cam smiled, a big, wide, excited grin on his face as he sluiced the sweat from his body. 'I was just coming to find you after I cleaned up. I have news.' His eyes sparkled like blue sapphires. She hadn't seen him like this for a long while, steady and pulsing with vibrant life, purpose. This was the Cam who'd come to her father's house. This was the Cam who'd made love to her so ardently in the early days of their marriage. This Cam had control of his restlessness. Best of all, he was letting her in, just as she'd asked so many weeks ago. In that moment in the yard, everything was possible. Perhaps she'd been too hasty. Perhaps he wanted to stay in Little Trull, with *her*. Maybe she'd misjudged. Maybe she could be enough. Maybe she didn't have to let him go.

Cam came to her, his body glistening with water droplets, his shirt slung around his neck like a scarf. He took her hands, his gaze in earnest. 'There's word that a man has been found wandering the woods near Balaclava who might be Fortis Tresham.' His smile widened, his voice was full of joy at the thought of his friend having been found. 'Do you know what this means? Fortis could be alive!'

Pavia smiled for his sake. 'It is good news indeed.' She knew what this meant to him. But she also knew what it meant to them. It would be their death knell. Cam would be drawn towards hope. What hope was left here? She was suddenly, fiercely, jealous of Fortis, who hadn't the decency to be either alive or dead, but kept torturing her husband. Part of her resented she was not the cause of Cam's happiness, but she'd done nothing to earn his smiles. In her grief and turmoil, she'd pushed him away, isolated herself from their marriage.

He took her hand. 'There's more, but I need to discuss it with you.' His eyes were serious. He was being careful, Pavia realised. Of her. Of this tenuous truth. He'd been hopeful over Fortis before only to have his hopes dashed. Those emotional hills and valleys had left him scarred, unwilling to open up to others for fear of being crushed. 'Our commander needs me to go to the Crimea immediately, to confirm this man's identity.'

Pavia's smiled faded. 'In two weeks when your leave is up?' she clarified. This was the discussion they'd been putting off since their wedding. There were no more excuses to postpone it now.

'No, Pavia. I need to leave immediately, tomorrow if we can arrange it, or the day after. I'll need to stop in London and see Cowden before sailing. We'll need documents and things of that nature. I will be in London for a week before shipping out.'

She pulled her hands away from his grasp. Desperation and disbelief swamped her. She couldn't think straight. There was no time, not even to argue. 'So soon? Can't anyone else identify him? Someone who is already there? Surely, others in your troop would know him. Why do *you* have to travel all that way?'

'Because I knew him best. It's not only his physical description that matters. We can't assume it's Fortis because he has dark hair and blue eyes. Any number of men could have that—and who knows what this man looks like after living in the woods or a cave or who knows where for the last ten months? We have to test his memories, whatever memories he has. From all reports, he's incredibly discombobulated. Only I can do that if we're to prove anything beyond the superficial.' He reached for her hands again and she limply surrendered them. 'I know it's sudden. That's why I wanted to talk with you about it.'

'What's there to talk about? It seems you've already decided.'

'Do you mind? I know it's two weeks earlier than planned.' He hesitated over the last word.

'"Than planned"? Nothing has been planned. Were you leaving in August? We hadn't discussed *that*. Why would we discuss *this*? Were you just going to pack up and leave? Was I going to wake up one morning and you would simply be gone with no idea of when you were coming back? Or if you were coming back? Did you think to make me into a living man's widow like Avaline Tresham?' Her fear, her jealousy, were feasting hard now. Losing him was somehow different when she had been the one deciding to let him go instead of him simply leaving of his own accord. Abandoning her.

The tentative joy over his news dimmed in Cam's eyes and she hated herself for taking it, hated herself for not being the one to give it to him in the first place. His gaze was harder now, his voice quieter. 'I didn't think it mattered to you if I stayed or left. Does it?' Did she imagine there was a begging note hidden in his question? If she said she wanted him to stay, would he? Would he stay just for her? No, not for her. For honour. She did not want that. She'd asked too much of him for honour's sake already.

'Of course it matters. I want you to be happy.'

'And your happiness?' Cam pressed, searching her gaze for something she could not let him find.

'I don't want my happiness at the expense of yours. We've already tried that and seen how it works out. You're miserable. Do you think I don't notice how restless you are? How you ride yourself to weariness so you don't have to think, so you can fall in bed exhausted every night.'

'I have been working with Conall, looking for new pastures to expand the enterprise, expand our profits so you might have a rosewood table without scars. And, yes, sometimes I ride out to stay in shape, to keep my soldiering skills honed.' He smiled at the admission, but there was hurt behind it. 'Why did you think I was out riding, Pavia?'

There were too many answers to that: because she was not bearing him a child, because she'd pushed him away and given him no choice, because she'd not welcomed intimacy back into their bed, because he needed a purpose beyond her. So many reasons. If there'd been some hope for them, she might have voiced those reasons. But he was leaving and voicing them now would only cause an unnecessary fight.

'Conall will manage all right without you?'

'Oh, yes, I needed his partnership more than he needed mine. I was happy to ride out for him, save him the effort of doing it so he could be at home. So—' He stopped, but it was too late. She could fill those words in for him. *So Conall could be at home with Sofia and his son.*

It prompted the question she had to ask. 'If I were pregnant, would you still leave?' Would he choose Fortis Tresham over her anyway? It was a terrible truth to face even if she'd long suspected it.

'Do you really want to know the answer to that? There's no good answer I can give, Pavia. If I answer yes, then I am choosing my best friend over my family. If I answer no, I am admitting I believe Fortis is truly dead, that I failed him on the field. Either of those choices pain me.'

'Then be pained. I want to know.'

'Then, no, I would not be leaving. Satisfied? Does that make you feel better or worse?'

Worse. So much worse. It would be easier to be jealous of Fortis's claim to him. But there it was. The horrible truth she'd tried to ignore since this honour-bound farce began. It had all been about the baby for him. At least she knew she was doing the right thing in letting him go. He would have his old life back.

She gathered her courage. He'd asked for her opinion so she would give it. 'Then you have your answer. Since there is no baby, you should go.' She took a step backwards, intending to head for the house. She'd done what she'd come out here to do—set him free. 'I will help you pack. Mrs Bran and I will make lists of things you might need to get in London. I'll open a bottle of wine tonight so you have a proper send-off.'

Then she hurried inside before he could see her cry.

Chapter Twenty

Damn it, that wasn't what he wanted at all. Cam whipped the shirt from his neck and roughly pulled it over his head. He didn't want to be putting his shirt back on. If things had gone right, he'd have been going upstairs with her. But it had all gone very wrong. He didn't want a farewell dinner. He didn't want her helping him pack. He wanted her to want *him*, to want him to stay, to tell him not to go. He wanted his marriage back. Even at the expense of Fortis.

Cam kicked a rock with his boot and strode towards the stable, needing some space and privacy to think over what had just happened and what was going to happen. He took the curry brush from the stable boy and made to send him home to his family early. Then Cam remembered. The boy only worked a couple of days a week. He wouldn't be back until Thursday. Too late. Cam drew a shaky breath and steadied himself. This would be his first goodbye. He'd not expected it to happen so soon. In truth, he'd not expected it to happen at all.

'Sir, are you all right?' The boy peered at him in concern.

'Here.' He flipped the boy a coin from his pocket and tried for a smile. 'Thank you for your hard work. I know we only have three horses to look after and a modest barn, but you've done well keeping it clean.'

Cam stroked Hengroen's nose with a long caress. 'Looks like we'll be on the move again soon. Back to Sevastopol…back to Balaclava.' He patted the horse's side and began to brush. 'Maybe even back to Fortis.' The thought of going back, of finding his friend alive, should have filled him with unspeakable joy. The latter had. He'd read the telegram from London and ridden straight home, joy in his heart, and he'd let that joy spill out. He'd shared that joy with the one person he wanted to know. He wanted Pavia to celebrate the chance with him. After months of uncertainty and difficulty, here was proof that hope sprang eternal. They had lost their child, but maybe they would have Fortis back.

For a moment, the world was perfect again. He was with Pavia, a smile on her face, the joy of his friend's safety bubbling up in him. Then she had told him she would prepare a farewell dinner, that he should go. That there was nothing here for him. But she was here. Which meant that she didn't want him. She didn't want him to stay.

'She doesn't need me any more,' he told Hengroen. 'She doesn't need my protection, my presence.' His throat tightened up at the thought. He liked being needed. He liked taking care of people. It was what he enjoyed about being an officer—taking care of his men. It was what he'd enjoyed about making Great-Aunt Lily's house into a home with Pavia. He'd thought she'd enjoyed it, too. He'd thought they were building a marriage together, something that would last as they got to know one another. He'd been wrong.

He knew what these months had meant to him; he wasn't sure now that he knew what they'd meant to her. Had it all really just been about the baby for her? Was he nothing but an accessory to make her decent and her child legitimate? It had never seemed like that to him, certainly not in bed. She'd never acted as if bedding him was her duty, but her pleasure, and she'd begged him to let her into his world. She'd wanted to know everything about him. Was that it? Had he not given her enough? Had he given her too much? Was she appalled by the man she'd married and now this was a convenient way to separate herself from him? by sending him back to his world?

Cam swiped a hand across his brow, across his face, his sweat making for stinging tears. This was supposed to be a marriage of convenience. So why did the realisations hurt so much? Why did it matter if she didn't want him? He knew the answer. It was why he couldn't give up on Fortis and simply believe he was dead. He didn't want to give up on his marriage, on Pavia. Because walking away from people one loved was hard.

He loved her. He loved his wife.

The curry brush slipped from his fingers. Hengroen tossed his head at the interruption. 'Sorry, old chap,' Cam muttered, bending down to pick up the brush. He loved Pavia. Not just because she was the most beautiful woman he'd ever seen. She was more than a pretty face. He loved the way she burnt toast, the way she'd brazened out their poor excuse for a wedding, the way she'd bravely taken on this old, decrepit house and made it a home alongside him, the way she'd embraced his neighbours and made herself a part of the community. She'd been a girl born to privilege and she'd taken the loss of that privilege in her admirable stride. He'd had the rigours of the military to see him through the early domestic disappointment of the house. But she'd had only him and that had been enough, he'd thought. He'd been wrong. He hadn't been enough. He loved her, but she didn't love him, not enough anyway. She was too kind to say it; she'd married him because she had no choice.

He would make things right for her, of course, regardless of what she thought she needed or not. He would meet with his solicitor in London while he gathered the documents he needed for Fortis. He would make sure Pavia was cared for in his absence and in case that absence was of a more permanent variety. A soldier couldn't be too careful.

Cam gave Hengroen a final pat. He stood in the doorway of the stable, drinking in the sight of his home: the little lawn on either side of the gravel drive, the curtains gracing the windows as the sun lowered overhead, bathing the brick in soft pinks and blues. His house made sounds, too—the clink of dishes coming from the house told him Pavia had dinner on the table, the smell of warm bread wafted out into the evening. Leaving had never been like this—never sad, never regretful. The days before leaving had always been heady, busy times in the past, evenings filled with drinking and rowdy parties in taverns with his men. Did his married men feel like this? Hollow inside at the thought of being away from home, of wondering who would take care of their homes and their wives with them a continent away?

The candles on the dining room table flared to life. He could see them through the window. Time to go in, or Pavia's meal would be cold. He'd not come home thinking tonight would be the beginning of the end, but that's what it was.

'I think the emporium in Taunton will have socks even though it's summer.' Pavia sipped at the wine she'd opened for the occasion. 'I know there won't be any ready-made socks in Trull this time of year.'

'It's all right,' Cam cut her off gently. She'd been chatting all supper about the things he'd need. 'I have plenty of socks in my campaign chest in London at the barracks and the weather will be warm.'

'Still, you can't underestimate the importance of socks, warm weather or not. You'll get blisters in your boots if you wear them wet or sweaty.' She sighed and set down her wine glass. 'Then, I guess you really do have everything you need. There's not much for you to do, I suppose, but get on your horse and ride out.'

'There's you to look after.' Cam wiped his mouth with his napkin. Dinner had been an awkward affair, both of them knowing things were ending and yet both of them trying to pretend all of this was normal. Perhaps that had always been their problem—pretending things were normal; that it was normal an exotic dancer took a man to bed and didn't ask for payment, that it was normal that an exotic dancer turned out to be a tea heiress, that people defied their families and married strangers. Nothing had ever been normal for them, but they hadn't seen that. They'd chosen not to, and here, at the end of it all, they were still clinging to the idea that even this farewell was somehow normal.

'We should talk about arrangements for you while I am a way. You'll have the quarterly stipend from the alpaca investment. I will write a letter to Conall explaining how to deposit the money and make it available to you. You should be comfortable and have money for Mrs Bran's wages and the stable boy and the gardener. However, if you need anything, I will leave a letter of credit for you at my bank in London. Conall and Sofia, also, would help you if there were any problems that arose.'

He felt more in control giving instructions, but it was still difficult to talk around the tightness in his throat, a tightness the wine hadn't eased. Cam cleared his throat. 'I worry about the roof. We didn't get to it yet and I'm not sure how well it will weather another English winter. The two horses for the gig will need shoes before long. I can make arrangements for the farrier to come out in a couple of weeks.'

The instructions were a pitiful few. If he'd been in London, or if he'd been close with his family, she'd have somewhere to go. His family would take her in, fill her days. 'You'll be busy. I'm sure the ladies' circles will be thrilled to have you back.' She had not attended since the miscarriage and he hadn't pushed her, thinking she'd return to her routine in time. Now he wished he had pushed a little harder. He didn't want her to be lonely.

He cleared his throat again, wishing the tightness would go away. 'I will meet with my solicitor in London and update my will. If anything happens to me, you will get the title to this house and any wealth I might have. It won't be much, but it will be something until you can find your feet again. You can always turn to Conall and Sofia. They would take you in.'

'It's bad luck to talk of such things,' Pavia shushed him with a mortified whisper.

'It's bad luck not to plan for such things,' Cam retorted. 'I've seen too many men not make plans and not come back.'

Cam played with the folds of his napkin and broached the other subject carefully, that of his return. 'If it really is Fortis, we could be home before Christmas as long as we start travelling in October or November at the latest.' That assumed, too, that he'd get leave to escort Fortis home. He could get that leave one way or another. He could always resign his commission. 'We could celebrate Christmas in London with the Treshams. It would be a joyous holiday indeed with Fortis returned to us.' He watched carefully for her reaction, his heart hoping for some flicker of happiness, for one of her smiles.

'Do you think it wise to take me to London? I'm not sure we'd be as welcome as you think,' was all she said.

'The Treshams would welcome us and that's all that matters. They are real friends.'

Cam shrugged. 'But if you'd rather not try on London yet, we can stay here in Little Trull. Country holidays have a special flavour all their own: a tableau at the church, wassailing in the snow if we're lucky to get any.' He eyed the banister leading upstairs through the door frame of the dining room. 'We could have a party here. I think the banister would look splendid draped in greenery and red bows.'

There was no response from her. Pavia merely looked at her plate and pushed her peas around with a fork. Cam pressed harder. 'I was thinking, when I came back, I'd resign my commission and focus on the alpaca with Conall, maybe even start a small herd of my own. We have the acreage for it and I'm not sure the land's good for anything else.'

That got her attention. 'Why would you do that? You love soldiering.' She gave a half-smile and a shake of her head. 'You've been restless these last weeks without it. I can't imagine being an alpaca farmer would entertain you for long.'

Cam held her gaze. 'Because you're here.' He paused, seeing the flaw in his assumption. Panic rose in his chest. He'd always assumed they'd have a chance to try again in time. Marriage was for ever. They could try as many times as they liked. He could not hide the urgency in his voice. 'Pavia, *will* you be here when I get back?'

The whole evening had been a nightmare, sitting there listening to Cam talk about provisions and plans as if a man outlined his own death every day. She couldn't bear to think of Cam dead. It was hard enough to think of him being gone and then to see that it wasn't enough to send him away. That this sacrifice she was making didn't free him. His sense of honour would bring him back to her when his duty was done and the trap would start all over for him. He would never allow himself to be free of her. She would have to do it for him.

'No, I don't think I will be. I was thinking of going to India, after all.' She kept her voice even and steady as she held his gaze. 'I'll leave as soon as I can make the arrangements and close up the house.'

Cam's eyes flickered infinitesimally. 'Shall I come to you there, then? The Crimea is halfway between England and India. It is no trouble and I'm sure someone else can escort Fortis home if it's necessary.'

'You needn't come to me at all.' Her heart was breaking. He would travel the world for her. If only his offer was made out of love for her and not out of his ever-present sense of honour and duty.

'You are my wife, Pavia. Does that mean so little to you?' His voice was stern as if he could command her submission. 'At the first sign of difficulty, you are willing take your father's offer?'

'It's a good resolution to our circumstances,' Pavia said defiantly, but she wavered inside. How long would she be able to hold this line?

Cam's face was grim. He was ferocious in adhering to his sense of duty. 'And what exactly are our circumstances?'

'A marriage of convenience, made with the protection of an innocent babe in mind. The babe is gone and that makes the marriage no longer convenient or even necessary.' She let herself be angry. Anger would be her best defence now, her best chance in setting him free.

'Is that all this is to you? Convenience?' Cam rose from his seat, tall and imposing in the small dining room. She rose to meet him as he circled the table. 'Would it make a difference to you if I said this marriage was more than convenience to me? Would it matter if I said I loved you?'

Pavia's eyes brimmed with tears. She shook

her head. It was too late for such sentiment to matter. 'No, because it's a lie. You loved the mother of your child. You loved the idea of being a father. I just happened to come along with that package. But all the things you loved are gone now.'

Cam's face was pale. She could see the physical effects of her words. They'd wounded him. 'Pavia, we can make another baby, we can still have that family.'

'No, Cam. I have to be more than the vessel for a man's children. And you deserve more than what marriage to me brings you.'

'Wherever you go, you will still be my wife.' Cam said staunchly, 'I won't divorce you.'

'I don't think you'll have to,' she replied honestly. 'All of our defiance has played into both our families' hands: a wedding that no one attended, a scandal that never was. No one outside of family knew we wed. No one knew I was…pregnant.' It was still hard for her to say. 'For all London knew, the Earl of Aylsbury's grandson danced with the Cit's daughter once at the Banfields' ball before the Season truly began. That's hardly a source of scandal. All your grandfather has to do is burn the marriage certificate and bribe the Church to do the same and the Lithgows of Little Trull will have vanished.'

Cam would ride off to war. She would sail for India. In time, even the residents of Little Trull would forget they'd been here. If she was lucky, she might forget, too, how it had felt to be Mrs Lithgow, the woman Cam held in his arms at night, the woman he made love to, the woman he'd made a garden for so that she might have shade in the summer, the woman he'd dreamed with, and for a brief time the woman he'd thrown everything over for. It would be painful to forget, but perhaps less painful than holding on to what she'd lost.

'A fantasy? Is that what this has been?' Cam reached for her and, in a moment of weakness, she let him draw her close as he used to. She breathed in the scent of him, all man and country soap. She closed her eyes and held on to it. She would pack him some of her oils in the morning; something to help him sleep, perhaps, or something to help with any headaches he might get. 'In the morning we wake up? Is that it? And it's all over? We go back to our old lives?'

'It's for the best, Cam. We loved the idea of something that doesn't exist any more,' Pavia whispered, her fingers finding their way into his hair of their own volition.

Cam gave a fierce growl, his mouth hovering above hers in prelude to a kiss. 'Then tonight, I'm still dreaming. Tonight, you are still mine.'

'Yes,' Pavia whispered, breathless beneath his lips. 'We have until morning. One last time.'

Cam lifted her in his arms and carried her upstairs as he'd done on their wedding night. It would end then as it had begun.

Chapter Twenty-One

Life was more vibrant when it might be lost.
It was a truth of love and war. The morning
of battle was like that: the air crisper, the dew
wetter, the birdsong sharper, the joy in the colours of the sunrise sweeter. It was like that
now, carrying Pavia upstairs to bed. He'd carried her up these stairs in good times and in
bad. Tonight, every memory, every sense was
alert; the scent of her was strong in his nostrils,
the weight of her tangible in his arms, and all
around him the world was simply more: the
bed softer when he laid her down, her gaze
more intense when he stripped for her in the
candlelight, his hands shakier as he took her
gown from her, revealing her inch by inch in
a reverent homecoming. It had been too long
since they'd been together like this. His fault.

He should have seduced his wife long before this when it might still have mattered.

'I've always loved looking at your body,' Cam whispered. He kissed the tips of her breasts, the valley of her navel, the nest of dark curls at her thighs. He feathered those curls with his breath, his tongue finding the core of her. Tonight he would give her everything, all the pleasure his body had to offer, with his mouth, his tongue, his hands, and, in return, he took his own pleasure in each mewl, each purl of delight, each nuance of her body as she bucked and arched against him until at last he rose up over her, and joined himself to her in deep, shuddering thrusts that drove them both to pleasure's brink and over it. She cried out and he collapsed against her, holding her tight as if by doing so he could hold back time itself.

It was a ritual he repeated three times that night, dozing only briefly to wake and want her again. He had no intentions of letting the night steal the last hours of his fantasy in sleep. But even Cam Lithgow wasn't immune to the needs of the body. Sleep could not be avoided entirely and neither could exhaustion, but it was a replete fatigue that swept over him, a sense of satisfaction that had been absent in the last weeks, as he held Pavia in his arms in the wee hours of the morning. 'Why did we break, Pavia?' He dared the words in the dark.

'Because we were never whole to begin with, Cam,' came the whispered reply. This was an anomaly, a time apart from the regular time line of their lives. This wasn't supposed to have happened. It was hard to remember their imperfections in the aftermath of perfect love-making. He did sleep then, conceding the short hours before morning to exhaustion.

Too soon, dawn woke him with the grey fingers of first light tugging at the corners of his eyelids. He resisted the pull to wakefulness, knowing what it would mean. The euphoria of the night could linger as long as he kept his eyes shut. He played that game as long as he could, remembering. But finally he had to concede to the morning. Last night belonged in the past, but today belonged to the future.

Cam opened his eyes and the world went grey and flat. The sharpness that had marked every scent, every touch, every sound of the night was gone. Beside him, Pavia was oblivious in sleep. He was tempted to wake her and reclaim a piece of the night, but that only postponed the inevitable. The future was waiting, Fortis might be waiting. He and Pavia had said and done all that was left to do between them in the night. No sense in rehashing it now when it could do no good.

Cam dressed quickly and silently in his uniform and gathered his shaving kit and essentials. It was all he needed to take with him. Everything he needed to return to duty waited for him in London. But everything he wanted was in this room. He risked a last glance at the bed where she slept, dark hair spread on a white pillow. Even after he'd dressed, the urge to undress and take her again thrummed through him with unwelcome persistence. He summoned the strength of his perseverance. It was best to be off now, while she slept. When she woke she would have what she wanted. He would be gone. She could start over and he would simply find a way to keep going.

Cam was gone. There was an emptiness in the room that could be felt long before she opened her eyes. She'd dreamed of hoofbeats fading in the distance. Perhaps those had been real. She had missed him! Pavia's eyes flew open, her body shaking off the shackles of sleep in a sudden upright surge, a wave of panic and regret swept her. She'd not meant for him to leave without saying goodbye. She glanced about the room, her eyes falling on her little kit of oils. She hadn't mixed any for him! She'd meant to do it in the morning, to have them ready for him at breakfast as a last gift and now it was too late. He should have woken her.

But he hadn't. Had he not wanted to say goodbye? Was he that anxious to be on the road? To be away from all of this? From her? He'd been saying goodbye all night and she had, too, with their bodies. What did it matter if they said the words now? It could hardly change anything, nor should it. She took her thoughts fiercely in hand. This was what she wanted for him because it was what he wanted for himself, what he deserved. He deserved to go search for his friend. He deserved to be set free from this honour-sprung trap of marriage now that there was no honour to preserve.

Downstairs, she heard the arrival of Mrs Bran, the heavy *thunk* of a cast-iron skillet. Soon afterwards, the scent of frying bacon wafted up to her. Cam's favourite and a reminder of all that needed to be done today. There would be people to tell, explanations to be made, starting with Mrs Bran.

Already, Pavia started to concoct her story. She would have to let everyone know the Major had been called back to duty a few weeks earlier than expected. She would have to pretend it didn't matter. What was two weeks when it was bound to happen anyway? She'd have to close up the house and pretend she was excited to follow him to London. It was mostly true. She was going to London, but not to follow him there. Yet the lie was necessary. Mrs Bran would never believe she was going to stay with family, not after the last scene with her father. There was a time when Pavia wouldn't have believed it either. She dressed and went downstairs to face the future.

Staying busy was her saving grace throughout the week, otherwise Pavia was certain she'd have spent the days in tears. Packing up the house was akin to laying a loved one out for a funeral, preparing for a final goodbye. Everywhere she looked in the house there were reminders of Cam. In the dining room, where she attempted to eat breakfast but failed, it was the rosewood table. In the kitchen, where she told Mrs Bran of the sudden change in plans, it was the butcher block where they'd made love. In her sitting room, it was the fireplace and the stories he'd told her of snuggling there in an old chair with Aunt Lily. Even the garden was a reminder of him. There was no escaping him. His mark was indelibly etched on this home. She hoped leaving it would ease the sense of loss.

The bedroom was the worst. She'd saved it for last, for just that reason. It was not the bed and the countless memories there, or the memory of how the room had first appeared to her that dark night of her arrival, that drew her tears, but his clothes. They smelled of him. She could remember each time he'd worn them: the shirt from the house-warming, his riding clothes. All of them held memories. And he'd left them. He would not need them where he was going. It seemed the perfect divide between their life here and his 'real life' in the military. He'd left them behind as assuredly as he'd left her behind. Pavia shook out a shirt and folded it. She would pack them and send them to London, to his grandfather's. Mrs Bran would find it odd to have them left behind. And, Pavia reasoned, Cam would need them when he returned to England.

He would return. She couldn't think otherwise. Last night's discussion over supper had nearly undone her. She couldn't bear to think of him dying so far from home. If he did, that would be her fault, too. She'd sent him away, thinking to do right by him. What if she was wrong? What if she was sending him to his death instead?

Mrs Bran poked her head into the room. 'I think everything is done. Are you sure you wouldn't like me to stay tonight?'

Pavia summoned a smile. 'No, I'll be fine and there's no need to come in the morning. I'll have the stable boy drive me in the gig and I'll be gone early.'

'Well, then...' Mrs Bran humphed, emotion catching up with the older woman '...I won't say goodbye, because you'll be back when the Major's tour is over and we'll be pulling the covers off all the furniture soon enough.'

'Yes, of course, Mrs Bran. Thank you. I'll walk you out.'

Downstairs was ghostly, even more so once Pavia had seen Mrs Bran off. The hutch that had held her mismatched dishes was empty. The furniture cloaked in holland covers, looking like spectres themselves. Pavia trailed a hand over the white sheets. Most unnerving, though, was the speed at which it had all been accomplished. It had only taken a week to dismantle all she and Cam had built here. It might have been accomplished more quickly, but she'd wanted to linger. Perhaps she hadn't quite given up hope that she'd hear his horse in the drive, that he would return. But this wasn't a fairy tale.

Pavia looked about the house. She'd been right. This house held no trace of the Lithgows having been here. They were already vanishing. Cam was gone, the house was closed. Tomorrow, the gig and horses would be taken to the livery for care and keeping after she was dropped off in Taunton for the train. The barn would be empty; the house would be deserted. By tomorrow, the Lithgows of Little Trull would vanish completely.

Pavia Honeysett was home. Within moments of raising the wood-carved jaguarhead knocker on the town house, she was surrounded by servants; one to take her bag, one to see to her trunks down at Paddington Station, one to pull her a bath, another to set out tea, one to tell her father.

'Ah, Pavia! You're back.' Her father held out his arms in an expansive, welcoming gesture as if she were returned from a holiday. There was no trace of the acrimony that had marked their previous visit. 'Your mother is out shopping, but she will be thrilled. Shall I send a messenger for her?'

'No.' Pavia's smile was polite but cool. 'You and I have business to discuss first.'

'This way, then, darling girl, we can do it over tea out the back.' It was her father's rendition of the prodigal's return. Tea was laid out in a splendour of cakes and biscuits amid her mother's fine china on a table overlooking the expansive Honeysett town garden with its well-manicured grasses, red roses and pristine, weed-free paths. Her garden in Little Trull paled by comparison, yet part of her cried out there'd was no other place she'd rather be than on her little bench in that garden.

'Is our second cup of tea too early for business?' her father asked congenially, reaching for another cake.

'No, not at all.' She was surprised he'd waited that long. Perhaps he'd learned not to rush her, or perhaps he guessed this would not be an easy discussion. 'As you may have deduced, I have lost the baby. It happened shortly after your visit, in fact. Now, I want to discuss India. I would like to take you up on your offer to spend a few years away. I'd like to leave as soon as possible.'

'Leave? You just got here.' Her father gave a friendly laugh, but it didn't ring true. None of this rang true: the amiable greeting, the tea in the garden instead of meeting in his office. He leaned forward, conspiratorially. 'Now that there is no baby to worry about, why leave at all? Why not stay and enjoy society?'

'I like it there,' Pavia argued.

'It's hot.'

'My uncle's palaces are in the hills and full of cool breezes.' And waterfalls, like the one outside the village in Little Trull. She couldn't afford to think about that now or she would lose her courage.

'It's dangerous. Tigers, cobras, all nature of stinging deadly bugs.' None as lethal as the man sitting across from her.

'You offered me a deal. I want to go.' Pavia returned the conversation to its original import, but she had a dreadful sense of foreboding about this. Had the offer been real or merely a trap to lure her back to town? Away from Cam? Not that the last mattered at this point.

'Lithgow has left you, hasn't he?' Her father's eyes were sharp now. 'Aylsbury must have got to him, after all, not that there was any doubt. It was only a matter of when.'

'He has been recalled to duty, that is all.' Pavia stiffened. 'I will not have him maligned in my presence. He is a good man who has been sorely used.'

'And yet you want to leave him?' her father prodded.

'It's what is best for him. Without the child, the marriage was a mistake.' But she misunderstood what her father had meant by 'leave'. What she had meant to imply temporarily, her father meant as permanent.

'I'm glad to hear you say that, Daughter.' He winked. 'I know someone else who will be glad to hear you're back in town. The Marquis has been missing you.' He waved a hand. 'We told him you were rusticating in the country for a while. He was very disappointed to hear that you'd left.'

Pavia pulled her hand away, appalled at the suggestion. 'You courted the Marquis on my behalf? I was married, Father, and pregnant, at least then.' More than that, he'd made plans for her. He wasn't going to wait for three years before trying again at a title.

'The marriage is nothing. I thought I explained myself in Little Trull. Aylsbury and I will have it annulled immediately.' He patted her hand. 'Everything will be fine in a few days and you'll be free to marry the Marquis. With a special licence, we can do it before the

Season ends.' He offered a benevolent, patronising smile as panic welled within her. This was the source of his good mood. He'd already bartered her off, hedged his bets as it were.

Pavia thought quickly. She rose and set down her napkin. 'Cam and I do not wish to have the marriage annulled.'

'Is that so?' Her father's dark gaze was impenetrable as he struck a match on the sole of his shoe and lit a cigar. Did he believe her? 'Perhaps I should ask the Major himself. I hear Lithgow is in town, preparing for the Crimea. Word at the clubs is that he's requested to have his tour extended.'

That boded ill for her. He couldn't wait to get away and stay away, apparently. 'We need some time to readjust after the loss of our child and he needs time to sort through his options with his military career. Everything has been so sudden.' It was a bald-faced lie, but it was the only bluff she had. As long as she was married to Cam, she had her freedom. She could not be bartered off.

'Then that's what I'll ask the Major when I meet with him.' Her father blew out a satisfied smoke ring. 'I can't have him abandoning my daughter like Tresham did with his wife. It would have been better to cut her loose than to leave her hanging on alone for years.'

Pavia schooled her features to show none of her inner turmoil. 'If you'll excuse me, I would like to lie down and rest before Mother comes home.' She had to get to Cam first and beg him to corroborate her lie. Without his protection, she was trapped, traded off into another marriage. To a man who wasn't Cam. By the time she reached the top of the stairs, her initial reaction had ebbed, replaced by the new reality of her life. She could not run to Cam and assume he'd be her bulwark. She'd pushed him away, told him there was no reason to be together. All for his own good, but now for *her* own good, she needed him back and she didn't know if he would come. Perhaps this time, she'd lost him for good and the realisation sickened her.

Chapter Twenty-Two

The note came for him in the midst of a bustling late afternoon at White's as Cam sat over drinks with the Duke of Cowden, discussing how to proceed with the Fortis situation. 'Probably just more orders from Raglan.' Cam took the note and the interruption from the footman good naturedly. The week had been peppered with interruptions like this one, full of excited notes from headquarters over the development and the possibility of bringing home a duke's son.

'I hear there's talk of a promotion for you,' Cowden put in as Cam unfolded the paper. 'For valour and persistence in the field. Some are even calling for a title.'

'It's just talk at this point.' Cam shrugged. Those same people had also called for his being sent home when that persistence had proven inconvenient and embarrassing to them. People were fickle creatures, changing with the wind. He looked down at the note, his nonchalance turning into something more complex, elation and anger rolled into a complicated combination of emotions. Pavia needed help. More specifically, Pavia needed *him*.

'Not bad news, I hope?' Cowden stilled, his features paling. Cam blamed himself for the fear suddenly scrawled across the older man's face. He needed to be more careful with his own emotions, always remembering that, to Cowden, 'bad news' could only be about Fortis, another hope dashed, another reminder that Fortis was dead and nothing was going to change that. He knew too well the hills and valleys the Treshams had been through since October. He'd crested those emotional hills himself.

'Nothing, Your Grace. I am sorry to have disturbed you.' Cam folded the paper and put in his pocket, but not out of mind. She was here, in London, and already in trouble. Part of him, the instinctive part, wanted to run to her, wanted to walk out of White's and go to her side. But another part of him, the part that was still reeling from their separation, cautioned against such impetuosity. She'd cast him off. She'd shunned their marriage. She needed to look elsewhere for assistance.

'You're a thousand miles from here, Camden. If I were a betting man, I'd say it was something to do with your orders. Eager, are you, to be back with your troops?' Cowden chuckled confidentially. 'Or are you wishing you were back in Little Trull with your new wife?'

The surprise was enough to draw Cam back to the present. 'How do you know about that?' So much for his grandfather's theory the marriage was invisible.

The Duke shrugged. 'I hear things.'

'From whom?' How widespread was this knowledge?

The Duke laughed. 'From Conall, of course. He wrote and told me about your partnership. He also mentioned you'd brought your lovely wife to visit.' Cowden's eyes softened. 'He told me about your loss as well. I am sorry, dear boy.' He reached out a fatherly hand and placed it over Cam's. 'Since you won't say anything on the subject, I will. Is this really the best time for you to go back to Balaclava?'

'There's no question of that,' Cam answered resolutely. 'My leave is up in a couple of weeks. My duty here is done. My men are waiting and

Fortis needs me. I owe Fortis to be underway as soon as possible. And you.'

The Duke scowled. 'There will be no talk of owing. You owe us nothing. We don't even know that the man in question is Fortis. You could be haring back for another wild goose chase. I can send Ferris. He can go.' The Duke sat back in the tall leather chair and signalled for another round of drinks.

'There's a reason young couples go on a honeymoon. It's to give them time to become accustomed to one another, to the rhythms of living together. It's been barely five months for you and your bride. That's hardly enough time for you to know one another, let alone to weather loss and yet you've had to do both under a cloud of uncertainty and a decided lack of support from your families.' Cowden raised his eyebrows meaningfully. 'It's no wonder that you're here and she's there and soon the Crimea and months apart will be between you.' He tapped his finger on the table, giving Cam time to think as fresh drinks were delivered. When the footman left, Cowden said, 'I wouldn't go if I were you.'

That was pretty blunt. 'We need time, Your Grace.' It was the lie he'd told himself all the way to London. They needed time. Pavia needed space. He would find her after the business with Fortis was over and things would be different. They'd have a second chance. He'd convince her he loved her. That had been his mistake. He'd not told her he loved her when he should have. He'd assumed she'd known. When he had told her, it had been too late. She saw the words as patchwork done in haste. She'd only sent him away because she understood his loyalty to Fortis and because she felt she'd trapped him in a life not of his choosing. That was when he was feeling charitable. Other times, he was brutally honest with himself. All the time and space in the world wouldn't change the fact that she wouldn't have chosen him if she hadn't been desperate.

Cam tossed back his drink. She was desperate again. The note proved his more brutal thoughts were right. She'd written out of desperation. Otherwise, she'd not have turned to him. Just as she would not have turned to him the first time.

'You're the not the first man driven to drink over a woman.' Cowden eyed the disappearing drink with mild disapproval. 'I would have thought you'd learned a little something from Fortis, though. He left when things became difficult with Avaline.' He sighed and spread his hands wide. 'I don't know what things. He never said. But he left, thinking time and distance would solve their problems. In a way it did. They never saw one another again. The longer they were apart, the less inclined they were to retrieve their relationship. Is your marriage not worth fighting for, Cam?'

'A man can't always fight alone, Your Grace.' *As long as there's a 'we',* he'd once told Pavia. There wasn't a 'we' any more, just him.

A shadow fell across the table. 'Ah, my boy, I heard you were back in town.' The Earl of Aylsbury leaned elegantly on his cane, managing to make ageing look like a fashionable feat. 'And, Cowden, how good to see you. Congratulations on the news of your son.' He turned back to Cam. 'Your trunk arrived at Aylsbury House yesterday, full of your civilian clothes. I don't imagine you'll need them at the moment, just thought you'd like to know.'

He lowered his voice and drew Cam aside. 'Seems your "wife" is back in town and living at her father's. All's well that ends well, hmm? We can all throw off this misfortunate interlude. I'll start the proceedings for an annulment right away. It'll be taken care of before you return from the Crimea.' He winked. 'It's always good to have someone at Lambeth Palace in your pocket. A little money and an unfortunate fire, and there will be no proof there ever was a wedding. The both of you can be married to other people by Christmas. Caroline will look lovely in winter white and Honeysett has the Marquis dangling on a golden chain.' He smiled coldly and clapped Cam on the shoulder. 'I hope you'll have time to call before you ship out.'

His grandfather sauntered on to meet other friends and Cam took out his pocket watch, his hand trembling with emotion; Pavia to marry another! And against her will. So this was the trouble Pavia was in. He had just enough time to make her rendezvous. 'Cowden, if you'll excuse me?' He'd no more said the words and sent for his horse than an exclamation brought the club surging to the windows in excitement. A dray had overturned, blocking the street to horse and carriage traffic. He'd never make to the rendezvous point in time on horseback. He'd have to go on foot and he'd be late, even if he ran.

Cam tore through the chaotic crowd, his mind equally riotous. What would he do when he got there? Did he help her? Did he let her use him again? Did he even have a choice? This wasn't just about Pavia. It was about him, too. He wasn't about to stand aside and let others dictate the status of his marriage. She couldn't marry another unless she were free to do so and the last time he checked neither of them were. No one, not even the Earl of Aylsbury, was going to take his wife from him.

Cam wasn't coming. Pavia paced the lawn outside the Queen's Temple in Kensington Gardens, hiding her agitation behind the ruffles of a white parasol. She couldn't wait much longer. She'd told her maid she'd be back by five o'clock. If she wasn't, her maid would sound the alarm. Her mother would worry and her father would be suspicious. She risked much with this meeting. A virtuous girl would not be out alone. Her father would scold her over what the Marquis might think if he found out. He might do more than scold her. In truth, she feared what her father would do to ensure the match. He had an important ally these days in the Earl of Aylsbury. Together, between the Earl's power and her father's money, they could cloak many sins.

Pavia turned to make another pass of the building, disappointment growing. Was Cam just late or was he simply not coming? Had he got her note and dismissed it? Had he decided in the week he'd left Little Trull that he was indeed better off without her? What man wanted to be tied to a woman who insisted she had no use of him? Until she did. But this meeting today wasn't just about needing his help. It was about *them*. She'd been wrong to dismiss his love, to not believe in it, and now she'd put them at risk by playing into her father's hand. Now she just had to convince Cam of that, if she ever saw him again.

'Pavia Honeysett, I hear you have need of my services,' Cam drawled from behind her.

She turned, relief making her weak. 'You came!' She stepped towards him, impulsively. It was too easy to want to throw herself in his arms. She stopped, seeing the wariness of his shuttered blue eyes. 'You don't trust me. That's my fault,' she said carefully.

'Maybe I don't trust myself when I'm with you.' Cam's reply was dry. 'You are in distress about marrying the Marquis?' His tone was cool, at odds with his appearance. His face was red and sweaty, his cravat undone. His horse was nowhere to be found.

'I am in distress about what my father's delusions will do to us,' she amended. 'How did you get here?'

'I ran most of the way, found a hack eventually. I wouldn't recommend it in boots.'

'Come inside the temple with me. We can talk in private and it's cooler.' Pavia held out her hand, but Cam didn't take it. Still, he'd run across London for her. That had to be a good sign.

'To marry the Marquis, I have to be free of my first marriage. My father and your grandfather are going to destroy it. There will be no record of it except our word against theirs.'

Inside, the temple undulated through three empty, cool, stone rooms. The place was deserted this time of day and they were alone.

'He's a good man. What is the distress?'

'I don't love him.'

'That hasn't stopped you before.'

'I don't recall you ever being mean, Cam. You know we had other circumstances to consider in the beginning.' He wasn't making this easy for her. She'd hoped he'd meet her halfway, that he would have been happy to see her the way she was happy to see him.

'When I told you I loved you, you offered to help me pack. Forgive me if I don't find that a resounding endorsement of your affections.' He was as cold as these stones today.

Pavia whirled about, arms crossed. 'This

isn't going how I hoped it would. Two men want to wreck our marriage for their own personal gain. Will you do nothing to stop them?'

'How do I stop them when I could not stop my own wife from leaving?'

'You left first.' He could not put all of this on her plate.

'Because you pushed me away. You told me to go after Fortis. Pavia, be fair.' Cam pushed a hand through his hair, a weary gesture. 'What would you have me do? I ship out in two days.'

'Make our marriage public knowledge.' She strode the length of the smaller chamber as she explained. 'Everyone needs to know we're wed. Your grandfather's influence over us comes from the fact that our marriage is secret at the moment. He can disavow it, see it erased, because there is no one to contest him, no one to be appalled at how he is violating the sacrament of marriage by pretending ours doesn't exist.'

Cam nodded. 'So, a belated announcement in *The Times*?'

'Yes, and tell all your friends. The more who know, the better. Your grandfather despises a scandal. He'd be horrified to do anything that attached one directly to his name. He can't be caught bribing officials at Lambeth Palace.'

'Then what, Pavia? We are publicly husband and wife. I think this brings us back to the question I asked you that last night in Little Trull.' His voice was husky as he leaned against the wall, his arm bracketing her head. 'Will you be here when I get back?'

Pavia licked her lips. 'No, because I will be with you. You are not leaving me behind.' This was the harder selling point of her plan. She could see resistance form behind his eyes. He'd want to protect her.

'Balaclava is a war zone. It may not be safe.'

'Other wives do it,' she argued.

'This is crazy, Pavia.'

'Love is crazy, Cam.' She reached up to kiss him then, a soft, sweet, lingering kiss as she caressed his jaw. It felt good to be back in his arms. More than that, it felt right. 'I don't deserve you.'

His hands were in her hair pulling out the pins. 'We both made mistakes. I was so set on being a father I didn't understand how it made you feel, as if you had no value except as the mother of my child.'

'I've never had value, Cam.' It was getting harder to talk between kisses, but she had to say this, had to share this. 'I've been defined my whole life by my fortune and my face.

Until you came along, but by then, how could I believe it? How could a stranger want me for me?'

'I'm not a stranger any more, Pavia,' Cam whispered against her neck, her back against the wall, his hand sliding up beneath her skirts.

'What are you doing, Cam?' Pavia gasped, half-alarmed, half-thrilled at the illicit nature of their activity.

He kissed her hard, his finger sliding into her until she moaned her pleasure into his mouth. 'I am making you a promise. I will come for you in two days' time and this time it will be for ever. On the day we sail an announcement will be in *The Times* and the world will know. That you are my wife for now and for always.'

Chapter Twenty-Three

The plan was simple. She would simply walk out the front door and leave. There would be no fanfare, no trunks, no secret supplies to usher off to the docks. Nothing would go wrong. Cam's ship sailed on the evening tide. With them on board. It was a litany Pavia repeated multiple times in the hours that remained. Never had two days crawled by at such a pace. A snail would have been faster.

Pavia looked up from her letter writing, studying the little clock on her desk. One o'clock. Just two hours to go. She ran through the plan again. She would leave the house with her maid or other escort, it didn't matter who, which was fortuitous since her maid had taken ill last night and wouldn't be able to accompany her. She and the escort would walk a few blocks. Pavia would exclaim she'd left something behind and send them back for it. At which point, she'd hail a hansom and be off. She would meet Cam at a tavern on the docks and from there they'd go to his ship. The only trick was the speed with which it all needed to happen. She could not leave the house too early in case she was missed before the boat sailed and there was pursuit. Three o'clock would be just enough time to account for traffic should she encounter anything out of the ordinary.

Pavia stared at the incomplete note. She needed to finish it. The clock was truly running now, at last. The note was for her mother. She would leave it behind in her room. Pavia needed her to understand. Cam was the right man, a life with him was the right life wherever it led them. She had nearly thrown that away. If she didn't go with him now, there wouldn't be another chance. This was the right decision, but being right didn't make it an easy one. She wished it could be accomplished in another way. Since it couldn't be, since her father and the Earl were set on making them choose between each other and family, it had to be this way. She refused to give up Cam.

The thought of Cam bolstered her courage. She imagined him overseeing the organisation of supplies this morning, writing out orders, directing men, his gold hair blazing beneath the sun. She would be with him soon. She finished her note and changed into the walking ensemble she would take with her. Cam had promised to have a trunk of essentials waiting for her. She wouldn't be without clothes, but this would be her last dress from home. When she'd left the first time, she'd had a trunk of her things with her. She took a final look around her room. No, not 'home'. This wasn't her home any more, it hadn't been for five months now. Her home was with Cam. *Wherever* that was.

Pavia walked down the stairs, gloves in hand, as if it were any other day for an outing. Her pulse raced, though, because while it had to look like any other day for an outing, it wasn't. The footman waiting to escort her rose from his seat in the hall. There was only her father's office to walk past. As usual, she reminded herself. She walked past that room every time she went out. He hardly ever noticed.

'Hatchard's today, I think, Rosman,' she said to the footman, proud of the casual tone in her voice when she felt anything but casual. 'There's a new novel I'd like to get.'

'Very good, Miss Honeysett.' His hand was

on the door knob. She smiled. She was very
nearly there. Just three more steps.

'Pavia? Is that you? Can you spare me a
minute?' Her father's voice seemed to boom
like cannon in the hallway. Pavia froze, rapidly assessing her options. Should she make a
run for it? Breeze past the footman, down the
steps and out the front gate and into the streets?
If she could make it that far, she might stand
a chance. But her father had guards posted
around the property to keep people out. Today
those guards would keep her in. If she didn't
make it to the street, she wouldn't make at all.
Running would tip her hand. Perhaps it would
be best to continue normally.

'Yes, Father?' She stood in the doorway of
the office, hoping her choice not to enter fully
communicated her need for urgency, a shorter
conversation.

'Come in, sit down. Your mother and I have
something to discuss with you.' He gestured
to a chair by the desk.

'Now?' She smiled. 'When I am on my way
to Hatchard's? I've been home all day.' She
tried to tease him, tried to appeal to her mother
with a look.

'This is important, Pavia.' His dark eyes
were sombre. Her laughter and teasing had no

effect. 'I've heard a troubling rumour that must be dealt with. You met a man secretly two days ago.' He studied her, looking for a reaction. She kept her features neutrally confused, letting a small furrow form on her brow.

'I don't understand, Father.' Although she did. Someone had discovered where she'd gone and told her father. Or her father had had her followed. Or Cam had been followed. She wouldn't have put it past his grandfather to have men watching Cam. She folded her hands in her lap, a chill starting low in her stomach. Her father knew. That made him dangerous. She had to get out of this room.

'I believe I do.' Her father steepled his hands on his desk. 'It comes down to two things, Pavia. Either the servant lied and it will cost them their position. I will not tolerate false-hoods about my family bandied about. Or, you did indeed meet a man, which is not out of the realm of possibility. That you had to do it in se-cret suggests it wasn't the Marquis. If I had to wager on it, I would say you arranged a meet-ing with Major Lithgow.' Her father looked at the clock on his desk. 'Lithgow ships out today, in two hours. How convenient you were going out just now.'

'I think you've put together quite a few tentative links, Father,' Pavia replied coolly. 'He is my husband—why should I need to meet with him in secret? I should be able to meet with him any time and any place I choose. May I ask which servant this was? Perhaps it is someone looking to make trouble or looking to earn your favour.'

Her father looked beyond her to Rosman. 'Bring us the maid.' He gave her a sly smile. 'Neither, Daughter, which is why I feel certain I have the right of it.'

Rosman brought in Margaret, sobbing and trembling. 'I am sorry, miss. I tried not to say anything, honestly, I tried.' The poor girl looked sleepless, worn down, her eyes puffy. She'd not been ill last night. She'd been bullied.

Pavia glared at her father. 'You forced her into confessing something—anything. You threatened to take her position. Did you also threaten to turn her out without a reference? That is despicable. Coercing servants with no power. Reneging on a deal with your daughter to send her to India. These are not ethical actions of conduct.'

'Oliver, what is this?' her mother broke in. 'Is this true? Did you promise Pavia she could go to India? Did you force this girl to a confession?' Her mother's dark eyes flashed with fire. She rose. 'Is there no honour left in you, Oliver?'

'Sabita, wait. India was predicated on Pavia needing to hide a baby. That was a condition that no longer existed.' Her father tried to placate her mother. He turned back to her, hoping to build the righteousness of his case. 'You were going to run away with Lithgow today. Again. Don't deny it. Why do you persist in doing things that displease your family and his?'

'Because I love him and he loves me.' Pavia pleaded with her mother, 'Surely that means something, Mother. Reason with him.'

Her father laughed. 'Marriage isn't for love, Pavia. It's for alliances. Did your mother teach you nothing? Did life at your uncle's court or our life here in London teach you nothing?'

'Excuse me, I will be going.' Pavia stood up and moved swiftly, hoping the element of surprise would buy her enough time to reach the door, the hall, the entry, that perhaps her mother would intervene.

'Rosman, detain her, please.' Her father's order was crisp and sharp. Rosman moved to block her exit and return her to her chair.

Her father smiled coldly. 'Pavia, we are not done. You will not be leaving this house. Rosman, have the front door locked and alert my men on the grounds. No one is leaving.'

'Oliver, this is madness,' her mother warned, but it had no effect. If he was willing to override her mother, then Pavia was truly on her own.

Real panic came to Pavia. They might as well have locked her in her room. She was being trapped, held against her will, and now the clock that had moved slowly for two days was racing its way around the hour.

'I can see in your eyes that I was right. You were meeting Lithgow.' Her father's features were grim. 'He loves you? Are you sure?'

'I am sure.'

'Shall we wager on that?' He opened his desk drawer and pulled out a piece of thick parchment. 'Your wedding certificate against his imminent arrival. If he comes for you, you may go with him. If he does not, we'll burn the proof you were ever married and you'll wed the Marquis.'

Pavia blanched and her father scoffed. 'Not so sure now? It's easy to say you'll risk all for love, it's much harder to do it. Perhaps you'll thank me for this one day. I am doing you a favour. A man who won't come for his bride isn't worthy of his bride.' He gestured for another footman. 'Be ready shortly, I want to send a message to Aylsbury. Perhaps he'd like to join us.' Then he glanced at the clock. 'Four-thirty, shall we say, Daughter? In an hour we'll know what your Major is really made of.'

'I already know,' Pavia said staunchly. 'He'll be here.' But her father only smiled like a cat with cream. Her stomach sank. She knew that look. He didn't just think he'd win, he thought he already had. Dear lord, panic gripped her anew. In her haste to make the wager, what had she missed?

Cam snapped his watch shut, eyes riveted on the taproom door. Pavia was late. Beside him, Ferris Tresham tried to offer consolation. 'Maybe she's stuck in traffic. She's not that late. It's only four o'clock.'

'We don't have time to spare,' Cam barked at his friend. 'This is the military. The boat leaves on a schedule. If the tide turns, we'll be de-layed.' His stomach was a mass of knots. He'd vacillated from elation to worry constantly the last two days. Should he have let her go back to her father's house? Should he have taken her away that day in the park? What if someone found out what they'd planned? He'd tried to be discreet in acquiring items for Pavia, but had he given his plan away with those purchases?

'Major, this has come for you.' A young subaltern held out a note and saluted.

'Thank you.' Cam unfolded the paper, foreboding growing. He scanned the short lines and passed the note to Ferris, his insides tightening. She wasn't coming. She'd changed her mind. He tried to hold on to reason. That couldn't be true. Two days ago she'd been terrified to be left behind. 'What do you make of this?'

'I am sorry, old chap.' Ferris looked up from the note with solemn concern.

'That's it? The woman you love tells you she's not coming and you just accept that? Would you have accepted that from Anna?' Ferris had only been married a scant year. Surely, there was still some romance left in his soul.

Cam stood up, restless with inaction. 'Something must have happened. Every time she's changed her mind, or pulled away from me, it has been her attempt to protect me, to sacrifice for my supposed better interest.' He slapped the table. 'Don't let the boat sail without me. We can wait an hour without losing the tide if we have to.' Didn't she realise by now that she was his greater good? His better interest? He was going nowhere until he heard the denial from her own lips.

'Cam, wait, what are you doing?' Ferris rose, confused. 'How do I keep a ship in port?'

'Make something up.' Cam was halfway to the door, already running. 'Tell the Captain we're waiting on late supplies. I don't care. I am going to get her.' In the street, he hailed a hansom. 'Fast as you can, good man, to May-fair. Bruton Street.'

The driver grumbled. 'Traffic's at a snail's pace today.'

'Do you what you can.'

Cam gave up on the hansom with five streets to go. He could cover the distance faster on foot. It was nearly four-thirty. They'd never make it back to the ship in time. He hoped Ferris had a creative excuse ready for the captain.

The town house was eerily still, Honeysett's guards manning the gate as if it were the royal palace. 'Let me through!' Cam barked with militant authority. The front door opened before he reached the steps. Honeysett standing in the frame. 'What are you doing here?'

'I am claiming my wife,' Cam answered, aware that the guards had closed ranks behind him.

'She does not wish to be claimed. Did you not get her note saying she changed her mind? Seems a life of following the drum is not for her after all. No surprise there, she was raised for better.'

For a moment, old doubt surfaced. Pavia was raised for better. Perhaps she had indeed decided to stay behind, to pursue a future with the Marquis. He pushed the doubt aside. 'Then let her tell me herself.'

'Cam, is this any way to behave?' Aylsbury stepped forward at the door. 'You're making a spectacle out of yourself.'

'I could say the same for you, Grandfather.' Cam smelled a conspiracy now. Game was afoot. 'Lowering yourself to visiting the home of a businessman? Do you let Honeysett call the shots?' He could not see beyond the two men, but if they were here, on their front step, trying so desperately to send him away, then it was a surety that Pavia was within.

His grandfather hated scenes. Well, Cam would give him one. Cam raised his voice. 'Pavia, I am here! Come out! I want to speak with you!'

'Will you hush?' his grandfather scolded, the old man's head wildly thrashing around to see if the neighbours were watching yet.

'Invite me in, let me speak with Pavia,' Cam bargained. 'I'd hate to force my way in, but I will do it. I think your neighbours would find a contretemps on the front lawn very entertaining.' That was bravado speaking. He would take out some of Honeysett's guards, but he wouldn't get them all, there were simply too many.

'Pavia!' he called out again, another scenario coming to him. Perhaps she'd been forced to write the note. What had these men held over her head if she refused to send it? Or had she not sent it all? Was the note a forgery?

'Cam!' A shriek followed the reply. It was all Cam needed to leap into action. His wife was inside, against her will from the sound of things. He sprang up the steps, using his speed and strength to barrel past the two men. If she was being held against her will, things had gone too far. It was past time to be polite even to his grandfather.

Pavia was on the stairs, struggling against two footmen, her hands wrapped about the banister, using it as an anchor. She kicked and fought to stay downstairs, to stay visible. So that was their play—Pavia was supposed to have been out of the way, locked in a room upstairs. She looked up and saw him. 'Cam!'

'I'm here!' His sword was out as he raced towards Pavia. 'Unhand my wife, immediately!' The sight of the blade was enough to deter the footmen. They fell back. He was beside her. 'You didn't send the note, did you?' It seemed impossible based on these circumstances that she would have.

'No, I sent nothing. What note?' She was breathless, her arms about his neck. 'You came. I thought I would never see you again, that you would sail without me, that I would lose you for ever. They were going to destroy the marriage certificates.' She was babbling, crying as she clung to him, confirmation that something far worse had happened in this house.

'Stay with me and behind me, Pavia.' He gripped her hand, leading her towards the door, towards her father and his grandfather, his sword in one hand, Pavia's hand in the other. Her father stepped forward to meet him, a pistol in his hand.

Dear God, would her father shoot Cam simply to widow her? Guns beat blades every time for speed. 'Cam,' Pavia murmured a warning. But Cam stood his ground.

'You both have interfered enough. This ends

today. Pavia Honeysett is my wife.' Cam's attention shifted to his grandfather. 'An announcement to this effect will be printed in *The Times* evening edition, publicly acknowledging our marriage. You cannot erase it now without causing a public scandal. I am leaving this house with her by consent or by force, it matters not which to me.'

A clock chimed the half-hour somewhere in the house. 'You gave your word, Father,' Pavia spoke. 'I won our wager. Cam came, despite your best efforts to convince him otherwise. Love really does conquer all.'

Her father would not relent. 'You will not take my daughter from this house again.' The gun stayed trained on Cam and for a moment Pavia feared he would fire. Not to kill, she realised. He was too keen of a strategist for such a mistake. He would never survive murdering an earl's grandson in cold blood. Aylsbury would not allow such a thing. But he could maim and for a military man like Cam, that would be just as deadly.

Pavia appealed to Aylsbury. Perhaps he would be her unlikely ally if it meant saving Cam. 'You can't possibly allow a man to hold a gun on your grandson?' she scolded, but the old man was stoic in his response.

'I am waiting for him to see reason. He will be safe the moment he steps away from you. If he is shot, it will be on his own head.' Good lord—Pavia's heart sank—they were both mad with revenge. What a pair the Earl and her father made, the two of them so drunk on the need for power and control they couldn't be logical. What was she to do against two such men? She needed an ally.

There was movement at the doorway to the office. Her mother stood there, her quiet dark eyes ablaze with an old fire. 'If there's to be any shooting done, it won't be in my entrance hall.' She strode forward, putting herself between Cam and the pistol. 'I have been silent too long, thinking you'd come to your senses on your own, Oliver.'

Pavia watched transfixed as her unassuming mother's hand curled confidently, without hesitation, over the barrel of the pistol as she spoke. 'Put the gun away, Oliver. You can't force a victory—you can't win this. This is not a competition for tea-leaf crops or access to trade routes. Are you really willing to shoot this man because he loves your daughter? Where's the logic in that?' She turned the gun barrel aside. 'There used to be a time when I loved to watch you compete, to go after what you wanted. It was what I first loved about you. Then your ambition began to eat you alive. I waited and hoped it would pass, but it has only spread. Your ambition threatens all of us now—your daughter's happiness and even your own marriage is about to be sacrificed to your avarice. Oliver, you have enough. You have more money than any one man can spend in a life time, you have a family that would like to love you if given a chance. Don't you remember how it used to be between us? Before you were corrupted by greed? Let Pavia claim her happiness and let me find the man I used to love.'

Pavia watched in riveted fascination as the gun lowered, her father's eyes fixed on her mother, his attention no longer on her and Cam. 'But, Sabita, it was all for you.' Her father's stern brow knit in confusion. 'So that you would be accepted, so that you would not regret leaving your family, your home, your country, so you would never regret the marriage your brother arranged for you.'

Her mother's hand smoothed the wrinkles from his brow, her voice soft like it used to be when Pavia was young and had a nightmare. 'Shh, Oliver. All I ever needed, wanted, was you, just as you were, just as you can be again.'

There were unshed tears in her father's eyes.

Pavia had never seen him cry before, never seen him broken before. But, no, that was wrong. He was not broken now. Her mother had not broken him. Her mother had reclaimed him. Love had reclaimed him. It was almost like watching a metamorphosis before her very eyes. Pavia felt Cam's arm about her. She glanced his way to see his own gaze downcast, for privacy, for respect, to give her parents the moment. Love had conquered even her father's hard heart. But not Aylsbury's.

'Grandfather, will you step aside? We have a boat to catch.' Cam sheathed his blade. It could be of no more use. There were more powerful forces at work here than weapons.

The Earl huffed. 'Sentiment is rubbish. You'll never be welcome in my home again, Camden.'

Cam nodded. 'I'm not sure I ever was. The only home that matters to me is the one Pavia and I will make. Mrs Lithgow, your ship awaits. This way, if you please.'

Pavia beamed up at him, relief and love flooding her. 'I do please. Mr Lithgow, lead on.'

The cabin was small, but it was private, thank goodness. She and Cam had put that privacy to good use the moment he was free of his duties above deck. Pavia levered up on her side, her hand stroking her husband's chest with idle drawings. 'I didn't think you'd come and it would be my fault. I had pushed you away once. I thought you'd doubt me and believe I had decided not to want you, not to want us.' There was still a fragility between them. They had to learn each other all over again, or perhaps for the first time, or maybe *still*.

Cam kissed her forehead. 'You needn't doubt again. I will always come for you.' He pushed back her hair, his hand soft at her cheek. 'Now, what was this about a wager with your father?'

'He bet our certificate against you showing up. If I won, he'd let us walk out of there together, if I lost, I had to let him erase the marriage.' She held his gaze. 'I never want to feel that way again, as if the world depended on you walking through that door.' She hesitated. 'But I think I probably will because that's how it feels to love someone the way I love you.'

He drew her to him and she revelled in the feel of his body against hers, skin to skin, mouth to mouth as the ship rocked beneath them. 'I know, because I feel the same way, every time I look at you,' He whispered. Cam gave her a long kiss that stirred her at her core. 'We'll keep each other safe, Pavia, I promise.'

She gave a soft laugh. 'When I looked out at the taproom that first night, I thought I only needed a man, that any man would do. But I was wrong, Cam Lithgow. I needed you.' From the look in his eyes and the press of him against her leg, he needed her, too. Maybe fairy tales did exist after all.

Epilogue

The Crimea—one month later

'Are you nervous?' Pavia reached for Cam's hand, wanting to lend him support as they waited in the big, notably empty white tent. Moments ago it had been filled with officers of all ranks eager for a glimpse of the man who might be Fortis Tresham. But Cam had insisted the first meeting be private.

Cam shook his head and threaded his gloved fingers through hers. 'No. Once, I might have been. Once, my life had centred on finding Fortis. I couldn't accept that he was gone. But now, it is merely one part of my life, not the sum of it.' He squeezed her hand. 'What will be, will be.'

He looked handsome in his dark blue uniform, his broad shoulders filling out the long officer's greatcoat with its polished buttons. Handsome and intimidating, some would say. But not Pavia. He was simply the man she loved and the man who loved her in return. She would follow him everywhere, anywhere. She'd followed him here to the Crimea. It was muddy and cold— even Cam's status as a major didn't afford them many luxuries: a bigger tent and better food, perhaps, but not protection from the elements. Still, she'd done her best to make that tent welcoming and there was the joy at the end of every day of lying down beside him on the bed she'd cobbled together out of cots and a hay-stuffed mattress, knowing they were together. That was enough. For now.

A cold wind cut through the tent and Pavia shivered despite the warmth of her wool cloak. 'It's a different kind of cold here, isn't it?' Cam smiled in commiseration. 'But we'll be going home before long, just as soon as this piece about Fortis is resolved.'

Pavia couldn't keep the surprise from her face. 'Home? To Little Trull?'

'Yes.' Cam grinned. 'I was going to surprise you later, but now is as good of time as any. I have resigned my commission, effective immediately. This is no life for us. Coming back has made me see that.'

Pavia's joy faded. 'But you love the military.'

Cam shook his head, stalling her worries. 'I *loved* the military, past tense. Now I have some things I love more: my wife, my marriage, the home we're making together. It's time for a new direction in my life.' He smiled his assurances. But Pavia wasn't convinced.

'And your search for Fortis?' she asked quietly.

'I can't spend my life chasing ghosts. It steals too much from the future. For me, that search ends today no matter what happens.'

'What will you do with yourself?' She could hardly imagine her active husband content with puttering around the garden *all* the time.

'Conall and I have plans for the alpaca syndicate. I shan't be bored, my dear.' His eyes twinkled. 'Perhaps you might like to invest?' Her father had written begging forgiveness and promising to transfer her rightful dowry to them when they returned. Cam had insisted she keep the dowry, her own money to use as she chose.

'I should think not right away.' Pavia gave him a coy glance. 'I might not have time.' She bit her lip, debating. It hardly seemed the place for her news, yet the moment seemed right. They were on the brink of a new start with Cam leaving the military behind and her news would be a new start as well. 'I have a surprise for you, too. I was going to save it, but I want to tell you now, before anything else happens.' She drew a quick breath, holding Cam's eyes with her own. She didn't want to miss a moment of his reaction. 'I'm pregnant. *We* are having baby.'

They were going to be parents. Absolute joy shrunk Cam's world to the woman beside him. All thoughts of Fortis, of his final mission, were gone, obliterated. He drew Pavia into his embrace, holding her close, her face shining up at him as they shared this moment. 'Nothing could make me happier,' he whispered. Or more complete. That completion was the source of his happiness. Pavia made him whole, his children made him whole. He bent to steal a kiss. Any interlopers could be damned. He loved his wife. He would not pretend otherwise.

'Ahem. Major.' A pink-faced corporal shifted uneasily on his feet at the entrance. 'He is here, sir.'

Cam straightened, gathering his thoughts to the present. 'Send him in, then.' Surreptitiously, he felt Pavia's gloved hand slide back around his, her touch the living promise she'd made to him the night he'd confessed all to her. She was beside him in all ways today. He did not have to face the hope or disappointment of this moment alone. No matter what happened, they would go home to Little Trull and build the life they'd dreamed together. What more could a man ask for?

The corporal moved aside and a tall man stepped through the entrance, stooping to fit beneath the flap. He straightened and met Cam's gaze evenly with sharp blue eyes the colour of glaciers. Cam was careful to give nothing away as he studied the newcomer; tall, dark-haired, he carried himself with a sense of authority. He waited, letting the other man speak first.

'They tell me my name is Fortis Tresham,' the man offered at last. His voice was hoarse, perhaps from illness or from cold, both were common in these parts.

'Who do *you* say you are?' Cam replied evenly, keenly aware of Pavia's hand in his, lending him much-needed strength.

Ice-blue eyes never wavered. 'I don't know.'

There was pain and shame beneath the prideful response.

Cam's heart went out to the man. How terrible not to know oneself. For all the grief he'd known, he could not imagine the grief of not remembering one's own name, one's family, one's beloveds. Cam slid a glance at his wife. There was much he might forget, but he'd never forget her. Pavia was his heart, his north star. With her, he would always find his way home.

* * * * *

MILLS & BOON

Coming next month

HIS CONVENIENT HIGHLAND BRIDE
Janice Preston

Lachlan McNeill couldn't quite believe his good fortune when he first saw his bride, Lady Flora McCrieff, walking up the aisle towards him on her father's arm. Her posture was upright and correct and her figure was... delectable. The tight bodice and sleeves of her wedding gown—her figure tightly laced in accordance with fashion—accentuated her full breasts, slender arms and tiny waist above the wide bell of her skirt. She was tiny, dwarfed by her father's solid, powerful frame, and she barely reached Lachlan's shoulder when they stood side by side in front of the minister. True, he had not yet seen his new bride's face—her figure might be all he could wish for, but was there a nasty surprise lurking yet? Maybe her features were somehow disfigured? Or maybe she was a shrew? Why else had her father refused to let them meet before their wedding day? He'd instead insisted on riding over to Lochmore Castle, Lachlan's new home, to agree the marriage settlements.

Their vows exchanged, Lachlan raised Flora's veil, bracing himself for some kind of abomination. His chest loosened with relief as she stared up at him, her green eyes huge and wary under auburn brows, the freckles that speckled her nose and cheeks stark against the pallor of her skin. His finger caught a loose, silken tendril of coppery-red hair and her face flooded pink, her lower lip trembling, drawing his gaze as the scent of orange blossom wreathed his senses.

She is gorgeous.

Heat sizzled through him, sending blood surging to his loins as he found himself drawn into the green depths of her eyes, his senses in disarray. Then he took her hand to place it on his arm and its delicacy, its softness, its fragility sent waves of doubt crashing through him, sluicing him clean of lustful thoughts as he sucked air into his lungs.

He had never imagined he'd be faced with one so young...so dainty...so captivating...and her beauty and her purity brought into sharp focus his own dirty, sordid past. Next to her he felt a clumsy, uncultured oaf.

What could he and this pampered young lady ever have in common? She might accept his fortune, but could she ever truly accept the man behind the façade? He'd faced rejection over his past before and he'd already decided that the less his wife ever learned about that past, the better.

Continue reading
HIS CONVENIENT HIGHLAND BRIDE
Janice Preston

Available next month
www.millsandboon.co.uk

LET'S TALK
Romance

For exclusive extracts, competitions and special offers, find us online:

[f] facebook.com/millsandboon

[y] @MillsandBoon

[o] @MillsandBoonUK

Get in touch on 01413 063232

For all the latest titles coming soon, visit
millsandboon.co.uk/nextmonth

COMING
SOON!

We really hope you enjoyed reading this book. If you're looking for more romance, be sure to head to the shops when new books are available on

Thursday 21st March

To see which titles are coming soon, please visit

millsandboon.co.uk/nextmonth